"Do you need money?"

His hand swept the room. "You light fires only for show. You have no flowers. And there is the matter of your servants...."

Would he tell the creditors and reporters? If word of her true situation escaped, all of England would know the shocking state of her finances.

"I don't need money." Lydia felt her cheeks heat. "Would that not mean I was in your keeping? Do not mistresses accept money from their...patrons?"

"I offer it without obligation."

Adrian said this so sincerely she almost believed him. It made no sense that a near stranger, a known rake, would offer her money without expecting something in return.

For a moment he looked as if he would cross the room to her, but instead he turned and walked to the door. She twisted away, not wishing to watch him disappear out of her life.

His voice came from behind her. "I am your friend, Lydia. Remember that."

She spun back around, but he had gone.

* * *

Scandalizing the Ton
Harlequin® Historical #916—October 2008

Diane Gaston

Scandalizing
THE TON

TORONTO • NEW YORK • LONDON
AMSTERDAM • PARIS • SYDNEY • HAMBURG
STOCKHOLM • ATHENS • TOKYO • MILAN • MADRID
PRAGUE • WARSAW • BUDAPEST • AUCKLAND

ISBN-13: 978-0-373-29516-6
ISBN-10:   0-373-29516-2

SCANDALIZING THE TON

DON'T MISS THESE OTHER
NOVELS AVAILABLE NOW:

#915 THE MAGIC OF CHRISTMAS
Carolyn Davidson, Victoria Bylin, Cheryl St.John

Three festive stories with all the seasonal warmth of the West—
guaranteed to keep you snug from the cold this Yuletide!

#917 HALLOWE'EN HUSBANDS
Lisa Plumley, Denise Lynn, Christine Merrill

All is not as it seems for three lucky ladies on
All Hallows' Eve. The last thing they expect from the
mystery of the night is a betrothal!

#918 THE DARK VISCOUNT—Deborah Simmons

A mysterious gothic mansion haunts Bartholomew,
Viscount Hawthorne, but it is also the new home of his
childhood friend Sydony Marchant. The youthful bond they
once shared is lost—will one stolen kiss be enough to rekindle
that intimacy and help them unravel the shadows of the past?

Chapter One

Once the finest ornament of the *beau monde*, a beauty so astounding and sublime a man would kill to possess her hand in marriage, the notorious Lady W— mourns her murderous husband in secret. How much knowledge did she possess of her husband's villainous acts?
—*The New Observer*, November 12, 1818

"Leave me this instant!"

A woman's voice.

Adrian Pomroy, the new Viscount Cavanley, barely heard her as he rounded the corner into John Street. Not even halfway down the road he saw the woman stride away from a man. The man hurried after her. They were mere silhouettes in the waning light of this November evening and they took no heed of him.

Adrian paused to make sense of this little drama. It was most likely a lovers' quarrel, and, if so, he'd backtrack to avoid landing in the middle of it.

"One moment." The man kept his voice down, as if fearing to be overheard. "Please!" He seized her arm.

"Release me!" The woman struggled frantically to pull away.

Lovers' quarrel or not, Adrian could not allow a woman to be treated so roughly. He sprinted forwards. "Unhand her! What is this?"

The man released the woman so quickly she tripped on her long hooded cloak. Adrian clasped her arm before she fell, holding her until she regained her balance. From the mews nearby a horse whinnied, but otherwise it was quiet.

The man backed away. "This is not as it appears, sir. I intend no harm to the lady." He raised his hands as if to prove his words.

The lady? Adrian assumed he'd rescued some maid from a stableman's unwanted advances, but the woman's cloak was made of fine cloth, and the man was dressed more like a tradesman than a stableman.

Adrian turned to the lady. "Did he harm you, ma'am?"

"No." The hood of her cloak shrouded her face. "But I do not wish to speak to him."

The man stepped forwards again. "I merely asked the lady a few questions—"

"I will not answer them," she cried from beneath her hood.

Adrian had the advantage of size on the man. He straightened his spine to make certain the man knew it. "If the lady does not wish to speak to you, that is the end of it."

"Let me explain, sir." The man stuck a hand in his pocket and pulled out a card. He handed it to Adrian. "I am Samuel Reed from *The New Observer*."

Adrian glanced at the card. "You are a newspaper reporter?" He had read the new London paper, quite recently, in fact.

The man nodded. "All England wishes to know Lady Wexin's reaction to the events surrounding her villainous husband. I am merely requesting the information from her."

"Lady Wexin?"

Adrian regarded the cloaked figure with new interest. Adrian had just called upon his friend, the Marquess of Tannerton.

Tanner had shoved *The New Observer* article about Lady Wexin under Adrian's nose not more than half an hour ago.

His friend, Tanner, had recently returned from Scotland with a new wife and news about Lord Wexin that had consumed the newspapers ever since. Truth to tell, Tanner's marriage had shocked Adrian more than the tale of murder, betrayal and death that involved the Earl of Wexin.

Lady Wexin interrupted Adrian's thoughts. "Do I take it by your silence that you agree with this man, sir?" She stood with one hand braced against a garden wall. "Do perfect strangers have a right to know my private matters?"

Adrian still could not see her face, but he recalled the *ton* beauty very well. What gentleman would not? Adrian had never been formally presented to Lady Wexin, but they had occasionally attended the same society gatherings. Years ago Tanner and Adrian had briefly included Wexin among their set, but that had been before Wexin's marriage.

"You owe this man nothing, my lady." Adrian gave her a reassuring smile. "He will trouble you no further."

According to Tanner, Lady Wexin was an innocent party in the perfidy that had so titillated the gossip-lovers. The newspapers had indulged the public's seemingly insatiable appetite for the scandal by speculating about Lady Wexin's part in it. Wexin might be dead, but his wife was not.

Lady Wexin let go of the garden wall. "I shall be on my way, then." She turned, her cloak swirling around her. She took one step, paused, then resumed walking.

Adrian frowned. She was limping.

Mr Reed's gaze followed her as well. He appeared to be considering whether to pursue her with more questions.

Adrian clapped him on the shoulder. "Best you leave, Mr Reed."

Mr Reed's eyes flashed. "This is a public street, sir."

Adrian smiled, but without friendliness. "Nonetheless, you

do not wish to be in my bad graces." He glanced at Lady Wexin, now fumbling with a key in the lock of a garden gate. "The lady looks as if she's had enough to deal with today. Leave, sir."

Reed hesitated, but eventually his gaze slid back to Adrian.

"Leave, Mr Reed." Adrian repeated, quietly but firmly.

Reed bowed his head and nodded. He cast another look at Lady Wexin before strolling to the corner and disappearing from sight.

Adrian walked quickly over to where Lady Wexin still worked the lock. "Let me assist you."

She waved him away. "I can manage."

He gestured to her legs. "You are standing on one foot."

She averted her face. "My—my ankle pains me a little. I believe I twisted it, but I assure you I can manage." The lock turned and she opened the gate. When she stepped into the garden she nearly toppled to the ground.

Adrian hurried through the gate and wrapped an arm around her. "You cannot walk."

The hood of her cloak fell away, fully revealing her face, only inches from his own.

Her skin was as smooth and flawless as the Roman sculpture of Clytie that had once captivated him in the British Museum. Unlike cold white stone, however, Lady Wexin's cheeks were warm with colour. Her lips, shaped like a perfect bow, were as pink as a dew-kissed rose. Adrian had often appreciated her beauty from across a ballroom, or from a box away at Covent Garden, but, this close, she robbed him of breath.

"Is this your house?" he finally managed.

She edged out of his embrace, but continued to clutch his arm. "Of course it is."

He smiled. "Forgive me. Yes, it must be."

She looked over her shoulder. "I must close the gate. Before they see."

"Before they see?" He followed her glance.

"More newspaper people. They loiter around the house, looking for me."

Ah, now it made sense why the lady entered her house through the garden gate. It did not explain why she had been out alone. Ladies did not venture out unless accompanied by a companion or a servant.

Adrian closed the gate with his free hand.

"I need to lock it." She let go of him and tried to step away, again nearly falling.

Adrian reached for her again and helped her to the gate. "I'll walk you to your door as well."

"I am so sorry to trouble you." She turned the key and left it in the lock.

Adrian kept his arm around her as they started for the house. When she put the slightest weight on her ankle, he felt her tense with pain.

"This will not do." Adrian scooped her up into his arms.

"No, put me down," she begged. "You must not carry me."

"Nonsense. Of course I must." Her face was even closer now and her scent, like spring lilacs, filled his nostrils. She draped her arms around his neck, and he inhaled deeply.

"See? I am too heavy," she protested.

Too heavy? She felt as if she belonged in his arms.

He smiled at her. "Do not insult my strength, Lady Wexin. You will wound my male vanity." He made the mistake of staring into her deep blue eyes, now glittering with unspent tears, and his heart wrenched for her. "You must be in great pain," he murmured.

She held his gaze. "It hurts not at all now."

He could not look away.

Somewhere on the street a door slammed and Lady Wexin blinked.

Adrian regained his senses and carried her the short

distance to the rear door of the townhouse. Voices sounded nearby, riding on the evening breeze.

"The door will be unlocked," she murmured, her hair brushing his cheek.

He opened the door and brought her inside. To the left he glimpsed the kitchen, though there were no sounds of a cook at work there. He carried her down the passageway and brought her above stairs to the main hall of the house.

It was elegantly appointed with a gilded hall table upon which sat a pair of Chinese vases, devoid of flowers. Matching gilded chairs were upholstered in bright turquoise. The floor was a chequerboard of black-and-white marble, but no footman stood in attendance. In fact, the house was very quiet and a bit chilly.

"Shall I summon one of your servants?" he asked.

"They—they are all out at the moment, but you may put me down. I shall manage from here."

He looked at her in surprise. "All out?" It was odd for a house to be completely empty of servants.

She averted her gaze. "They have the day off." She squirmed in his arms. "You may put me down."

He shook his head. "Your ankle needs tending." He started up the marble staircase, smiling at her again to ease her discomfort. "By the way, I ought to present myself. I am—"

She interrupted him. "I know who you are."

Adrian's smile deepened, flattered that she'd noticed him.

He reached the second floor where he guessed the bed-chambers would be. "Direct me to your room."

"The second door," she replied. "But, really, you mustn't—"

It was his turn to interrupt. "Someone must."

Her bedchamber was adorned with hand-painted wallpaper, bright exotic birds frolicking amidst colourful flowers. A dressing table with a large mirror held sparkling glass bottles, porcelain pots and a brush and comb with polished silver handles. Her bed was neatly made, its white coverlet gleaming and its many pillows plumped with what he guessed was the finest down. The room was chilly, though, as if someone had allowed the fire in the fireplace to go out.

He set her down on the bed, very aware of her hands slipping away from his neck. "I'll tend the fire."

"Really, sir. You need not trouble yourself." Her voice reached a high, nervous pitch.

"It is no trouble."

He removed his hat, gloves and topcoat and crossed the room to the small fireplace, its mantel of carved marble holding another empty vase. To his surprise, the fire had not died out at all. It was all set to be lit. He found the tinderbox and soon had a flame licking across the lumps of coal.

He returned to her. She had removed her cloak and clutched it in front of her. Adrian took it from her hands and draped it over a nearby chair. It contained something in its pocket. Adrian felt a purse, heavy with coin.

He turned back to her and their eyes met, hers still shimmering with tears.

He touched her arm. "Are you certain you are not in pain? You look near to weeping."

She averted her gaze. "I'm not in pain."

He knelt in front of her. "Then let me have a look at that ankle. If it is broken, we will need to summon a surgeon."

She drew up her leg. "A surgeon!"

"A surgeon would merely set the bone," he said, puzzled at her alarm.

Her hand fluttered. "I was thinking of the cost."

"The cost?" Concern over the cost was even more puzzling. Adrian gave her a reassuring smile. "Let us not fret over what is not yet a problem. Let me examine it first."

She extended her leg again and Adrian untied her half-boot. He slipped off the shoe, made of buttery soft white kid, and held her foot in his hand, enjoying too much its graceful shape.

She flinched.

He glanced up at her. "Am I hurting you?"

"No," she rasped. "Not hurting."

He grinned. "Tickling, then. I'll be more careful." He forced himself to his task, feeling her ankle, now swollen. His hand slipped up to her calf, but he quickly moved it down to her ankle again, gently moving her foot in all directions.

She gasped.

"Does that hurt?" he asked her.

"A little," she whispered. "I—I should not be allowing you to do this."

Indeed. He was enjoying it far too much, and desiring far more.

He cleared his throat. "I believe your ankle is sprained, not broken. I predict you will do nicely in a day or two." He did not release it. "I should wrap it, though, to give you some support. Do you have bandages, or a strip of cloth?"

Her eyes were half-closed. She blinked and pointed to a chest of drawers. "Look in the bottom drawer."

Adrian reluctantly let go of her leg and walked over to the chest. The bottom drawer contained neatly folded under-clothing made of soft muslin and satiny silk as soft and smooth as her skin.

His thoughts, as if having a will of their own, turned carnal, and he imagined crossing the room and taking her in his arms, tasting her lips, peeling off her clothing, sliding his hands over her skin.

He gave himself an inwards shake. He would not take advantage of this lady. Her peace was disturbed by reporters hounding her for a story, and her whole world had been turned head over ears with news of her husband's crimes. And his death.

He frowned as he groped through her underclothing, finally coming up with a long thin piece of muslin.

He returned to her and knelt again. "I must remove your stocking."

She extended her leg.

He slipped his hands up her calf, past her knee, until he found the top of her stocking and the ribbon that held it in place. He untied the ribbon and rolled the stocking down and off her foot. Her skin was smooth and warm and pliant beneath his fingers.

Adrian quickly took the strip of cloth and began to wind it around her ankle.

"Did you study surgery?" she asked, her voice cracking.

He looked up and grinned at her. "I fear it is horses I know, not surgery."

She laughed, and the sound, like the joyful tinkling of a pianoforte, echoed in his mind.

He tried to force his attention back to the bandage, but she leaned forwards and gave him a good glimpse of her décolletage. "Are you so gentle with horses?"

He glanced back to the bandage and continued wrapping, smoothing the fabric with his other hand.

"What is your name?" Her tone turned low and soft.

He glanced up. "I thought you said you knew me."

"I do not know your given name," she said.

"Adrian." He tied off her bandage and reluctantly released her.

"Adrian." She extended her hand. "I am Lydia."

He grasped her hand. "Lydia."

Lydia's heart raced at the feel of his large masculine hand enveloping hers. His grip was strong, the sort of grip that assured he was a man who could handle any trial. She now knew better than to make judgements based on such trivialities as a touch, but she could not deny he had been gentle with her. And kind.

It seemed so long since she'd felt kindness from anyone but her servants.

And even longer since she'd felt a man's touch, since her husband left for Scotland, in fact. It shocked her how affected she was by Adrian Pomroy's hand on hers. He warmed her all over, making her body pine for what only should exist between a husband and wife.

She took a breath. She'd always loved that part of marriage, the physical part, the part that was supposed to lead to babies…but she could not think of that. It was too painful.

It was almost easier to think of her husband. The Earl of Wexin.

The newspapers wrote that her husband had killed Lord Corland so that Wexin could marry her. Lord Corland's death had been her fault.

She gripped Adrian's hand even more tightly, sick that Wexin's hands had ever touched her, hands that had cut a man's throat.

She thought she'd loved Wexin. She'd trusted him with everything—the finances, the decisions, everything. But she had not known him at all. He'd betrayed her and left her with nothing but shame and guilt.

Her happiness had been an illusion, something that could not last, like the baby that had been growing inside her the day Wexin left.

The cramping had started the very next day after he'd gone, more than a month ago now, and she'd lost that baby like the two others before.

She swallowed a sob. Now she had nothing.

"Lydia?"

She glanced up into Adrian's eyes, warm amber, perpetually mirthful, as if his life had been nothing but one long lark.

He smiled, and the corners of his eyes crinkled. "You are squeezing my hand."

She released him. "I am sorry."

He stood and took her hand in his again. "It was not a complaint. You look troubled." He lifted her hand to his lips, warm soft lips. "You have been through a great deal, I suspect. I will act as your friend, if you will allow me."

Her senses flared again and her breathing accelerated. "If you knew how I need a friend."

He smelled wonderful. Like a man. And she felt his strength in his hands, in his steady gaze. She took a deep breath and reached up to touch his hair, thick and brown with a wayward cowlick at the crown that gave him a boyish appeal.

His eyes darkened and the grin disappeared, though his lips formed a natural smile even at rest.

This man pleased women, it was said. He was a rake whose name was always attached to some actress or opera dancer or widow. Well, she was a widow now and her whole body yearned to be touched, to be pleased, to be loved.

She spoke, but it was as if her voice belonged to someone else. "You can do something for me, Adrian. As a friend."

He smiled again. "You have but to ask."

She wrapped her arms around his neck, and with her heart thundering inside her chest, she brought her lips near to his oh-so-tempting ones. "Make love to me."

She felt his intake of air and watched his lips move. "Are you certain you want that?" he whispered.

"Very certain," that voice that only sounded like hers said. Before she could think, she closed the distance between them, tasting his lips gently at first, then more boldly.

He tasted lovely, but this kiss was not enough, not nearly enough. She opened her mouth and allowed his tongue to enter, delicious and decadent. She slid as close to the edge of the bed as she could, as close to him. She pressed herself against him, loving the feel of his firm chest against her softer one.

While his tongue played with hers, she worked the buttons

of his coat and waistcoat. He parted from her long enough to shrug out of them. She pulled his shirt over his head and ran her hands over his muscular chest. She'd not known a man's muscles could really be as sculpted as the statues of antiquity, nor as broad. No wonder women wanted to be his lover.

"Turn around," he murmured.

She twisted around so he could reach the hooks at the back of her dress. He made short work of them.

She pulled her dress over her head, and he untied the laces of her corset with the practised ease of a lady's maid. Lydia felt a *frisson* of excitement at the prospect of coupling with a skilled lover. She had never even kissed a man besides her husband.

Her corset joined the growing pile of clothing on the floor, and Lydia made quick work of removing her shift. She wanted—needed—to feel her skin against his, but he held her at arm's length and caressed her with his gaze.

Her breathing accelerated. She reached for the buttons of his trousers.

He smiled and his hand rose to stroke her cheek. "I was merely savouring you for a moment."

He stepped back and pulled off his boots and trousers. Lydia removed her remaining shoe and stocking, taking in his naked body through half-closed eyelids.

He was indeed a magnificent man.

And an aroused one. Her eyes widened. Here must be another reason he pleased women so well.

Lydia extended her hand to him and pulled him towards her, making room for him on her bed, pulling the blankets away as she did so. He joined her and covered her with his body, warming her—she had not realised she'd been so very cold. His hands stroked her with exquisite gentleness, relaxing her in places she'd not known she'd been tense. She stretched, arching her back like a cat. He closed his palms over her breasts and need consumed her.

She grasped his neck and pulled him down to her lips again, wanting him to breathe his strength into her. She longed for him to join himself to her. She longed not to feel so alone. So betrayed. So abandoned.

He broke the kiss and, as if reading her mind, took charge, moving his lips down her neck, tasting her nipples. Then he slid his hand to her feminine place and slipped his fingers inside her.

She had never experienced such a thing. Wexin had never done anything like this with his fingers. The intensity of the pleasure stunned her. Adrian seemed to know precisely where to touch, how to touch, until she was writhing beneath him, moaning in a voice that sounded more primal than her own.

Her climax burst forth inside her, so intense she cried out and clung to him as the waves of pleasure washed over her, and washed over her again.

When it ebbed, confusion came in its wake.

"But what of you, Adrian?"

Her husband always saw to his own pleasure first. She did not know her pleasure could come in such a different way.

He held her face in his hands. "We are not finished, Lydia."

She took in a ragged breath.

He lay beside her, his head resting on one hand, the fingers of the other hand barely touching her skin, but stroking slowly and gently until she forgot her confusion and became boneless and as pliant as putty. To her surprise, her desire grew again, but less urgent than before.

His lips traced where his hands had been, his tongue sending shafts of need wherever he tasted her. He touched her feminine place again, with such gentleness she thought she might weep out of sheer bliss. It still seemed it was her pleasure, not his, that guided his hand. He made her feel cherished, revered.

"Adrian," she murmured, awash in this new sensation.

Slowly, very slowly, her desire escalated, until again she writhed with need.

"Now, Lydia," he whispered into her ear.

He climbed atop her again and stared into her eyes as he slowly slipped his entire length into her, each second driving her mad with wanting. Lydia gasped as he began to move, still slow and rhythmic, like the intricate moves of a dance. She moved with him, but the pace he set kept the ultimate pleasure just out of her reach. He moved with such confidence, she gave herself over to him, trusting he would bring her to where she so very much wanted to go.

His pace quickened and her need grew even greater. The sound of their breathing filled the room, melding together like voices singing a duet.

Her release burst forth and she saw stars brighter than at Brighton. She thrilled when his seed spilled into her. They pressed against each other, moaning with a pleasure that burned away her desolation.

Gradually the pleasure waned, but left in its wake a delicious feeling of satiation.

He slid off of her and lay next to her, breathing hard. "Lydia," he whispered.

"Mmm," she murmured, snuggling against him.

She must have fallen asleep, but the knocker sounding on the townhouse door woke her with a start. She heard voices outside.

The newspaper people. Would they never stop hounding her? She sat up, covering herself with the bed linens and realising what she had just done.

She'd begged the dashing Adrian Pomroy, who conquered women more easily than Napoleon had conquered countries, to make love to her. And he had obliged.

"There is no one here to answer your door," he said.

She groped around for her shift. "I do not want my door

answered." Covering her mouth with her hand, she squeezed her eyes shut. "They must not see you here." Finally her fingers flexed around the muslin of her shift. She pulled it on over her head and climbed off the bed. "You must get dressed." Hopping on one foot, she tried to gather his clothes. "Leave here by the rear door." She twisted his shirt in her hands. "The gate. You cannot lock the gate." She shook her head and reached for his waistcoat. "Never mind the gate. The servants will be here soon and they will lock it behind them."

He seized her arm. "Lydia, calm yourself. They will not see me."

It was not only the reporters or creditors fuelling her alarm. Her own wanton behaviour had shocked her much, much more.

She shoved the shirt and waistcoat into his hands.

He dressed as quickly and efficiently as he had undressed. Buttoning his waistcoat, he said, "I will call upon you tomorrow."

"No!" she cried. She forced herself to sound rational. "You cannot come here again, Adrian. If you are seen here, there will be more scandal." She hopped over to the chest of drawers and pulled out a robe of Chinese silk. She wrapped the robe around her. "Please, just go."

He strode over and enfolded her in his arms, pressing her ear against his beating heart. "Be calm," he murmured. "Your troubles will vanish soon."

She wanted to laugh hysterically. Once she had believed that troubles were what other people experienced, but she knew differently now. Now it seemed trouble would follow her to the end of her days.

"I'll lock your gate and throw the key back into the garden." He released her, but placed one light kiss on her forehead. "And I will return."

"You must not return," she pleaded.

He flashed a smile before walking out of the bedchamber. She hobbled to a room at the back and peered into the garden, telling herself she just wanted to be certain he left by the rear of the house. She could never allow him to call upon her, but she could gain one last glimpse.

He, no more than a shadow now, appeared in the garden and crossed to the back gate with a long-legged stride. When he reached it he turned back towards the house and lifted his face to the upper windows. With a gasp, Lydia jumped back, although she doubted he could have seen her. Slowly he turned back to the gate, opened it a crack, and peeked out before walking through, out of her sight.

Out of her life.

Chapter Two

What magic allure does the Lady possess, to turn a man to such desperate acts? Who will her next victim be, this Siren, this daughter of Achelous, who sings men to their deaths?   —*The New Observer*, November 12, 1818

Adrian entered White's gentlemen's club, his senses still humming, the lovemaking with Lydia still vibrating through him so powerfully he wondered if others could sense it.

He felt strong and masculine and completely devoid of the amorphous discontent with which he'd been lately plagued. It had vanished when he had walked into Lady Wexin's life. Adrian fought the impulse to turn around and retrace his steps to John Street, to scale the walls of her garden if necessary, to enter her house, and repeat the lovemaking that had stirred his senses to such heights.

The footman stationed at the door of White's greeted Adrian with undisputed normality, chatting about the weather while assisting Adrian out of his coat. Adrian glanced over to the bow window, but no one sat there. He made his way through the club to the coffee room.

Several men nodded a greeting, and Adrian had to suppress

a smile. They had no idea that he'd just left the bed of one of London's most beautiful, and now most notorious, women. And they would never know of it.

A voice called from across the room, "Cavanley! Over here. Join us."

Adrian glanced around, expecting to see someone summoning his father, but it was his father who was waving to him from a table in the corner of the room. Adrian rubbed his face in dismay. He, not his father, was Cavanley now.

Since Adrian's father had inherited the title Earl of Varcourt from a distant and elderly cousin who had very recently passed away, Adrian now had the use, by courtesy, of his father's lesser title of Viscount Cavanley. Inheriting his father's titles with all their rights, responsibility, and property would only occur upon his father's death. At present, he merely gained the privilege of being called Viscount Cavanley. Adjusting to the new appellation was more difficult than he'd anticipated.

The new Earl of Varcourt waved with more vigour, signalling Adrian to join him. His father sat with the Marquess of Heronvale and Heronvale's brother-in-law, Lord Levenhorne.

Adrian crossed the room and greeted them. "Good evening to you." He bowed to each in turn. "Lord Heronvale. Lord Levenhorne. Father."

His father gestured for him to sit. "What are you drinking, son?"

"Port will do," Adrian responded.

His father clicked his fingers to a nearby footman. "Port for Lord Cavanley," he cried in a loud voice.

At least his father had no difficulty using his son's new title.

The new Lord Varcourt turned back to Adrian. "Are you bound for the card room?"

Adrian's father relished his son's success at cards, boasting that Adrian's winnings would eclipse the family fortune one of these days. An exaggeration, of course, although Adrian did often win.

"Not today," he replied.

His father beamed and turned to Heronvale and Levenhorne. "It is said my son won a bundle off Sedford the other night."

Adrian drummed his fingers against the white linen tablecloth. "The cards were good to me."

The loss must have hurt Sedford, Adrian thought with some guilt, but he guessed Sedford would be in the card room again tonight, drinking just as heavily, losing just as swiftly. Sedford would be better off if he spent more time at his wife's musicales, even if they were deadly affairs.

"They say Sedford played foolishly." Levenhorne drained his glass and signalled the footman for another drink. "I'm sick to death of reckless card players and the problems they cause others."

"I'd heard the man enjoyed cards a great deal more than his skill at them ought to have permitted," Heronvale said.

Adrian glanced from one to the other. "You have lost me. Do you speak of Sedford?"

"Of Wexin," his father explained. "We were speaking of Wexin before you arrived. Levenhorne stands to inherit his title, you know."

Levenhorne rolled his eyes. "Of course, I must wait the blasted ten months to see if Wexin's widow produces an heir. Ten months during which I could be solving problems that are likely to be mine and will only become worse for the wait."

Adrian straightened in his chair.

The law gave a peer's widow ten months to give birth to an heir. As next in line to inherit, Levenhorne had no choice but to wait.

Levenhorne gave a dry laugh. "It is fortunate Wexin died, is it not? Things would be in even more of a mess if he'd been hanged for treason."

Seizure of the title, forfeiture of the property—all would have been possible had Wexin been convicted and hanged. It was complicated, indeed, but Levenhorne could not know how truly complicated. Tanner had confided to Adrian that Wexin shot himself, but Tanner had convinced the Scottish officials to declare Wexin's death accidental. "To minimise the scandal and ease Lady Wexin's suffering," Tanner had explained. It also vastly simplified the settling of Wexin's estate.

"Ah, the drinks have arrived." Levenhorne looked towards the footman who approached the table carrying a tray. He grabbed his glass, shaking his head. "Wexin's debts are staggering. The man owes money all over town." He took a fortifying drink. "Or I should say, owed money. He was damned reckless in his spending. Or perhaps it was Lady Wexin who spent like an empress. The trustee has clamped down on her, I tell you."

"Indeed?" Adrian's interest increased.

Levenhorne shrugged. "Her father will pay her debts, I suspect, although he will be none too pleased when he discovers the townhouse he purchased as a wedding gift is now mortgaged to the hilt."

Adrian's father spoke up. "I heard Strathfield was on a tour. His son as well. Headed to Egypt and India."

Strathfield was Lydia's father and as wealthy as any man could wish.

"True." Levenhorne waved a dismissive hand. "Let her depend on her sister, then." Lydia's sister had married quite well. "I'll be damned if I'll use my own funds."

Adrian frowned.

Heronvale broke in. "Her sister's husband has refused any contact, my wife tells me." He sipped his drink. "In my opinion Lady Wexin deserves our pity, not our castigation. The newspapers are brutal to her."

Adrian's father grinned. "Did you see the caricature in the

window at Ackermann's? It shows her and Wexin standing with a clergyman while Wexin hides a long, bloody knife. One had to laugh at it."

Adrian failed to see the humour. He tapped on his glass. "Tanner told me Lady Wexin knew nothing about Wexin killing Corland. In fact, Tanner told me that Wexin's motive was to have been kept confidential."

Tanner had been on the run with the woman fugitive whom Wexin had framed for Viscount Corland's murder. The newspapers called her the Vanishing Viscountess and, at the time, her name filled the papers like Lydia's did now. Tanner had married her in Scotland, and she and Tanner were the ones who had exposed Wexin.

"Who divulged that he'd killed Corland before the man could ruin his chance to marry her, I wonder?" Heronvale frowned. "Someone present at the inquest, I suppose."

Adrian's father laughed. "Come now. Who could resist? Tanner is a fool to think such delicious gossip can be silenced."

Heronvale looked at Adrian. "Tanner is certain of her innocence?"

Adrian bristled at the question. "He assures me she had nothing to do with her husband's crimes."

Levenhorne lifted his glass to his lips. "I am not so certain. The papers speculate she knew what Wexin was about."

Adrian gripped the edge of the table, angry at this man's insistence on believing the worst of Lydia. Had he not heard Adrian say that Tanner had proclaimed her innocence? Did they believe a newspaper over a marquess?

Another worry nagged at him, one that explained the unlit fire and the absence of servants, if not the purse full of coin.

"How severe was Wexin's debt?" Adrian asked Levenhorne.

Levenhorne leaned back in his chair. "He was in dun territory, both feet in the River Tick. The whole matter of his estate is a shambles. The executor is Lady Wexin's brother, who is on that bloody tour of Egypt or wherever." He shook his head in disgust. "Mr Coutts, the banker, you know, is the trustee. He had the audacity to ask me for funds, which I refused, I tell you."

Adrian glanced away. Poor Lydia! Adrian could not simply walk away from her difficulties without assisting her, could he?

Lydia sat up in the bed where only two hours before she'd made love with a man she barely knew, one of London's most profligate rakes. She wrapped her arms around herself, remembering the passion of his lovemaking, the delightful pleasures he had given her. His reputation as a lover was deserved, well deserved.

She blushed. Her life was a shambles, a mockery, a laughing stock. She was a widow who could not grieve, a lady who could not pay her debts, a daughter who could not run to her parents. Only God knew where her parents or brother might be. Greece. Egypt. India. She'd written to all the places on their itinerary. Her sister, merely a few streets away, had been forbidden to help her. Forbidden to see her. And what was Lydia doing? Tumbling into bed with the handsome Adrian Pomroy.

Her maid knocked and entered the room, carrying a tray. "Cook said tomorrow we will have soup, but tonight there is but cheese and bread. I've brought you wine. We seem to have a lot of wine."

Her husband had a great fondness for purchasing the very best wine. Perhaps she could sell it. How would one go about selling one's wine? She must discuss the idea with her butler.

She smiled at her maid. "It is good of you to bring my meal above stairs, Mary."

When the other servants had left, Mary, one of the housemaids, had begged to stay and act as Lydia's lady's maid. The girl took her new duties very seriously.

Mary set the tray upon its legs so that it formed a bed table across Lydia's lap. "I ought to have been with you, my lady." The girl frowned. "I told you not to go to the shops alone."

But Lydia needed to go to the shops. Had she not, they would have had no money at all. She'd taken several pieces of her jewellery to Mr Gray on Sackville Street and he had given her a fair price.

"Do not fret, Mary," Lydia responded. "I would have twisted my ankle had you been there or not." That odious newspaperman would not have allowed a mere maid to deter his pursuit, but events would have transpired very differently if Mary had been there when Adrian had come to the rescue.

She must not think of him.

"You deserved a visit to your mother." Lydia's voice came out louder than she intended. "Is she well?"

"Indeed, very well, my lady, thank you for asking." The girl curtsied. "My brothers and sisters are growing so big. Mum expects them to go into service soon. She is making inquiries."

"I wish I could help them." Once Lydia might have given Mary's siblings a recommendation, but now a connection to the scandalous Lady Wexin was best hidden.

"They'll find work, never you fear," said Mary, plumping the pillows.

Would Mary be able to smell Adrian upon the linens? Lydia could. She felt her cheeks burn again and turned her face away, pretending to adjust the coverlet.

"Lord knows how you got yourself home and up the stairs," Mary went on. She peered in the direction of Lydia's foot, even though it was under the covers. "You even wrapped your ankle." She looked pensive. "And managed to undress yourself."

"I wanted to get in bed." Lydia's cheeks flamed. How true those words were!

She glanced quickly at Mary, but the girl did not seem to

notice any change in her complexion. Lydia would be mortified if even her loyal Mary discovered her great moral lapse.

Mary straightened the bedcovers again and stepped back.
"Is there anything else I can do for you, my lady?"

Dixon, her butler, and Cook would be waiting for Mary below
stairs where they would share their meal in the kitchen, the other
warm room in the house. "You took the purse to Dixon, did you
not? Was there enough to pay the household accounts?"

"I gave him the purse, my lady, but I do not know about
the household accounts. Shall I ask Mr Dixon to come up to
speak to you?"

Lydia shook her head. "I would not trouble him now.
Tomorrow will do." Let her servants enjoy an evening of
idleness. Goodness knows the three of them had toiled hard
to keep the house in order and to take care of her, doing the
work of eight. Lydia missed the footmen, housemaids and
kitchen maid she'd had to dismiss. The house was so quiet
without them.

Mary curtsied again. "I'll come back for the tray and to
ready you for bed."

Lydia gazed at the girl, so young and pretty and eager to
please. Mary would be valued in any household, yet she'd
chosen to remain with Lydia. Tears filled her eyes. She did
not know if she could ever pay her, let alone repay her. "Thank
you, Mary."

Mary curtsied again and left the room.

Adrian's father lingered after Heronvale and Levenhorne
took their leave, both hurrying home to dinner with their
wives. "What diversion awaits you this evening, son?"

Adrian tilted his chin. "None, unless I accepted an invitation I no longer recall."

His father looked at him queryingly. "No visits to a gaming
hell? Or, better yet, no lusty opera dancer awaiting you after

her performance? A young buck like you must have something exciting planned."

Adrian finished his second glass of port. "Not a thing."

"You are welcome to dinner, then. Your mother and I dine alone this evening. I am certain she would be pleased to see you." His father stood. "Come."

Why not? thought Adrian. A glance around the room revealed no better company with whom to pass the time, and he had a particular dislike of being alone this night.

As they strolled through the streets of Mayfair where all the fashionable people lived, Adrian was mindful that he'd walked nearly this same route before. The Varcourt house, part of his father's new inheritance, was on Berkeley Square, only a few roads away from Lydia's townhouse on Hill Street.

And the garden gate he'd carried her through on John Street.

"You are quiet today," his father remarked.

Adrian glanced over at him, realising he had not uttered a word since they'd left White's. "Forgive me, Father. I suppose I was woolgathering."

His father's brow wrinkled. "It is not like you at all. Are you ill? Or have you got yourself in some scrape or another?"

"Neither." Adrian smiled. "Not likely I'd tell you if I were in a scrape, though."

His father laughed. "You have the right of it. Never knew you not to get yourself out of whatever bumble-broth you'd landed in."

It was perhaps more accurate to say Tanner always managed the disentanglement, but Adrian's father probably knew that very well.

"What is it, then, my son?" his father persisted.

Adrian certainly did not intend to tell his father about his encounter with Lady Wexin. Likely his father would see it as a conquest about which he could brag to his friends. Adrian was not in the habit of worrying over the secrecy of his affairs, but Lady Wexin's name had been bandied about so unfairly, he had no wish to add to the gossip about her.

Adrian did wish he could explain to his father the discontent he'd been feeling lately. His father would in all likelihood pooh-pooh it as nonsense, however.

His father seemed to believe there could be no better life than the one Adrian led, spending his days and nights gambling, womanising and sporting. Adrian had lately wished for more than horse races or card games or opera dancers, however. He was tired of having no occupation, no purpose, of feeling it would take his father's death to bring some utility to his existence.

Adrian's discontent had begun about a year ago when he'd accompanied Tanner on a tour of his friend's estates. He'd marvelled at Tanner's knowledge of his properties and the people who saw to the running of them. Adrian had learned a great deal about farming, raising livestock, and managing a country estate during that trip, more than his father had ever taught him. Adrian's restlessness had increased recently after learning of Tanner's sudden marriage. He did not begrudge his friend's newfound domestic happiness; surprisingly enough, he envied it.

His father came to an abrupt halt. "Good God, this is not about some woman, is it? Do not tell me. I'll wager it is Lady Denson. The word is she is quite enamoured of you, as well any woman would be."

An image of Lydia flew into Adrian's mind, not Viola Denson, who had indeed engaged in a flirtation with Adrian, but one in which he could not sustain an interest.

"Not Lady Denson," he replied. "Nor any woman, if you must know."

And it seemed his father always wanted to know about Adrian's romantic conquests. He told his father as little as possible about them.

If his father were paying attention to more than Adrian's love life and gambling wins, he'd recall that his son had asked to take over some of the family's lesser holdings. He'd thought it proper to ease his father's new burdens of all the Varcourt properties, but the new Earl of Varcourt would have none of it. "Plenty of time for all that," his father had said. "Enjoy yourself while you can."

Adrian glanced at his father, a faithful husband, excellent manager, dutiful member of the House of Lords. His father might glorify the delights of his son's bachelorhood, but, even without those delights in his own life, his father was a contented man.

Unlike Adrian.

Adrian attempted to explain. "I am bored—"

His father laughed. "Bored? A young buck like you? Why, you can do anything you wish. Enjoy life."

He could do anything, perhaps, but nothing of value, Adrian thought. "The enjoyment is lacking at the moment."

"Lacking? Impossible." His father clapped him on the shoulder. "You sound like a man in need of a new mistress."

Again Adrian thought of Lydia.

"Find yourself a new woman," his father advised. "That's the ticket. That Denson woman, if she wants it."

Typical of his father to think in that manner. His father had inherited young, married young and lived a life of exemplary conduct, but that did not stop him from enjoying the exploits of his son.

"Do not forget," his father went on, "your friend Tanner's marriage has deprived you of some companionship, but you'll soon accustom yourself to going about without him." His father laughed. "Imagine Tanner in a Scottish marriage. With the Vanishing Viscountess, no less. Just like him to enter into some ramshackle liaison and wind up smelling of roses."

Indeed. Under the most unlikely of circumstances Tanner

had met the perfect woman for him. Why, his wife was even a baroness in her own right, a very proper wife for a marquess.

Adrian's father launched into a repeat of the whole story of Tanner's meeting the Vanishing Viscountess, of aiding her flight and of them both thwarting Wexin. Adrian only half-listened.

Adrian glanced at his father. The man was as tall, straight-backed and clear-eyed as he'd been all Adrian's life. Even his blond hair was only lately fading to white. He did not need Adrian's help managing the properties or anything else.

Adrian was nearly seven and thirty years. How long would it be before he had any responsibility at all?

"Did you know Wexin's townhouse is on Hill Street?" he suddenly heard his father say.

"Mmm," Adrian managed. Of course he knew.

"Strathfield purchased it as a wedding gift. Nice property. There's been a pack of newspaper folks hanging around the door for days now. I agree with Levenhorne. Those newspaper fellows know a thing or two about Lady Wexin that we do not."

Adrian bristled. "Tanner says—"

His father scoffed. "Yes. Yes. Tanner says she is innocent, but when you have lived as long as I have, son, you learn that where one sees smoke, there is usually fire."

There was certainly a fire within Lady Wexin, but not the sort to which his father referred.

They reached Berkeley Square. His father stopped him before the door of the Varcourt house. "When your mother gives the word, you must give up your rooms and take over the old townhouse. She is still dithering about what furniture to move, I believe, so I do not know how long it will take."

Splendid. Adrian had wanted an estate to manage. He would wind up with a house instead.

Samuel Reed stood among three other reporters near the entrance of Lady Wexin's townhouse. His feet pained him, he was hungry, chilled to the bone and tired of this useless vigil. The lady was not going to emerge.

"I say we take turns," one of the men was saying. "We agree to share any information about who enters the house or where she goes if she ventures out."

"You talk a good game," another responded. "But how do we know you would keep your word? You'd be the last fellow to tell what you know."

The man was wrong. *Reed* would be the last fellow to tell what he knew. He was determined that *The New Observer*, the newspaper he and his brother Phillip owned, would have exclusive information about Lady Wexin. He'd not said a word to the others that he'd caught the lady out and about. She'd been walking from the direction of the shops. Why had she gone off alone?

He glanced at the house, but there was nothing to see. Curtains covered the windows. "I'm done for today," he told the others.

"Don't expect us to tell you if something happens," one called to him.

Reed walked down John Street, slowing his pace as he passed the garden entrance. He peered through a crack between the planks of the wooden gate.

To his surprise, the rear door opened, though it was not Lady Wexin who emerged but her maid, shaking out table linen.

Reed's stomach growled. It appeared that Lady Wexin had enjoyed a dinner. He certainly had not. He watched the maid, a very pretty little thing with dark auburn hair peeking out from beneath her cap. Reed had seen the young woman before, had even followed her the previous day when she'd gone to the market. For the last several days, Reed had seen only this maid and the butler entering and leaving the house. He'd surmised that Lady Wexin had dismissed most of the servants.

He'd been able to locate one of Lady Wexin's former

footmen, but the man refused to confirm whether or not other servants had left her employment. The man had refused to say anything newsworthy about Lady Wexin, but perhaps a maid might have knowledge a footman would not.

He watched her fold the cloth and re-enter the house. A carriage sounded at the end of the street, and he quickly darted into the shadows until the carriage continued past him.

He glanced at the moonlit sky. Time to walk back to the newspaper offices, get some dinner and write his story for the next edition, such as it was.

If only he could identify the gentleman who had come to Lady Wexin's aid. He could make something of that information. The man was familiar, but he did not know all the gentlemen of the *ton* by sight. He'd keep his eyes open, though, and hope to discover the man's identity soon enough.

Chapter Three

The scandalous Lady W— walks about Mayfair without a companion...or was it her intention to rendez-
vous with a certain gentleman? Beware, fine sir. Recall
to what ends a man may be driven when Beauty is the
prize... —*The New Observer*, November 14, 1818

Sheets of relentless rain kept indoors all but the unfortunate
few whose livelihood forced them outside. Adrian was not in
this category, but he willingly chose to venture forth with the
rain dripping from the brim of his hat, the damp soaking its
way through his topcoat and water seeping into his boots.

He turned into Hill Street, watchful for the reporters who'd
lounged around Lady Wexin's door the previous day when
he'd made it a point to stroll by. As he suspected and dared
hope, no one was in sight.

To be certain, he continued past the house to the end of the
street and then back again. Not another living creature was about.

Apparently there were some things a newspaper reporter
would not do in pursuit of a story, like standing in the pouring
rain in near freezing temperatures. Adrian was not so faint of
heart. What was a little water dripping from the brim of his

hat, soaking his collar and causing his neck to chafe? A mere annoyance when he might see Lydia again.

Still, he wished he might have brought his umbrella.

Adrian strode up to the green door of the Wexin townhouse and sounded the brass lion's-head knocker.

No one answered.

He sounded the knocker again and pressed his ear against the wooden door. He heard heels click on the hall's marble floor.

"Open," he called through the door. "It is Pomroy. Calling upon Lady Wexin."

"Who?" a man's muffled voice asked.

"Pomroy," Adrian responded. He paused. He'd forgotten again. "Lord Cavanley," he said louder.

He heard the footsteps receding, but pounded with the knocker again, huddling in the narrow doorcase so that only his back suffered the soaking rain. He planned to knock until he gained entry.

Finally, the footsteps returned and the door was opened a crack, a man's eye visible in it.

"I am Lord Cavanley, calling upon Lady Wexin." Adrian spoke through the crack.

The eye stared.

"On a matter of business." Adrian reached into his pocket and pulled out a slightly damp card. He handed it through the narrow opening. "Have pity, man. Do you think I wish to stand out in the rain?"

The eye disappeared and, after a moment, the crack widened to reveal Lady Wexin's butler. The man was of some indeterminate age, anywhere from thirty to fifty. He did not wear livery and possessed the right mix of hauteur and servitude that befitted a butler. Adrian liked the protective look in the man's eye.

"Be so good as to wait here a moment, m'lord." The butler bowed and walked away, his heels clicking on each step as he ascended the marble stairs.

Adrian remembered carrying Lydia up those flights of stairs.

His gaze followed the butler, puzzled as to why the man had not taken his coat and hat, but left him standing in the hall like a visiting merchant.

Adrian removed his hat and gloves as puddles formed at his feet on the marble floor. The gilded table still held its vases, and the vases were still empty of flowers.

Finally the butler's footsteps sounded again as he descended and made his unhurried way back to Adrian. "I will take you to Lady Wexin."

Adrian handed him his hat and gloves and removed his soaked topcoat carefully so as to lessen both the size of the puddles and the amount of rainwater pouring down the back of his neck. He waited again while the butler disappeared with the sodden items, daring to hope the man might lay them out in front of some fire to dry a bit.

When the butler returned, he led Adrian up the stairs to a first-floor drawing room. Even standing in the doorway, Adrian could feel the room's chill. There was a fire in the fireplace, but Adrian guessed it must have just been lit.

Lydia's back was to him. She stood with arms crossed in front of her, facing the window that looked out at the rain.

"Lord Cavanley," the butler announced.

She turned, and her beautiful sapphire eyes widened. "You!"

The butler stepped between her and Adrian.

She waved a dismissive hand. "It is all right, Dixon. I will see this gentleman."

Frowning, the butler bowed, tossing Adrian a suspicious glance as he walked out of the room and closed the door behind him.

Adrian was taken aback. "I announced myself to your man."

She shook her head. "But you are Mr Pomroy."

He realised the mistake. "Forgive me." He smiled at her. "You must not know me as Cavanley."

"I certainly do not!" She stepped forwards and gripped the back of a red velvet chair. Her forehead suddenly furrowed. "Did…did your father pass away? I confess, I did not know—"

He held up his hand. "Nothing like that." He caught himself staring at her and gave himself a mental shake. "Well, a cousin of his passed away, but he was quite elderly and had been ill for many years. My father inherited the title, Earl of Varcourt, so his lesser title passed to me." Good God. He was babbling. He took a breath. "How is your ankle?"

Stepping around the chair, she stared at him as if he had just sprouted horns. "It troubles me little."

"I am glad of it," he said. His voice sounded stiff.

She walked closer to him and his breath was again stolen by her beauty. Her golden hair sparkled from the fire in the hearth and lamps that he suspected had also been hastily lit. While the rest of the room faded into greyness, like the rainy day, she appeared bathed in a warm glow, as if all the light in the room was as drawn to her as he was. She wore a dress of rich blue, elegantly cut. Its sole adornment was a thick velvet ribbon tied in a bow beneath her breasts. A paisley shawl was wrapped around her shoulders, the blue in its woven print complementing her dress and her eyes.

She cast her gaze down. "Why do you call upon me, sir, when I asked that you not do so?" Her voice was steady, but no louder than a whisper.

Once Adrian might have cheekily proclaimed that he could not resist calling upon her, that her beauty beckoned him, that the memory of their lovemaking could never be erased. Once he would have presented reasons why their affair ought to continue, needed to continue, and that he was there because he could not stay away.

Those sentiments were true, but his decision to call upon her involved another matter. Still, it stung that she looked so wounded and angry. "Did you think it was my father who called upon you?"

"I did," she admitted.

He stiffened. "You would have allowed my father entry, but not me?"

"I would."

He shook his head, puzzled. "But why?"

She glanced away. "I thought perhaps your father was on an errand for Lord Levenhorne. He and Levenhorne are friends." She glanced back at him. "They are friends, are they not?"

"Indeed." All the *ton* knew they were friends.

She went on. "Levenhorne is my husband's heir, and I thought perhaps it truly was a matter of business, as you told Dixon it was."

Adrian did not miss her accusing tone. He had told the butler that one lie. Although, in a way, it *was* business.

He took a breath, releasing it slowly before speaking, "I did not mean to deceive you, Lydia. I merely wished to see you."

Her eyes flashed. "I cannot believe you thought I would welcome this visit." She snatched a newspaper from a table. "Did you not read this? That reporter connects us."

He had indeed read *The New Observer* and every other newspaper that mentioned the notorious Lady W. "The reporter did not name me. I fully comprehend that you do not wish any contact between us to be known. I would not have come but for the rain. I knew the weather would drive the reporters away from your doorstep."

She gave a mirthless laugh. "Do you think it matters to me that the man did not name you? It is *my* name that suffers! I am linked to a gentleman. There will be no end to what will be written about me now." She threw the paper back on the table.

"I merely responded to your need," he retorted. "I refuse to apologise for it."

"My need?" Her voice rose.

"Yes," Adrian shot back. "That man was attacking you. I could not walk by and do nothing."

"Oh." Her shoulders slumped. "That need. My need for rescue, you meant."

He realised that she'd thought he meant the other needs they'd indulged that day.

Their gazes connected and it seemed as if those needs flared between them again, like the hiss of red coals about to burst into flame. He wanted to cross the room, to touch her and re-ignite the passion that was burning inside him, as real as the thumping of his heart, the deep drawing of his breath, the pulsing of blood through his veins.

However, his purpose in calling upon her had not been to indulge in that pleasure again, to enjoy each other as they had done before, although Adrian could see no harm in it. Society rarely censured a widow for such conduct as long as she acted discreetly, and he could be very discreet.

Of course, she was not just any widow. She was society's latest scandal.

"Lydia." The sound of her name on his tongue felt as soft and smooth as her ivory skin. "I have no wish to see you harmed in any way. I will keep our association secret."

She laughed. "Do you think I believe in secrets, Adrian?" She stepped closer. "I have been hurt by secrets. Those kept and those divulged."

She was so close Adrian's nostrils scented lilacs. Her eyes, however, were filled with pain and accusation.

He wanted to assure her he was a good sort of man, with a good proposition for her if she would only listen to him.

"My husband kept secrets from me," she went on, lifting her gaze to his. "What makes you think I can trust anything you say?"

He had no answer.

He forced himself to look directly into her lovely face.

"Please know, dear lady, that I speak truly when I say I have no wish to hurt you, no wish to ever hurt you." He gave her a wan smile. "I told you before that I would act as your friend. I came here as such."

"A friend." Her gaze softened.

She stepped forwards and touched his arm. Even through his layers of clothing, the contact seared him with need, a need he knew he must deny. When he looked in her eyes, though, he saw a yearning to match his own.

"Lydia," he whispered.

Lydia thought she must have gone completely mad. She gazed into his eyes and was content to be caught there, like a leaf caught in a whirlpool that pulled it into its depths.

She ought to send him away now. She ought to forget what she'd done two days before, wantonly bedding him, a man well known for his conquests of women.

He had acted nothing like she'd supposed a rake would act. He had never pushed himself on her, never spoke words of seduction. She had pushed herself on him, in fact. *She* had been the one who'd spoken words of seduction. And she felt herself about to do so again.

Her hand on his arm trembled against the fabric of his coat, damp from where the rain had soaked through. She had only to move her hand away and let him go.

Instead, she raised her hand to his face and lightly grazed his cheek.

God help her, she *was* weak. And wanton.

From the moment of seeing him framed in the doorway, her body had craved the return of his touch, the passion of his lovemaking.

She traced her finger from his temple to the perpetually upturned corner of his mouth. He remained still, giving her the power to choose if she wanted more or not. She almost wished he would seize her now, take her by force. Even though his eyes darkened and his breathing accelerated, he still waited for her to choose.

What harm would it do? she thought. What harm to have his arms around her again, to have his practised touch drive away the worries that seemed to double and triple with each passing day? She was lonely. What harm to pass time with him? He knew the same people, attended the same entertainments. She missed being a part of it all more than she would have guessed.

But what she missed most was what a man could give her, what Adrian had given her. If the newspapers only knew what a wanton woman she'd turned out to be, a woman who bedded a man merely because he'd been kind. She shuddered to think what would be written of her if they knew.

She let her hand fall away.

Adrian's gaze turned puzzled. He did not say a word. He did not move. He would leave if she told him to, she knew.

Or he would stay.

Her choice.

She stepped closer to him, her aching ankle reminding her how he had so gently tended it. What had come after his gentle care now consumed her. His kiss. What his touch had aroused in her.

What harm to feel that delight one more time? What harm?

Lydia slid her hands up his chest until her arms encircled his neck. The hair at the nape tickled her fingers and his collar felt cool and damp. She rose on tiptoe and tilted her face to him, letting him know she'd made her choice.

He groaned with a man's need and bent forwards, placing his lips on hers, tentatively, as if he still would permit her to change her mind.

She did not want to change her mind. She wanted her body to sing with the pleasure he could create. She wanted to be joined to him, like one. She wanted to not be so terribly alone.

He drew away slightly, then crushed his lips against hers with a man's command. The effect was exhilarating.

His kiss, familiar but new, deepened. Her lips parted and their tongues touched, the sensation intimate and delighting.

He pressed her to him, and she could feel the evidence of his arousal beneath his clothing. That womanly part of her ached with desire to feel his length inside her again. She wanted him to sweep her away, to make her forget everything but him.

Her heart pounded wildly.

She'd once forgotten everything but Wexin. Wexin's kisses—chaste compared to Adrian's—had once made her feel secure in a future of happiness, but Wexin, while kissing her, had the stain of blood on his hands, the murder of a friend.

Lydia pushed hard against Adrian's chest and backed away. The look he gave her was wild, heated, aroused and confused.

She put a hand to her forehead. "Forgive me." She dared to glance into his eyes. "Forgive me. I cannot do this. I must not."

He breathed heavily, and it seemed to her he was fighting to keep calm.

"Lydia." His voice was so low she seemed to feel it more than hear it. "Why deny this passion between us?"

She stared at him. How could she explain that she could never again allow a man to have that sort of power over her?

"I must deny it." Her voice sounded mournful and weak. She must never again be weak. She lifted her chin. "Please leave, Adrian. Do not return." She walked behind the chair again and clutched its back.

"Lydia." His eyes pleaded.

She held up a hand. "Do not press me, Adrian." She took a deep breath. "I have enough worries."

He turned and started to walk away. Lydia did not know which feeling was the greater: relief at his departure, or sorrow.

Before he reached the door, he stopped and turned back. "Before I walk out, tell me something, Lydia."

She waited.

He looked directly into her eyes. "Do you need money?"

She inhaled sharply. "What makes you think I need money?"

His hand swept the room. "You light fires only for show. You have no flowers. And there is the matter of your servants—"

"I have servants," she retorted. Well, three servants, but he need not know the number was so small.

Would he tell the creditors and reporters? If word of her true situation escaped, all of England would know the shocking state of her finances. Even Levenhorne and the men at the bank did not know how bad it was, how close they'd come to having nothing to eat.

"I came here to offer you help," he said. "How much money do you need?"

"I don't need money." She felt her cheeks heat. "But if I did, I would not take yours."

His brows rose. "Why?"

"Why?" She gave a nervous laugh. "Would that not mean I was in your keeping? Do not mistresses accept money from their…patrons?"

His eyes creased at the corners. "I make the offer as a friend, nothing more."

She glanced away. Truth was, she still needed money for the most pressing debts. It would buy her time until her parents returned and her father could help her. At present, her only hope was that her sister could find a way to help her, to get money to her without her husband's knowledge. Lydia had sent Mary to pass on a letter through her sister's maid.

"I do not need your money, Adrian," she whispered.

"I offer it without obligation."

He said this so sincerely, she almost believed him, but she'd believed Wexin, a murderer who professed to love her, who bought her trinkets, while spending every penny of her dowry. It made no sense that a near-stranger, a known rake, would offer her money without expecting something in return.

"It is not your place to help me," she told Adrian. She blinked. "*If* I needed help, that is." She squared her shoulders and forced herself to look directly into his eyes. "Please leave now, Adrian."

For a moment he looked as if he would cross the room to her, but instead, he turned and walked to the door. She twisted away, not wishing to watch him disappear out of her life.

His voice came from behind her. "I am your friend, Lydia. Remember that."

She spun back around, but he had gone.

Chapter Four

All eyes are on Kew Palace this day where the Queen
remains gravely ill, her physicians declaring the state of
her health to be one of "great and imminent danger"
—*The New Observer*, November 15, 1818

Samuel Reed lounged in the wooden chair while his brother,
Phillip, the manager and editor of *The New Observer*, sat
behind the desk, his face blocked by the newspaper he held
in front of him.

"We must find something more interesting than the
Queen's illness for tomorrow's paper, else we'll be reduced
to printing handbills and leaflets like Father."

Their father had been a printer with no ambition, except to
see how much gin he could consume every night. It was not
until the man died of a drunken fall from the second-storey
window of a Cheapside brothel that Samuel and Phillip could
realise their much loftier ambitions: to publish a newspaper.

They were determined to make *The New Observer* the
most popular newspaper in London, and Samuel's stories
about Lady Wexin had definitely set it on its way. Each
London newspaper had its speciality, and the Reed brothers

had deliberately carved out their own unique niche. Not for them political commentary or a commitment to social change. The Reed brothers specialised in society gossip and stories of murder and mayhem, the more outrageous the better.

"Anything interesting in the out-of-town papers?" Samuel asked.

"Not much…" Phillip's voice trailed off.

Like all the newspapers, they freely stole from others, often passing the stories off as their own. Every day Phillip perused the out-of-town papers looking for the sort of sensational and unusual stories that fitted their requirements.

The New Observer had other reporters besides Samuel to provide shocking or remarkable items from all around London, including the seediest neighbourhoods. Fascination with the most lofty and with the lowest, that was what the Reed brothers banked upon.

Samuel rose and sauntered towards the window. At least the rain had passed. The previous day had been nothing but rain, and, therefore, precious little news.

"Here's something." Phillip leaned forwards. "Fellow in Mile End set a spring gun to shoot at intruders. Except his own feet tripped the wire and he shot himself. Died from it."

"That's reasonably interesting."

"Not to the fellow who died." His brother laughed.

Phillip picked up another paper and read. "The spinners are still rioting in Manchester." He rolled up the paper and tapped it on the desk. "What news of Lady Wexin?"

Lady Wexin guaranteed profit.

"Nothing from yesterday because of the rain." Samuel examined the grey sky. "If you send someone else to watch her house today, I will set about discovering the identity of the gentleman who came to her aid."

Phillip grinned. "The gentleman who rescued her from you, do you mean?"

Samuel returned the smile. "I mean precisely that."

Samuel had a plan to scour St James's Street where White's and Brooks's were located. Whether this fellow be Tory or Whig, he'd walk down St James's Street to reach his club.

Phillip crossed his arms over his chest. "Her Majesty the Queen is doing poorly. We need some detail about her illness that the other papers do not know."

Another priority of the paper was royal news, and the Reed brothers would not make the same mistake as Leigh and John Hunt, who went to prison for printing a mild criticism of the Prince Regent in the *Examiner*. *The New Observer* lavished praise on the royals.

"Do not send me to Kew Palace, I beg you." Samuel was eager to pursue what he considered his story. Lady Wexin.

"I would not dream of it." His brother waved his hand. "Hurry out there and find your gentleman."

Samuel soon found himself strolling back and forth on St James's Street, trying to look as if he had business there. He'd been strolling in the vicinity for at least an hour and was prepared to do so all day long, if necessary, until he laid eyes upon the gentleman who had come to Lady Wexin's assistance.

Samuel had done a great deal of thinking about why the lady would have ventured out alone that day. When he had first spied her, she'd been walking from the direction of the shops, but it was quite unlikely that a lady would visit the shops in the afternoon. That was the time young bucks lounged on street corners to watch gentlemen with their less-than-ladylike companions saunter by.

It was more likely Lady Wexin had been calling upon someone, but who? Samuel had not known her to make social calls since her husband's story became known.

Samuel's scanty exclusive—knowledge that she'd been

out and about alone and knowledge that a fine-looking gentleman had come to her aid—still gave him an edge over the other reporters who wasted their time watching her front door. All he needed was the tiniest piece of new information. Samuel was skilled at taking the tiniest bits of scandal and inflating them larger than any hot-air balloon.

Samuel reached the corner of St James's and Piccadilly, sweeping Piccadilly Street with his gaze.

Carriages and riders crowded the thoroughfare, and the pavement abounded with men in tall beaver hats and caped topcoats. Curses to that Beau Brummell. Gentlemen dressed too much the same these days because of him. Samuel searched for a man taller than average, one who carried himself like a Corinthian.

Such a man appeared in the distance. Samuel shaded his eyes with his hand and watched him for several seconds. He decided to come closer. Samuel crossed Piccadilly and walked towards him, holding on to the brim of his hat so the man would not see his face.

Within a foot of the man, Samuel's excitement grew. This was the one! His instincts never failed.

Samuel walked past the gentleman and doubled back as soon as he could, quickening his step. If he could follow close behind, perhaps he would hear someone greet the man by name.

To Samuel's surprise, the gentleman turned into New Bond Street. Samuel almost lost him when several nattily attired young fellows, laughing and shoving each other, blocked his way. His view cleared in time to see the man enter the jewellers Stedman & Vardon.

Jewellers?

Already Samuel had begun spinning stories of why the gentleman should enter a jewellery shop, all of them involving Lady Wexin. He preferred learning the real story. True stories had a way of being more fantastic than anything he could conjure up.

Samuel wandered to the doorway of the shop and peeked in. The gentleman spoke to the shop assistant and suddenly turned around to head back out the door. Samuel ducked aside as the man brushed past him.

Samuel ran inside the shop. "I beg your pardon," he said. "Who was that gentleman?"

The shop assistant looked up. "The gentleman who was just here?"

"Yes. Yes." Samuel glanced towards the door. He did not want to lose track of the man.

"Lord Cavanley, do you mean?"

"Cavanley!" Samuel's voice was jubilant. "Thank you, sir." He rushed out of the shop in time to catch a disappearing glimpse of the gentleman.

Lord Cavanley. Samuel did not know of a Lord Cavanley, but it should be an easy matter to learn about him.

Samuel hurried to catch up. He followed Cavanley to Sackville Street where he entered another jewellery shop. Puzzling. Perhaps Cavanley was searching for the perfect jewel. He did not, however, even glance at the sparkling gems displayed on black velvet beneath glass cases. He merely conversed with the older man with balding pate and spectacles. The jeweller, perhaps? In any event, the man seemed somewhat reluctant to speak to this lord.

Finally the jeweller nodded in seeming resignation and said something that apparently satisfied Cavanley. The men shook hands, the jeweller bowed, and Lord Cavanley strode out the door. Samuel turned quickly and pretended to examine something in the shop window next door.

After Cavanley passed by him, Samuel entered the shop. He smiled at the jeweller. "Good day to you, sir. I saw you with Lord Cavanley a moment ago. Did he make a purchase?"

The jeweller's eyes narrowed. "Why do you ask?"

Samuel dug into his pocket and pulled out his card. "I am a reporter for *The New Observer*. I am certain my readers would relish knowing what lovely object Lord Cavanley purchased."

The man frowned and the wrinkles in his face deepened. "His lordship purchased nothing, so you may go on your way."

"He purchased nothing?" Samuel, of course, had already surmised this. "Then what was his purpose here, I wonder?"

The jeweller peered at Samuel from over his spectacles. "Wonder all you wish. I am not about to tell you the business of a patron, am I now?"

Samuel gave the man his most congenial look. "I assure you, kind sir, our readers would relish knowing where a man with such exquisite taste in jewellery would shop. I dare say one mention of your establishment in our newspaper will bring you more customers than you can imagine."

"Hmph." The jeweller crossed his arms over his chest. "I am more interested in keeping the customers I have, thank you very much. Telling the world what they buy from me will not win me their loyalty."

"Sir—"

The man held up a hand. "No. No more talking." Another customer, more finely dressed than Samuel, entered the shop. "I must attend to this gentleman. Good day now. Run along."

Dismissed like an errant schoolboy.

Samuel bit down on a scathing retort. He might have need of this jeweller at a later time and he'd best not antagonise him. Back out on the pavement, he scanned the street for Lord Cavanley, but too much time had passed and the man was gone.

Samuel pushed his hat more firmly upon his head and turned in the direction of *The New Observer* offices. He planned to learn all he could about this Lord Cavanley. He'd start with old issues of their rival newspapers saved for just such a purpose.

* * *

Adrian dashed to a line of hackney coaches. "Thomas Coutts and Company on the Strand, if you please." He climbed in and leaned back against the leather seat.

At that last shop Mr Gray had confirmed what Adrian had suspected. Lydia had sold her jewels.

A lady did not resort to selling her jewels unless she was in desperate need of money. No matter her protestations to him, she was skimping on coal and candles, he was certain of it.

It rankled Adrian that Levenhorne and Wexin's trustee, a banker of considerable wealth, would allow an earl's wife to exist in such poverty. If her parents and brother were abroad and her sister forbidden to assist her, to whom could the lady turn for help?

Adrian had no connection to her, nor any obligation. It would certainly be commented upon if he stepped forwards to assist her, but assist her he would. In secret.

He smiled as the hackney coach swayed and bounced over the cobbled streets. At least he'd found something of interest to occupy his time. Solving the puzzle that was Lydia and easing her troubles seemed a better purpose than seating himself at a card table, checking out good horseflesh or, God forbid, entangling himself with Viola Denson. It mattered not one whit to Adrian that no one would know of it, least of all Lydia.

Although a part of him would not mind having Lydia look upon him with sapphire eyes filled with gratitude.

He shook that thought away. The coach passed Charing Cross as it turned into the Strand, and Adrian had a whiff of the Thames. He mulled over his plan until the hack stopped in front of Thomas Coutts and Company, a bank favoured by aristocrats and royalty. Adrian climbed down from the hack and paid its jarvey. He entered the bank.

In the marbled and pillared hall Adrian approached an attendant and identified himself. "I wish to speak with Mr Coutts. He is expecting me, I believe."

Earlier that morning Adrian had sent a message to Mr Coutts, telling of his intention to call.

The attendant escorted him to a chair and returned shortly to lead him to Mr Coutts's office.

As Adrian entered the room, the old gentleman rose from his seat behind a polished mahogany desk. "Ah, Lord Cavanley."

Adrian extended his hand. "Mr Coutts, it is a pleasure. Thank you for seeing me."

Coutts gestured for Adrian to sit. "Your note indicated that you wished to discuss Lord Wexin's estate?" The man looked wary.

Adrian smiled. "On behalf of a friend."

Mr Coutts nodded. "It is a trying affair, but I suspect there is little I might do for you. Allow me to direct you to Wexin's solicitor, who is tending to the entire matter."

"I would be grateful."

"Delighted," said Mr Coutts. "And how is your father? And the Marquess of Tannerton?"

Adrian responded, accustomed to people asking him about Tanner. In fact, in this situation, he'd counted upon it. Mr Coutts scribbled the direction of Wexin's solicitor on a sheet of paper and handed it to Adrian.

The solicitor's office was close by and Adrian quickly found the building and entered. A moment later he had been admitted to the man's office.

The solicitor was a younger man, near Adrian's age, but obviously trusted with a great deal more responsibility. His desk was littered with papers that he hurriedly stacked into neat piles at Adrian's entrance.

"I am Mr Newton, my lord," he said.

Adrian shook his hand and explained his purpose, stress-

ing it was at the behest of a friend that he inquired about Lady
Wexin's financial affairs.

Adrian's intention was to imply to Mr Newton that Lydia's
benefactor was Tanner, not Adrian. It was widely known that
Tanner was a generous man, the sort of man who would assist
Wexin's widow. No one would suspect the frivolous Adrian
Pomroy of such a thing.

"I am certain you understand that my friend—" Adrian em-
phasised the word *friend* "—does not wish his name to be
known. He fears the lady would refuse his assistance. My
friend would say, however, that it is the right thing for him to
do for her."

Because Tanner had been instrumental in exposing Wexin
as a murderer, it was not too much of a leap of the imagination
to think that Tanner might feel an obligation to assist Wexin's
innocent widow. In fact, Tanner would be very willing to assist
Lydia, if he knew she needed help. He was that kind of man.

Mr Newton blinked rapidly. "Of course, sir."

Adrian nodded. "The mar—my friend, I mean—" he
smiled "—sent me in his stead. He is anxious to discover if
Lady Wexin has any financial difficulty and, if so, charges me
to see it remedied."

"I do understand." Newton gestured to a chair and waited
for Adrian to sit. "Would you care for tea?"

"No, thank you." Adrian lowered himself into the chair.
"Tell me about Wexin's finances."

Newton rubbed his face. "Wexin's debts, you mean." He
peered at Adrian. "We speak in complete confidence, I presume."

"Indeed," Adrian agreed.

"Because even Lord Levenhorne does not know how bad
it is." Newton leaned over the desk. "There is nothing."

"Nothing?"

"Worse than nothing. The townhouse is mortgaged to the
hilt. There is only the entailed property, but even that is mort-

gaged, and it provides nothing to Lady Wexin. There is no money for Lady Wexin's widow's portion. I do not know how she is getting on. I have been unable to give her any funds at all." His hand fluttered. "She assures me she is able to manage, but I do not see how."

Adrian's chest constricted. "It is as I—we—feared." He straightened in his chair. "Tell us what needs to be done."

Newton pulled out a wooden box, opened the lid, and lifted out a handful of small pieces of paper, letting them flow through his fingers like water. "Gentlemen have sent their vowels." He picked up a stack of papers. "Shopkeepers have delivered their bills—"

Adrian had no interest in Wexin's debts. His purpose here was solely for Lydia. "What was the marriage settlement supposed to provide Lady Wexin?"

Newton closed the lid of the box. "In the event of Wexin's death, she was to receive the amount of her dower and the Mayfair townhouse."

Adrian could guess the value of the townhouse. "And the value of the dowry?"

"Nine thousand pounds."

Adrian leaned back and drummed his fingers on the mahogany arms of the chair. He calculated the sums in his head and leaned forwards again. "This is what I will do…" Adrian glanced up at Newton. "On my friend's behalf, I will assume the mortgage of the townhouse." Levenhorne said the house had been a gift from Lydia's father. Adrian would give it back to her. "And I will restore the dowry, but only under the stipulation that creditors are not to seek redress from Lady Wexin. Any debt must be attached to what was Wexin's."

Newton's jaw dropped. "Your friend would pay so much?"

"He can afford the sum." Adrian smiled inwardly.

It was a staggering amount, but one Adrian was well able to afford. For years he had kept his gambling winnings, and the investments made from them, separate from his quarterly portion. It had been a game he played with himself to see how much he could win and also how much he could afford to lose. His quarterly portion from his father was more than adequate for his other needs.

He'd done quite well at the game, quite well indeed, so well that he could restore Lydia's widow's portion, keep her in her London house and still have plenty of gambling money left over.

"My friend wishes the lady to have fifty pounds immediately and to have the townhouse in her name."

Newton nodded, his eyes still wide with disbelief.

Adrian pointed to the wooden box. "How many unpaid bills pertain to the lady's belongings or to the contents of the house?"

Newton riffled through the papers again. "I would have to do a careful calculation, but it is not as bad a debt as some of the others. Perhaps as much as two hundred pounds?"

"Those will be paid as well. I want—and my friend wants, as well—that Wexin's debts do not cause her any more suffering."

"I understand completely, sir." Newton's mouth widened into a smile.

Adrian returned the expression. "Need I add that no hint, no speculation as to the identity of her benefactor must ever be divulged to her? Or my small part in this?"

Newton gave him a level gaze. "It will be kept in complete confidence. I have been successful in keeping the extent of Wexin's debts from becoming public knowledge, and I certainly can keep Lady Wexin's affairs private."

Affairs.

The word sparked the memory of Adrian's very brief affair with Lydia, an affair she was loath to continue.

He supposed he was mad for bestowing a small fortune on a woman who wanted nothing to do with him. It was not like him to invest time or money in a lady who had no regard for him, but what would happen to Lydia if he did not assist her? He was investing in her happiness, a divergence from indulging in his own.

What's more, it was his money to do with as he wished. And he wished to do *good* with it, to feel a scant bit useful in this world. Besides, it gave him a new game to play, to see how long it would take to recoup the amount of money he had invested in Lydia. How many card games and horse races and other wagering would he have to engage in before he earned back the total amount? It was a game.

Nothing more.

Adrian and Newton completed all the arrangements and shook hands. When Adrian walked back to the Strand, the sun was peeking through the clouds. He headed in the direction of waiting hackney coaches, feeling both exhilarated and deflated.

The next morning from the drawing-room window, Lydia watched Mr Newton leave her townhouse. As soon as he stepped onto the pavement, he was accosted by a throng of newspaper men. Mr Newton pushed his way through them, waving a hand and shaking his head.

She breathed a sigh of relief. Mr Newton had not stopped to talk to the newspaper men. She ought to have known. Mr Newton had not breathed a word of how distressed Wexin's finances had been, and still were. It appeared Mr Newton would also not discuss this reversal of her misfortune, this restoring of her finances.

It was too remarkable to be true. Her widow's portion was restored and the house was securely hers. She had income and a place to live.

Lydia hugged herself and twirled around for joy. The news was too good to keep to herself a moment longer. She dashed out of the room and hurried down the stairs.

"Dixon!" she cried. "Mary! Oh, get Cook! I have something to tell you!"

Mary leaned over the second-floor banister above her. "What is it? What has happened?"

Lydia called up to her. "Come! I will tell you all." She flew down the stairs to the hall.

Dixon appeared from the back staircase, trailed by Cook wiping her hands on her apron and looking frightened.

Lydia ran up to the woman and gave her a squeeze. "Do not worry. It is good news."

"Good news from Mr Newton, my lady?" Dixon looked sceptical. There had, after all, been so much bad news from him.

Lydia clasped her hands together. "Oh, it is so unbelievable. It must have been my sister—"

Who else but her sister? Lydia had no indication that her letters had reached her parents. No one else knew of her distressed finances. No one but—

Adrian.

It was unthinkable that he would pay such sums. Ridiculous, even. Her sister's husband was extremely wealthy. Her sister must have convinced him to do this in secret.

"Tell us, m'lady," Mary cried.

Lydia took a breath. "Mr Newton informed me that someone—it must have been my sister—has restored my widow's portion and has signed the house and its contents over to me! Mr Newton assures me the interest on the six-per-cents will give us income enough!"

"Oh, my lady!" Mary exclaimed.

"May God be praised." Cook fell to her knees. "We can buy food!"

Lydia grabbed her hands and pulled her to her feet. "Food and coal and whatever we need!" She turned to the butler. "Will you find our servants, Dixon? Hire those who wish to return and pay the others what we owe them?"

Dixon beamed. "It will be my pleasure."

Still holding Cook's hands, Lydia swung her around in a circle. "Everything shall be as it was!"

Not precisely as it was, but so much better than she thought her future ever could be when she'd risen from her bed that morning.

Lydia gave Cook another hug. "We must celebrate today! I even have money to spend! Fifty pounds! We must fill the larder and celebrate!"

"I shall make a dinner fit for King George!" Cook cried.

Lydia swept her arm to include all of them. "We must eat together, though. I insist upon it. Just this once."

"May I suggest, my lady, that I bring up a bottle of champagne from the cellar?" Dixon asked.

"That would be splendid!" Lydia clapped her hands. "Champagne for dinner."

Dixon lifted a finger. "I meant immediately, my lady."

"Yes," cried Lydia. "Mary, find four glasses, and all join me in the morning room."

Lydia walked into the morning room, the small parlour off the hall, a room where callers were often asked to wait until they could be announced.

A sound sent her spinning towards the windows.

Outside the reporters, all abuzz, were all facing the house, craning their necks over the railings to try to see into the room.

With a cry, Lydia drew the curtains.

Her celebration did not include them.

Chapter Five

The certain gentleman, whom we have now identified as Lord C—, and with whom Lady W— was so recently linked, has lately visited several jewellery shops. Will the notorious beauty soon receive some adornment for her widow's attire?—*The New Observer*, November 17, 1818

"Oh!" Lydia threw down the paper and pounded her fist on the table. She picked up the paper again and reread the lines.

Lord C, *The New Observer* said, Lord C, with whom Lady W was so recently linked...

Lord Cavanley. The reporter had discovered it had been Cavanley who had rescued her.

"Ohhhhh." She squeezed her fist tighter. What else had the man discovered?

She read the account again. No hint of Lord Cavanley calling upon her in the rain and definitely no hint of the earlier time she'd spent with him. Adrian would not have betrayed her. Or so she hoped.

She looked through the other papers that Dixon had purchased for her earlier that morning. There was no news of her in either *The Morning Post* or *The Morning Chronicle*, only the silly mention of *Lord C* entering jewellery shops. Likely he was shopping for one of the other women with whom his name was for ever linked.

At least the newspapers said nothing of Mr Newton's visit.

"What is it, m'lady?" Mary bustled into the bedchamber, carrying one of Lydia's day dresses. "I heard you cry out. Is it your ankle?"

"No, not my ankle." Lydia spread her fingers and forced her voice to sound calm.

Mary had brought the newspapers and breakfast to Lydia in her bedchamber. In front of her on the small table were a plate of toast, a cooked egg and a pot of chocolate, the most sumptuous breakfast she'd had in weeks.

Lydia picked up a piece of toast. "I am mentioned in the newspaper again."

"About the money coming to you?" Mary's eyes grew wide.

"No, thank goodness." She bit into her toast.

Mary clucked her tongue. "Mr Dixon told you the doors and the walls were too thick. Those newspaper men could not hear us cheering, I am certain of it, m'lady."

Lydia swallowed. "So far, it appears you are right."

Mary pursed her lips. "What did they write about you?"

Lydia cast her eyes down. "My name is linked to a man, who will buy me jewels."

"They said such things?" Mary cried.

"One paper, that is all."

The maid's brows knitted. "But how can they make up such a story? It isn't right, m'lady."

Lydia gave her a wan smile. "I agree." She sighed. "I sometimes think they will never leave me alone."

Mary's expression turned sympathetic. She lifted the dress. "I brought the pink."

Lydia nodded. "That will do very nicely."

Any dress would do, because Lydia did not intend to go out,

nor to have callers. She could wear anything at all, anything but black. Lydia refused to wear black. She refused to mourn for Wexin, refused to even think his given name. He'd been a stranger, really, and one did not formally mourn strangers.

She took another bite of her toast. The jubilation of the previous day was dampened by reading her name in the paper once more.

And the connection to Adrian.

Lydia straightened her spine and took a fortifying sip of chocolate. She would forget all about that episode with Adrian. Soon the newspapers would find someone else with whom to attach her name.

She planned to spend the day perusing the household accounts. Now that she was in control of her money, she intended to spend wisely and never have to worry over money again. First she must learn the cost of ordinary things, such as lamp oil and beeswax and the food for their table. She must learn how to make a budget that included the servants' salaries, taxes on her menservants and the house, and whatever amounts she would be expected to pay throughout a year. It would be like assembling a puzzle, and she enjoyed assembling puzzles.

"My lady?" Mary laid the dress on the bed. "I thought I would go to the shops this morning to purchase the items you requested."

Lydia had asked for pins and also silk thread. She planned to embroider new seat covers for the dining-room chairs. She needed something to keep her fingers busy and to fill her time. To keep her from becoming lonely.

Mary turned to her. "Won't you come? You've not been out in ever so long."

Only a scant few days ago, Lydia thought, but Mary knew that outing had not been for pleasure.

Although Lydia had gained pleasure from it. She glanced at her bed and thought of Adrian.

Lord C in *The New Observer*.

"Not today, Mary." She shook her head, more to remove his image than to refuse Mary's invitation. "I fear I would be followed by the newspaper men."

Mary walked over to the window and peeked through a gap in the curtains. "They are still out there."

Lydia had already seen them loitering near her door.

"I suppose you cannot come with me, then," Mary said.

Lydia smiled at her. "You must purchase something for yourself when you are out. A length of fabric for a new dress, perhaps. Or a pretty hat. I will give you some extra coins."

Mary curtsied. "Thank you, my lady, but I could not—"

"I insist." Lydia stood. "Would you help me dress?"

Samuel stood shivering on the corner of the street where he had a clear view of Lady Wexin's side gate. He had already seen the butler hurry out. Samuel almost followed him, but made a snap decision to remain where he was. He really hoped the maid might come out next.

All the reporters knew that something had made the household jubilant two days previously, but none of them had discovered what it was. It had been noted that Mr Newton, Wexin's solicitor, had called and shortly after whoops of joy were heard. Perhaps the widow had come into more money, but coming into money when one was wealthy was not too interesting.

He needed something more.

The hinges of the gate squeaked, and, as Samuel had hoped, the trim figure of the maid appeared.

In Samuel's experience, maids knew everything that went on in a household and they could often be encouraged to talk about what they knew.

The maid headed towards Berkeley Square. If Samuel hurried, he could catch up with her, but he needed to detour so that neither she nor the other reporters saw him.

He walked to Charles Street and practically ran to Berkeley Square where he caught sight of her just as he'd hoped to do. Keeping a good distance between them, he followed her as she walked to the shops.

It was almost peaceful following her on her errands. Samuel watched her select threads and pins and pieces of lace. She did not hurry at her tasks, but instead examined all the wares at a leisurely pace, as if this excursion was merely for her own pleasure.

Instead of making him impatient, it seemed a treat to watch her. She had a trim little figure, a graceful way of walking, and a sweet way of smiling at the assistants in the shops. Her heart-shaped face was as pale as the finest lady's, fringed by auburn curls that escaped from her bonnet. Her lips were so pink they might have been tinted, but what intrigued him the most were her huge blue eyes.

She filled a large basket with her purchases, adding bouquets of flowers from the flower vendors until she looked more like a girl who had come from a stroll in a lush garden than a servant about her errands.

When she headed back towards Berkeley Square, Samuel realised he'd not found an opportunity to speak to her, although it somehow had not seemed like time wasted.

When she entered Gunter's Tea Shop, a confectionary in Berkeley Square, he saw his chance. Samuel hurried into the shop behind her.

"A lemon ice, please," she said to the shop assistant. "And six of those." She pointed to marzipan displayed under glass, perfect miniature pears and peaches and apples, confections made from almonds, sugar and egg whites.

He stood behind her, his heart beating a little faster. He could easily see over her head. She was no taller than the level of his chin. She turned and gave him the briefest glance with those big blue eyes. He nodded to her, and she turned away again.

The shop assistant produced the lemon ice and packed the marzipan into a box, tying it with string. The maid handed the shop assistant her coins. When she walked past Samuel he had a whiff of lemon from the lemon ice, but also a hint of lavender.

He stepped up to the counter. "A lemon ice, as well." He wanted to ask the shop assistant to be quick about it, but held his tongue.

The maid took her time leaving the shop, admiring the delectable fare displayed under glass on both sides of the aisle. He'd nearly had a chance to speak to her and still might if the shop assistant hurried with his lemon ice.

His quarry walked out of the door.

"Your ice, sir." The shop assistant handed over the dish.

Samuel threw down his coin and hurried out after the maid. As he'd hoped, she was seated on a bench near a tree, her basket beside her. He sauntered over.

He nodded to her again. "I see you, like me, could not resist a lemon ice even on this chilly day."

She glanced up, a spoonful in her hand, "That is so," she said softly. She shivered prettily as she swallowed it.

Samuel dipped his spoon in the treat, taking a generous portion and swallowing it at once. Pain seized his entire chest.

"Oh, that hurt," he gasped. "Did you ever do that? Swallow something cold and have it feel as if someone had punched you in the chest?"

She glanced at him, looking uncertain as to whether to speak to him. "You should take it a little at a time," she finally said.

After dipping his spoon into the ice again, he lifted it to show her the tiny portion before letting it slide slowly down his throat. He grinned at her. "That was a great deal more pleasant."

She glanced at him again and turned her attention back to her own lemon ice.

He took another spoonful. "I am Mr Samuel…Charles," he

said, taking the name of the street that had been his detour in following her. "I know it is forward of me to speak to you, but I am new to London. I do think it is so much nicer to share the eating of such a treat as an ice, than to eat it alone, do you not agree?"

She nodded ever so slightly and shifted in her seat, knocking the box of marzipan out of her basket.

Samuel picked it up and put it back in.

"Thank you, sir," she said, briefly meeting his gaze.

"Will you be eating all that marzipan alone?" he asked.

She smiled. "Oh, no, sir. It is my treat for my lady and the others."

"For your lady?"

She nodded again, but with less reserve. "I am a lady's maid, sir."

"Do you always bring your lady such delicacies?" He kept his tone soft and friendly. It was not difficult to do with such a sweet and pretty girl.

She smiled at him. "Oh, no, but it is my treat. We are celebrating today."

His brows rose and his heart accelerated. "Celebrating? And what do you have to celebrate? Something wonderful?"

Her smile widened and her eyes sparkled and, for a moment, Samuel forgot everything but how charming she looked. "We are celebrating good fortune!"

"Good fortune?" By his tone he encouraged her to go on.

She merely nodded happily and scraped the last of her lemon ice from her dish. She picked up the basket and stood.

He quickly finished his own ice. "Allow me to return your dish for you." He reached for it and his glove scraped hers.

"Thank you, sir." Her eyes caught his again.

He continued to peer into their depths. "Would…would you like to share a lemon ice again? I could meet you right here whenever you say."

Her expression turned serious, but she did not look away. Finally she answered him. "Saturday. Around one o'clock? I think my lady might not mind."

His smile was genuine. "I will be delighted. It…it pleases me to have a friend with whom to share my lemon ice."

Her lashes fluttered and her face flushed pink. Before he could say another word, she curtsied and hurried off.

Samuel watched her rush away before he returned the dishes to the tea shop. He had not wormed very much out of her, but more would come.

Saturday at one o'clock.

He was surprised at how much he looked forward to sharing another lemon ice with her.

Adrian opened his eyes to bright daylight illuminating his bedchamber. He twisted around in the bed linens to look at the clock on the mantel.

It was about to chime two o'clock.

He groaned and swung his legs over the side of the bed.

His valet appeared. "Do you rise now, m'lord?"

Adrian rubbed his face, wondering how his man always seemed to know the instant he awoke. "I suppose."

Dawn had been showing its first glimmer of light when Adrian walked home from the gambling den where he'd spent the night hours at a table of whist. His profits had not been spectacular, but, then, he had not been as keen at keeping track of cards. Too many other thoughts intruded.

Every win, every loss, was measured against the sum he had given to Lydia and, thus, he'd kept her constantly in his thoughts, distracting him, leaving him feeling unsettled.

Hammond stood next to the bed, holding his banyan so that Adrian had no choice but to stand and be assisted into the garment. He padded over to the basin, not surprised that the water in the pitcher was warm. How Hammond accomplished having warm water no matter what the hour of Adrian's rising was another unfathomable mystery.

Adrian splashed water on his face and brushed his teeth, then sat so that Hammond could shave him. Same as he had done the day before and the day before. Boredom was a dreadful thing. What did one do when that which once relieved boredom now merely added to it? Hammond left to prepare Adrian's breakfast while Adrian finished washing up.

He walked into his drawing room where Hammond had prepared a table for him with slices of cold ham, cheese, bread and jam. There was also a fresh pot of hot coffee and copies of the morning newspapers.

Adrian sipped his coffee while looking through the papers. He came to an article in *The New Observer*:

> *The certain gentleman, whom we have now identified as Lord C—, and with whom Lady W— was so recently linked, has lately visited several jewellery shops...*

Adrian sat up. *Good God.*

This was Reed's newspaper. Reed had identified him.

Adrian turned hot with fury.

The damned man had probably followed him, as well.

If Adrian caught Reed following him again, there would be hell to pay and he'd see Reed paid it.

How much did the man know? Adrian perused the column again and blew out a relieved breath. Reed thought he'd been purchasing jewels.

It was nearly half past three before Adrian ventured out. For wont of any other place to go, he headed towards White's. The air felt damp as if rain was in the offing, and other pedestrians on the street seemed to keep their heads down. To Adrian, the cold was bracing and it felt good to walk at a fast clip.

He was almost invigorated by the time he walked into White's, but, as soon as he stepped into the coffee room, he knew something was wrong.

The room was quiet and the gentlemen present were whispering among themselves or keeping their eyes downcast. Adrian saw Tanner sitting alone at one of the tables. He crossed the room to him.

"Who the devil died?" he asked.

Tanner looked up and gave him an ironic smile. "Actually, the Queen."

Adrian dropped into a chair. "My God. I was merely joking."

The Queen had been ailing for some time, and news of her condition was printed often in the newspapers. She'd been convalescing at Kew Palace for some time. Even lately, she'd been reported taking the sun in the garden.

"When did you hear?" Adrian asked.

"Not more than an hour ago." Tanner took a sip of coffee. "She died at one o'clock, it was said."

Adrian signalled the attendant. "Tea, please."

Tanner lifted a newspaper that had been lying on the table in front of him. "Did you see this?"

It was a copy of *The New Observer*.

"I read it."

Tanner twirled his finger. "Before news of the Queen arrived, they were all speculating about who was this Lord C *The New Observer* writes of."

Adrian kept his eyes steady. "*The New Observer* writes of a Lord C?"

Tanner tapped the paper. "It does. *Lord C—*, it said… *Lord C—, with whom Lady W— was so recently linked.*" Tanner grinned. "You don't suppose he means Lord Cavanley, now do you?"

Adrian made himself roll his eyes. "Of course, *you* would think of me. Not Lord Crawford or Carlisle or Crayden."

Tanner feigned being offended. "I would expect you would tell me before it appeared in the newspaper. I mean, we are friends and there is, of course, my recent connection to Wexin."

This was the moment that Adrian ought to tell Tanner the whole—only he could not quite bring himself to open his mouth.

"I was about to head off to Gentleman Jack's," Tanner said. "Come with me."

The moment passed. "Very well."

A good bout of fisticuffs would not hurt.

When they were outside, Adrian asked Tanner, "I know you have been concerned about Lady Wexin. What do you think this newspaper report means?"

Tanner shook his head in dismay. "I cannot know. After our return to London, Marlena and I sent Lady Wexin a note asking if we could call upon her, but she refused."

Adrian walked several steps in silence. Here was another moment for him to tell Tanner of his encounter with Lydia.

"How is Lady Tannerton?" he said instead. "I do hope she is well."

Tanner smiled, but it seemed to Adrian that the smile was meant for Tanner's wife. "She is splendid, Pom. She is splendid." He stared off into the distance for a moment before glancing back at Adrian. "Lady Heronvale has taken her under her wing. They are making calls to other ladies today."

"Good of Lady Heronvale."

Tanner turned pensive. "I suppose there will be much involved with the Queen's funeral. I wonder if Marlena will be up to all the pomp so soon."

After what Tanner's wife had been through already, Adrian suspected a royal funeral would seem like a simple ride through Hyde Park. "She'll do splendidly."

Tanner laughed. "Pom, I am so unused to this. I feel amazingly at loose ends. I have become so accustomed to being at her side."

Adrian, at least, knew precisely how it felt to be at loose ends.

He clapped Tanner on the shoulder. "Then it is good that I am with you. Let us beat each other to a bloody pulp at Gentleman Jack's, and we will both be certain to feel better."

Chapter Six

The Ceremonial for the Internment of her late Most Excellent Majesty Queen Charlotte of blessed memory, will take place in the Royal Chapel of St George at Windsor, on this day, Wednesday of the second day of December, 1818.   *—The New Observer*, December 2, 1818

Lydia stood at her window watching the carriages roll by. It looked as if the funeral procession for the Queen had begun in Mayfair, rather than Windsor. Most of the peerage, it seemed, would be in the procession for the Queen.

She felt apart from it all, separated from the life into which she had been born. It was true that wives and daughters of peers would not be greatly in attendance at the funeral, but they would have been intimately involved in conversations about its planning and would hear every detail of the ceremonial at the end of the day. She had no one with whom to converse about it.

One fine carriage after another rumbled by, the gentlemen wearing tall black beaver hats or plumed regimentals just visible through the carriage windows.

Would Adrian be among them?

Lydia groaned. She ought not to think of him, but with her empty days it seemed he came much too often into her mind. Even when she ventured to Piccadilly Street to browse in Hatchard's or to purchase jams at Fortnum and Mason, she found herself searching for him among the passers-by.

At least now she was able to walk to the shops unmolested. The reporters had vanished from her doorway when it became known that the ailing Queen had reached the end of her suffering. Lydia could not be glad the beloved Queen had died, but she was ecstatic that the reporters' attention had turned towards the King, the Prince Regent and the Royal Dukes and Princesses. The newspapers were filled with every step the royals took. Speculation was rampant about the Queen's will and the fact that she had only recently composed the document. Who would she remember in her will? And who would she leave out?

The Queen had always seemed like a formidable figure to Lydia. She had shaken in terror when she'd been presented to the Queen during the Season of her come-out. Lydia imagined all sorts of mishaps, like tripping on her skirt or losing one of the huge feathers she wore in her hair. When it had been her turn to be announced to the Queen, Lydia had been convinced she would faint, but somehow she'd made her approach and performed a graceful, if overly practised, curtsy.

The Queen had actually spoken to her. "Why, you are quite a beauty," Her Majesty had said. "Quite a beauty."

Lydia smiled at the memory of herself, so young and giddy and full of hope. It had been a time when she'd dreamed of love and marriage and children.

It had been a long time ago.

"Thank you, Your Majesty," she said aloud, curtsying again, just as she'd done that day.

Lydia had dressed in black today. She'd wear black to honour the dear Queen. She turned to leave her bedchamber and to make her way to the morning room where her breakfast would be served.

When she entered the corridor, the sweet sound of Mary humming a happy tune reached her ears. Lydia smiled.

Two weeks ago Mary had met a young man who'd put stars in her eyes and a skip in her step. Mary had seen the fellow only twice, when Lydia gave her permission to spend a little time to meet him at Gunter's, where they shared some treat together. Those two meetings had been enough to keep the girl humming through all the other days.

"You must be thinking of your young man," Lydia said when Mary came into view.

Mary blushed. "Oh, I suppose I should not hum on such a sad day. I do beg pardon, my lady."

"Do not be silly, Mary," Lydia scolded. "It is perfectly acceptable for you to be happy."

It was more than acceptable. It was the one bright spot in Lydia's life.

Mary beamed. "Well, I am very happy and that is the truth."

Lydia reached out and touched the girl's hand. "And I am happy for you."

Lydia turned to walk down the stairs. As she descended she heard Mary's cheerful tune again and almost felt like humming herself.

But a wave of queasiness came over her, so strong she almost missed a step. She grasped the banister to keep from falling.

She'd had such a feeling before, but that had been when she—

No. It could not be. It must not be.

"I'm hungry, that's all," she said aloud, although the thought of food made her stomach roil again. She pressed a hand to it and walked more slowly to the morning room.

She glanced at the food set out on a little table in a spot where the sunlight shone in from the window. The fare was simple. A pot of chocolate, a cooked egg, toast and jam, but her stomach rebelled at the sight. She took deep breaths and walked over to the window to wait for the nausea to subside.

There were still plenty of coaches rumbling by to entertain her. From this window it was easier to see the crests on the sides of the carriages. She recognised some of them. They were numerous enough to form a queue on her street, all waiting for the traffic to clear at South Audley Street, she supposed.

A fine shiny black town carriage came to a stop directly in front of her house. She examined the crest, but did not know to whom it belonged. Her gaze lifted to the window of the carriage. There staring back at her was Adrian. He nodded to her, and she quickly stepped back out of sight.

"By Jove, I believe that is Lady Wexin at the window." Adrian's father leaned over him to see better, but Lydia had already disappeared. "Did you see her?"

"I was not looking at the windows," Adrian lied.

He'd seen her. His stomach muscles had clenched when his eyes met hers, like some besotted whelp in his first infatuation, but she'd quickly stepped away when he acknowledged her.

The message was clear. She had no wish to see him, even by accident.

"I am certain it was she." His father leaned over him to get another look, but Adrian could have told him she would not show herself again, not while their carriage stood in front of her house. "Cannot mistake her. She is a beauty, that one. Can see why Wexin wanted her."

"Mmm," responded Adrian, not wishing to encourage this turn in their conversation.

It was merely his vanity that was wounded when she did not smile at him or nod in return, nothing more. Besides, not every woman he met wanted him. Why would they? He did not want every woman he met, including Lady Denson, the widow who seemed to appear at any society affair he attended.

"Did you hear?" His father chuckled. "Bets have been placed in White's book on the identity of this Lord C who was connected with Lady Wexin in the newspapers."

Adrian glanced over at him in surprise. "Indeed?" He'd hoped the story would have been forgotten in the wake of the Queen's death.

His father lifted a finger. "Odds are on Crayden, you know."

"Crayden?" Adrian should have been glad his father had not named him, but why Crayden, who was an impoverished Irish Viscount?

His father shrugged. "Word is he was a suitor of hers before Wexin. Never married. Needs the money from her dowry and a rich father-in-law as much as Wexin did."

It ought not to matter to Adrian, but this news depressed him, even though he knew he was the Lord C of *The New Observer*'s story. He also knew her financial situation was not likely to attract Crayden, if the man knew of it, that is.

Betting on her at White's didn't please Adrian either. He disliked this manner of attention on her. She did not deserve it. Wexin had been the villain, not Lydia.

Adrian had discovered that Lydia had hired back most of her servants. Or rather his valet had discovered it at Adrian's request. He had no idea how his man had accomplished it, but within a day Hammond had produced the information of how many servants had been dismissed originally and how many had returned. The number was sufficient to ensure her comfort.

He leaned back against the padded upholstery, trying to feel some satisfaction in having helped her.

The coach lurched forwards, the unexpected motion causing both father and son to grip the seats.

His father frowned. "I do hope the springs in this carriage are up to a trip of this length. I do not relish being jostled about."

This was Adrian's first ride in the elegant carriage bearing the Earl of Varcourt's crest. "It is a damned sight better than the last hack I rode in."

His father huffed. "Why you ride in those things is a mystery to me. Our old coach is at your disposal any time you require it."

"That is generous of you, sir." Adrian's father was always generous.

This carriage did have a tendency to sway to and fro in a manner as lulling as a ship in gentle waters. After leaving the busy streets of London, they lapsed into silence. His father dozed and Adrian lost himself in thoughts that seemed as unfocussed as his life. The day promised to be long and tedious, but it was their duty to be present at the Queen's funeral.

"When duty calls, a gentleman must always rise to do what is required of him," his father always said. And always added, "So enjoy life while you can, my son."

His father would deny it, but Adrian knew he relished doing his duty in whatever form it took, and probably had enjoyed it even from his youth, when he inherited the family title. Adrian's father was a man who could be counted upon to do what must be done, but he also tended to glorify what he'd missed, the chance to be a frivolous, pleasure-seeking youth. His father could not fathom how such trivialities could grow tiresome over time.

When they reached Kew Palace there was a jumble of carriages, cavalry and foot soldiers, royal grooms and pages. Also in attendance were the royal physicians and countless other members of the royal entourage. Somehow this multitude sorted itself into a dignified and orderly procession, moving solemnly towards Windsor and St George's Chapel.

The procession kept its snail-like pace the whole distance, reaching Houslow Heath shortly after noon and the chapel at seven in the evening. By that time most of the London carriages had turned off, making their way back to town. It was appalling how few peers actually endured the day long enough to attend the Queen's funeral service.

Adrian and his father endured it, as duty demanded. By the time their coach was again pointed in the direction of London, his father's energy had flagged and his rhythmic snores joined with the sound of the horses' hooves and the creaking of the coach's springs.

Adrian stared at the darkness outside, alone again with his thoughts.

What was there to look forward to in the weeks ahead? Within days London would empty, the *ton* fleeing to country houses or the Continent, places where they might find entertainment. With the official mourning of the Queen, the London entertainments would disappear. The theatres were already dark, and no one had hosted a ball or dinner or rout since the mourning commenced.

Adrian supposed he could accept his mother's invitation to spend Christmas at the Varcourt estate. No doubt several of his parents' friends would be in attendance. There would be card playing at night and perhaps he could ride in the mornings. There would be plenty of land to give his horse a good run.

Tanner had invited him to Tannerton, as well, but Adrian had already begged off. He knew Tanner would prefer to be alone with his new wife.

Perhaps he should travel somewhere, somewhere like… Paris.

Yes. Paris would be a novelty. Things were a bit gayer there now than they had been right after the war, he'd heard. More money was pouring in to the city each day. There were plenty of casinos he might visit, as well as the various sites of interest in the city.

Yes, he made the decision. He would go to Paris.

Anywhere to battle this cursed ennui.

Chapter Seven

The notorious Lady W— has gone back into hiding, no longer venturing to visit the shops on Piccadilly or to take walks in Hyde Park. All of London wishes to know why. Could she perhaps be in an interesting condition?
—*The New Observer*, April 11, 1819

Adrian sat in the dining room at the townhouse on Curzon Street. While he'd been in Paris, his father had written to him that the Pomroy house would be ready for him on his return. Adrian made arrangements for his belongings to be moved from his rooms near St James's Square, and wrote to tell the servants at the townhouse when to expect him. He'd entered the house he'd known as a child, just the day before this one. It continued to be a curious combination of familiar and strange. Adrian had slept in the room and on the bed he'd always known as his father's and was now seated at the head of the long dining-room table in what seemed like his father's chair.

His family's butler, a man hired by his father years ago, entered the room. "The newspapers, my lord." The butler even addressed Adrian in the same tone he'd always addressed Adrian's father.

"Thank you, Bilson." Adrian tried at least to sound like himself. He returned his coffee cup to its saucer and took the papers in hand.

He supposed he ought to send an announcement to the papers telling of his return. In fact, Bilson could see that it was done—one of the benefits of having more servants. He had even less to do.

The New Observer happened to be the newspaper on top. Adrian rolled his eyes. Bilson could forgo the subscription to the scandal sheet that had so maligned Lydia.

Adrian took a deep breath and dug his fork into a slice of cold beef. It made no sense to think of Lydia. He'd done an excellent job of forgetting her in Paris. Several high stakes' card games had taken his mind away.

Until he won, that is, and remembered he was replacing funds he had given to her. He had also met a few very pretty French *mademoiselles*, but he could not sustain an interest in them. He attributed this to his general malaise, not to comparing them to Lydia.

Adrian shook his head and skimmed *The New Observer*, its columns full of gruesome murders and titillating affairs.

His gaze caught on the words *the notorious Lady W—*.

Damned paper. What were they saying of her now?

He read on.… *All of London wishes to know… Could she perhaps be in an interesting condition?*

Adrian sprang to his feet, toppling the mahogany chair onto the carpet. "What the deuce is this?"

Bilson stepped in. "Is anything amiss, my lord?"

Newspaper still in hand, Adrian strode towards him. "My hat and gloves, Bilson, and be quick. I'm going out."

Bilson lost no time in retrieving the hat and gloves, and Adrian was on the street in less than a minute. He set a quick pace in the direction of Hill Street and Lydia's house, an easy walk away.

When he reached the street he saw several men clustered around.

Newspaper reporters.

He had half a mind to send them about their business, but that would certainly not remove her name from the papers. It would merely add his. He blew out a frustrated breath. He could not call upon her while the reporters watched who was admitted to her house. He crossed the street.

He thought about calling upon Tanner, but what would he say? Lady Wexin is with child and, if the child is not Wexin's, it might be mine?

Adrian wasn't ready to burden his friend with that information, especially as Tanner had written to him that he and Lady Tannerton were expecting a baby.

Adrian walked past Lydia's house. As he passed by, a gentleman approached it—Lord Levenhorne, holding a newspaper and wearing a determined look upon his face. He was almost immediately swarmed by reporters.

Adrian watched Levenhorne beating them off with his newspaper. Adrian decided to head to White's. With luck, Levenhorne would stop by there, and, when he did, Adrian would be present to hear all about his call upon Lady Wexin.

A soft light diffused through the curtains of the morning room and illuminated the page of the newspaper.

Lydia stared at the words. *Could she perhaps be in an interesting condition?*

A wave of nausea overcame her, not morning sickness this time, but a sickness of another kind. "How could they have discovered this?"

She'd secluded herself ever since the familiar symptoms emerged several months ago—aching breasts, inability to keep food in her stomach, heavy fatigue. Mary had noticed and knew from the start that Lydia was with child. Mary also had witnessed her last miscarriage and knew this child was not Wexin's. The maid had not asked the baby's paternity, though, and Lydia had explained nothing.

Five months had passed and Lydia's figure showed the telltale changes. The other servants now also knew her condition. Lydia trusted her servants had kept this secret. They had been as loyal and caring as a family, but perhaps one of them had slipped and said something to someone and someone had said something to *The New Observer*. Or perhaps that vile reporter, Mr Reed, had decided to make this up and accidentally hit upon the truth.

She heard the murmur of voices outside. Tiptoeing to the window, she peeked through the gap in the curtains. They were out there again, the reporters. She'd been totally free of them ever since the poor Queen had died and had hoped never to see them cluster around her door again. They were back this morning, gathering around a gentleman who flailed at them with a newspaper in one hand and his walking stick in the other.

Lord Levenhorne.

Lydia pressed a hand protectively against the rounded mound of her abdomen. She had never carried a baby inside her this long.

She ought to consider it a tragedy that she'd conceived a child from that one brief moment of making love with Adrian, but she could not. It was a miracle. *A miracle.* One last chance to have a baby. She did not expect to ever have another chance. She would certainly never marry again, even if some man wanted her. She would never again put her life and her future in a man's hands. She pressed her belly again, thankful this child was not Wexin's.

Still, she mourned the loss of his babies, the three little lives she'd been unable to hold inside her long enough. Every morning now, she woke expecting to feel that cramping, that spilling of blood, but this baby still grew within her. She could feel it flutter, blessedly alive.

She wished now she had written to her sister to give her the excellent news. Instead her sister would read it as gossip in the newspapers.

After her money had been restored to her, Lydia had sent her sister a letter of thanks. She'd heard nothing in reply, and her sister's maid told Mary there should be no more correspondence. Lydia still felt she ought to have written to her with the news of her pregnancy.

She wondered if her sister would contact her if she heard from their parents or brother. Lydia had heard nothing, which distressed her greatly. Surely if they were safe, one of their letters would have reached her by now, even if her letters had not reached them.

Lydia heard footsteps approach. She took in a deep breath. Lord Levenhorne could not upset her. Even the vile reporters could not upset her. Not when her baby moved inside her.

"Thank you, Adrian," she whispered to herself. "For such a gift."

Dixon entered the room, his expression distressed.

Lydia saved him from having to inform her who had called. "I know who it is, Dixon. I saw him through the window."

Dixon cleared his throat. "I shall tell him you are not receiving callers if you wish it."

Lydia gave him a reassuring look. "I will see him." She touched her abdomen. "This is no secret, is it, Dixon? He will have to know at some time."

Dixon's features softened. "'Tis no secret, my lady, but we cannot allow his lordship to cause you distress."

She was touched by his concern. "Do not fear. I shall manage nicely."

She followed Dixon out to the hall where Levenhorne paced back and forth. The moment he saw her, he started towards her. "Lady Wexin—"

She extended her hand to him. "How kind of you to call upon me, Lord Levenhorne."

He looked taken aback by the offer of her hand. He shook it, and belatedly gave her the bow politeness required of him.

Lydia turned to Dixon. "We'll have tea, if you please."

Levenhorne blustered, "This is not a social call—"

She swivelled back to her guest. "I would still serve you refreshment, sir. Let us go to the drawing room where we might be more private."

She led him up the stairway into the more formal drawing room with windows so high no reporter could see into them. She settled herself on a sofa and gestured to her guest. "Do sit, sir."

His eyes flashed with impatience, but he lowered himself into the chair opposite her.

"How is Lady Levenhorne?" Lydia made her tone polite, as if this were indeed a social call. "I have not seen her in an age. Is she in town yet?"

"She is well," he answered curtly. "She is in town."

Most of the *ton* would be in town. The London Season had commenced, as gay as always, since the Regent had ended official mourning for his mother after only six weeks.

"And the children?" Lydia asked.

Levenhorne waved a hand. "They are well. All of them."

"I am delighted to hear it." Lydia made herself look Levenhorne in the eye. "I confess, I had thought to see Lady Levenhorne before this. I had thought perhaps she would call on me."

It was bad manners to point out his wife's neglect—and his—but these people had hurt her. The Levenhornes were related to Wexin, after all. True, Lord Levenhorne had called after Wexin's death, but, like today, only to speak of the inheritance and to ask if she were increasing. Indeed, the only person who'd reached out to her in kindness had been Lady Tannerton, but Lydia had refused to see her. How could she face the widow of the man her husband had murdered, the woman he had framed for the deed?

Lydia felt her baby flutter inside her. She'd forgotten. One other person had called upon her and had been very kind.

Adrian.

Her butler accompanied the footman who carried the tea tray and set it on the table in front of Lydia. She knew Dixon had come out of worry for her.

"Thank you so much." She glanced at Dixon, hoping he knew she thanked him for his concern as well as the tea. "I shall let you know if I require anything else."

Dixon left the room and Lydia looked across at Lord Levenhorne. "How do you take your tea?"

He squirmed in his chair. "With milk. One lump of sugar."

Lydia busied herself with pouring his tea and then handed the cup to him so he was forced to take it from her. She watched him until he took a polite sip before pouring her own cup.

She was proud of herself. A few months ago she might have cowered in front of Lord Levenhorne. That had been when she'd had no money and no child to give her life purpose. He could not frighten her now.

She sipped her tea quietly, not making it easy for him to blast her with what the newspapers implied and her waistline verified.

He put down his tea cup and picked up the newspaper, now creased from having been folded in his hand. "Have you seen this?"

She blinked at him, pretending to be confused. "A newspaper?"

"Blast it," he swore more to himself than at her. "*The New Observer.* Have you seen it today?"

She did not answer directly. "What does it say that distresses you so?" Let him utter the words.

He glanced down at it for a moment, then he tapped it with his finger. "It says you are in an *interesting condition.*"

Lydia made herself laugh. She stood so that her skirt draped against her thickening middle. "I *am* in an interesting condition, as you can see, sir, but I have announced the happy event to no one."

"They know." He tapped the paper again. "It says Lady W."

She lowered herself back into her seat and picked up her cup of tea. "Oh, then it could not possibly be Lady Wilcox or Willingham or Warwick…"

"Come now, they must mean you." He pushed the paper towards her as if that would prove it. "What is the idea of this?"

"Of what?" She gave him her best ingenuous expression.

"Of your—your—your—delicate condition."

She placed a hand on her abdomen. "My baby, do you mean?"

"Of course I mean that!" he cried. "Why was I not told of it? Why must I learn of it from this scurrilous newspaper?"

Lydia took a sip of tea before answering him. "First of all, Lord Levenhorne, I am not at all certain you have learned of *my* condition from a newspaper. Surely your wife knows very well that I have lost other babies. If I preferred not to make any announcement until I was more certain I might carry this baby to term, I cannot see how you can fault me."

His face turned red and he bowed his head.

She went on. "I do appreciate that you have some interest in the information, sir." If she produced a son within ten months of Wexin's death, that son would inherit Wexin's title and estate instead of Lord Levenhorne. "I would have told you as soon as I believed the baby had a chance to survive."

Which was true, but it was also true that she'd wanted to keep the precious news to herself as long as possible.

Levenhorne grimaced as he lifted his head and met her eye. "You cannot tell me this—this—child is Wexin's."

She kept her gaze level, but her heart beat frantically inside her chest. "If my child is not born within the ten months, you have the right to make that statement to me, sir. Not before." She stood. "Do you have anything else you must say to me?"

He rose to his feet, still looking as if he wanted to chew her for breakfast. "You have not heard the end of this."

He might make all the accusations he wished. No matter what she knew to be true, the law stated that this child was Wexin's if born within ten months of his death.

It was not a huge risk she was taking. She'd conceived the baby only a month after Wexin's death; surely the baby would be born within the ten months. Her prayer was that she could hold the baby inside her long enough for the baby to live. Nothing mattered more to her than birthing a healthy child.

Levenhorne marched out of the room, and Lydia collapsed onto the settee.

"Well, that is done," she murmured, touching her belly where the child that was not Wexin's kicked inside her.

The baby that was Adrian's.

Adrian chose a table in White's coffee room with a clear view of the doorway. Should Levenhorne appear, Adrian would be the first person he encountered. There were very few gentlemen present at this hour, men who had no better place to eat breakfast and no better place to spend their time.

Like him.

He had checked the betting book on his way in. The wagering about which Lord C had been linked with Lydia seemed to have ended with the Queen's death and the exodus from town. His name was still not among the suggested Lord Cs.

He finished two cups of coffee and read all of the newspapers. He read a great deal more than he wished to know about the state of herring fishing as reported to the House of Commons. He read of a terrible fire in corn mills in Chester and of the trial of a former soldier who had robbed the White Horse Inn. The only paper that printed anything about Lydia's condition had been *The New Observer*, and the reporter had been Samuel Reed.

Adrian lifted his head every two minutes to see if Levenhorne had arrived. Eventually he glanced up, and Levenhorne indeed strode in the room, looking like thunder.

Adrian was ready for him. "Good God, Levenhorne. Come tell me what has happened."

The man looked no further into the room, but sat down across from Adrian, a crumpled newspaper in his hand. "Have you read this?" He waved the paper in Adrian's face.

"I've read several papers this morning." This was obvious as they sat in a pile next to his coffee cup. "Which one is that?"

"*The New* blasted *Observer*." Levenhorne signalled the servant who quickly took his request for coffee…and brandy.

"Ah, the gossip newspaper." Adrian responded. "Was there something of you in it?"

Levenhorne shook his head and opened the newspaper, jabbing it with his finger. "Not of me. Of Lady Wexin."

The servant brought his coffee and brandy, and Levenhorne downed the brandy in one gulp. Adrian waited for him to continue.

He added cream and sugar to his coffee and lifted the cup for a sip. "The newspaper said she was increasing. I have just come from calling upon her and it is bloody well true."

"Increasing." Adrian spoke in as non-committal a voice as he could.

"Increasing," repeated Levenhorne. "And if she produces a son within the ten-month period, the title and property go to him."

"And not to you." Adrian made himself take a sip of coffee.

"Not to me."

Adrian gave him what he hoped was a puzzled look. "But I thought you lamented this inheritance, saying Wexin had riddled it with debt."

The man grimaced. "That was before Mr Coutts persuaded me to fund some rather substantial repairs to the buildings on Wexin's estate and to finance the spring planting."

"Ah," Adrian said.

"Thing is, it is a good piece of property, worthy of the investment. Prime land. Could make an excellent profit." Levenhorne shook his head in dismay. "I had no intention of providing for Lady Wexin's brat, however. Let her father do that. I dare say he can afford it better than I."

"Has her father returned from his tour?" Adrian asked.

Levenhorne shook his head. "Not that I have heard. God knows what has happened to them. No one has heard from them, it is said." He bowed his head. "I'm afraid I was unforgivably rude to Lady Wexin. Said the baby could not be Wexin's."

Adrian took the creased newspaper in his hand and pretended to read it for the first time. "It says nothing of that here."

"I know." Levenhorne tapped his fingers on his coffee cup. "Besides, who else could have fathered the child? The lady is a recluse."

But not by her desire. Because the society whose darling she once had been had turned its back on her. And Adrian knew precisely who else could have fathered the child.

Levenhorne's eyes widened. "I say, Cavanley. You will say nothing of this, will you? I'd prefer no one knew I spent good money on that blasted estate. I probably ought not to have spoken so plainly."

Adrian waved a hand. "I'll speak of it to no one, you have my word."

Levenhorne stared into his coffee for what seemed like a long time. "The more I think of it, the more I think that baby is not Wexin's. Too much time has passed. Conception would have to have taken place in October before Wexin travelled to Scotland. She'd be six months along and, let me tell you, at six months, my wife's belly was always bigger than this lady's."

Adrian frowned. He knew nothing of such matters, but he did know that it had been almost five months to the day that he'd lain with Lydia.

Levenhorne pounded his fist on the table. "She's pulling a fast one on me, I'd wager on it, and she has my hands tied until the ten months is over. Crafty wench. There's not a blasted thing I can do about it." He sighed. "Except hope the baby comes late or she pushes out a girl."

Adrian made himself sit very still lest he launch himself over the table and put a fist into the other man's face.

This child, girl or boy, to which Levenhorne so scathingly referred, might be Adrian's, and Lydia did not deserve to be spoken of in such a coarse manner.

Adrian stood. "Forgive me, Levenhorne. I must be on my way."

Levenhorne glanced up at him again. "I have your word you will tell no one of our conversation?"

"You have my word."

Adrian walked out, collected his hat and gloves and left White's. He headed back into Mayfair, again walking by Lydia's house.

The reporters still clustered. He did not see Samuel Reed, the man who seemed to know more and do more damage than the others.

Adrian continued past the house. He decided he must gain entry in another way besides knocking upon her door in front of the London press. He'd return when daylight was gone, and somehow, some way, he'd speak to Lydia before the dawn of a new day.

Reed stood near Lady Wexin's side gate. Night was falling and he waited with anticipation for Mary to appear.

Sweet Mary. He liked meeting her this way, in secret, at a time he might pull her into a dark corner and steal a few kisses.

He liked it a bit too much, knowing he must eventually cut off the liaison. He just hoped he could do it without her discovering his true purpose for romancing her. Dear sweet Mary. He despised the idea of causing her that kind of hurt.

He heard the familiar creak of the gate and stepped out from the shadows. She ran towards him, propelling herself into his arms.

"Oh, Samuel, I am so glad to see you," she cried against his chest.

She was hatless and wore only a thin knitted shawl over her dress to ward off the evening's chill. He wrapped his arms around her tighter.

"I am glad to see you, too," he responded truthfully. She smelled so clean. Of lavender and soap.

She clung to him. "I have had the most wretched day!"

He kissed her on top of her head, his heart beating faster. "Tell me what has happened."

"Well, the reporters are back." She moved out of his embrace and rearranged her shawl. "One of them wrote something in the newspaper, and now they are all back."

"What did he write?" As if Samuel did not know.

Her hand fluttered to her forehead. "I do not know, really, but it upset m'lady."

He reached for her again. "Is that all it is? Newspaper reporters?"

She didn't fall back into his arms as he'd hoped. "And then his lordship came."

"His lordship?" Samuel felt a rush of excitement.

"Lord Levenhorne. He inherits Lord Wexin's estate." She paused. "Unless…"

"Unless what?"

She shook her head and her curls bounced around her face. "Oh, I do not understand all this. I just know m'lady is made unhappy by it."

He took her in his arms once again. "Do not fret, love. Is it about money? Wealthy people seem always to distress themselves about money."

She snuggled against him. "I suspect so. It is about the inheritance at any rate."

She felt so good next to him that he could hardly think and hardly wanted to. Mary had never actually told him Lady Wexin was going to have a child, but she'd skirted around the topic enough for him to guess.

Mary lifted her face and looked at him with her huge, trusting eyes. Samuel felt a twinge of conscience for pressing her. Enough for one night. He could concentrate on Lord Levenhorne next and just enjoy being with Mary for a while.

He dipped his head and touched his lips to hers, so soft and sweet.

Yes, he would enjoy these stolen kisses with Mary. He would enjoy them very much.

Chapter Eight

Does she hide out of shame? What would it be like, we wonder, Dear Readers, to carry the child of a murderer in one's womb? —*The New Observer*, April 11, 1819

Adrian watched the maid locked in the embrace of her lover. The two stumbled into the garden, still in each other's arms.

They had left the gate slightly open. Adrian stole over and peeked in. The lovers were headed for a far corner, away from the house.

Adrian had planned to knock at the front door, to be announced to Lydia properly even if the hour was unforgivably late, but one of the newspapers had left a young fellow watching the house, so Adrian had walked on by. He turned the corner just when the maid and her lover had wrapped their arms around each other.

It was all too easy. Adrian slipped through the gap in the gate and crept through the shadows to the back door. When he reached the door, it was unlatched.

He walked in, still intending to announce himself.

Sounds came from the kitchen, but when he peeked in, he could see no one. He continued to the stairs, climbing them as quietly as he could and opening the door a crack to see if anyone was in the hall.

Empty.

He ought to call out. Announce his presence.

Instead he climbed the marble stairs and saw a glow of light coming from the drawing room. Taking in a breath and holding it, he opened the door.

Lydia rose from a chair near the window, book in hand. An oil lamp on the table next to her gave more illumination than the waning daylight through the glass. The lamp lit her face with a soft glow, making her hair appear tinged with gold where the light touched it.

He had forgotten how lovely she was.

She gasped and dropped her book.

He stepped into the light. "Forgive me, Lydia, I know I intrude."

"Adrian!" Her voice was breathless. She took a step forwards as if glad to see him, but she quickly shrank back. "Why didn't Dixon announce you?"

"He does not know I am here." He gave a rueful smile. "I fear no one knows I am here. I truly did intrude, Lydia. I entered without anyone seeing me."

"Without anyone seeing you?" She picked up her book, closing it and placing it on the table.

"I entered through the back door." He did not wish to get the maid into trouble. "One of your servants stepped out for a moment, and I came in unseen." Saying it made him realise how outrageously he'd acted.

She looked rightfully indignant. "You *sneaked* into my house?"

"I know it sounds bad," he said with chagrin. "But there was a fellow watching the front door. From a newspaper, I expect." He paused, feeling as if he was not making sense. "Otherwise I would have knocked for admittance."

She held up a hand, stopping his explanation. "Never mind. Tell me why you are here when I asked you not to call upon me again."

"The newspaper this morning—" he began.

She swung away. "That—that—*horrid* paper."

In the low light and with her loose dress, he could not perceive any telltale changes signalling her condition. If anything, her figure appeared even more voluptuous than he remembered, as if she'd had enough food to eat.

"Is it true?" he asked.

She turned her head to him. "Is what true?"

He could think of no delicate way to say it. "Are you increasing?"

She blinked rapidly. "That is a very private matter, not one to discuss with a gentleman I hardly know."

He walked closer to her. "But it is how you know me that makes it my business. At least to ask."

Her breathing accelerated.

"Lydia?"

"You need not concern yourself, Adrian. I am well able to handle whatever my situation might be." She lifted her chin. "I am not as forlorn as when you first encountered me."

And he had been the one to take away her pitiable state, even if she would never know it. "I am glad of it."

She met his gaze steadily. "So there is no reason for you to come here."

She looked elegant and regal, even though her dress was a simple one more suited to morning. Her hair was piled in a loose knot on top of her head, tendrils escaping to caress her forehead and cheeks. He remembered how soft her curls had felt, slipping loose and luxuriously through his fingers. Even now he itched to pull the pins from her hair so that it would fall about her shoulders and he could grab a fistful in his hand.

He forced himself to his task. "Lydia, cut line. Are you going to have a child or not?"

He walked close enough to touch her. If he could place his hand on her belly he might feel for himself if a child grew within her. That would, he supposed, be even more of an intrusion than entering her house.

She raised her eyes to his, and he felt a jolt of attraction, the same attraction he'd been unable to resist when she'd asked him to make love to her. He waited for her to speak, his heart beating so hard, he thought she must be able to hear it.

She said nothing.

He tried again. "If the child is mine, Lydia, I will do my duty."

"Your duty?" Her voice rose. "What do you mean by your duty?"

His emotions were in a muddle about this, but he was enough of his father's son to know what was expected of a gentleman. "Marriage, if you should wish it."

"Marriage!" She spat out the word and quickly turned her face from him, silent for so long he had an impulse to prowl the room like a caged cat. Finally she cast her gaze upon him again. "Do you expect me to believe you would marry me?"

Why not? he wondered. "I am an honourable man, Lydia."

She gave a scoffing laugh. "You are a libertine, Adrian. Libertines do not marry."

Her words stung. "A libertine? And how is it you are so certain I am a libertine?"

"It is what people say of you. They call you a rake, at least, which is the same thing, is it not?"

He was not about to debate the differences between a rake and a libertine. His eyes narrowed. "You of all people should know not to give credit to gossip."

She glanced away, two spots of colour rising to her cheeks. "It is, nonetheless, all I know of you. I have no experience to tell me otherwise."

He waved his hand as if erasing that piece of conversation. "It matters not what you believe of me. If the child is mine, I will take responsibility, and that means marrying you, if that is what you desire."

Lydia glanced away, her muscles taut with anxiety. The *ton*'s most devil-may-care bachelor said he would marry her out of duty. She almost wished to laugh. The last thing in the world she desired was another marriage. She'd married once with stars in her eyes and look what a horror that husband had turned out to be.

But Adrian was not Wexin.

She darted a glance to him, so handsome, standing so tall and still. Masculine energy emanated from him, and, God help her, attracted her.

She'd be a fool to give in to the desire that pulsated inside her, a fool to entrust her life—and her child's—to any man.

She took in a fortifying breath. "There is no need for you to do anything, Adrian. There is no responsibility that I would hold you to."

He stepped away and bowed his head, seemingly lost in thought.

It would be so easy to simply lie and tell him the child was Wexin's, but she could not make herself say the words.

Think of what the newspapers would write about her if she married him and acknowledged the child as his. The world would know that she'd bedded a man before her husband was cold in his grave.

Her indiscretion had been the cause of this pregnancy. That made it her problem to handle, not Adrian's. If her child was born within the ten months stipulated by law, the child, son or daughter, would be considered Wexin's, but she would be in charge of her finances and her life.

She made herself look directly at Adrian again, even though looking at him made her heart leap and flutter and her body yearn for him. She could not forget how his hands had felt upon her, the softness of his lips, the firmness of his muscles. Her carnal urges flared into life and it was all she could do to keep from propositioning him again.

Dear God, she could not possibly want to couple with him again, not when she was hiding that this child was his.

"You need not have an attack of conscience or duty or whatever it is that men have," she said to him in an angry voice, although the anger was at herself for her weakness, not at him. "It is quite all right with me if you forget this matter."

He met her gaze and she thought she saw a wounded look in his eyes. "I have done nothing to deserve your bitter tone."

Her cheeks flamed at the truth of his statement, but she recovered quickly. "Nothing?" She hit him with the one dishonourable thing he had done. "I asked you not to call upon me again, and you break into my home like a thief."

"I did it to find out about the child," he shot back, taking a step towards her, coming so close she caught the clean scent of lime soap on his skin.

She held her ground with difficulty. "Is it so hard to believe that this baby is my husband's?"

His voice turned so low it vibrated inside her. "It is when I know there is a chance it is mine."

"Believe me, Adrian," she whispered, "it is not so easy for me to conceive a child that I would conceive after one time." At least it had not been that easy with Wexin. She softened her tone. "Take your leave. You have done enough by coming here. There is nothing I need from you."

To her surprise, he reached out to her and gently touched her arm. "Forgive me for not knowing. I have been abroad. They say you have been a recluse. Are you not going out at all? Is there no one who has renewed acquaintance with you?"

She was startled by his concern. Besides Lord Levenhorne calling today, and the occasional bank representative, no one but Adrian had called upon her. "No member of the *ton* wishes to see their name in the newspapers, I suspect."

He frowned. "You must not allow the newspapers to make you a prisoner in your house. Go where you please and ignore them."

He could say that with ease. He was not the one followed about, or stopped on the street and asked rude questions.

She glanced at his hand, still upon her arm, then back at him. "I am not certain I should heed advice from an intruder."

He did not take the hint and release her. "Then accept the advice as from a friend," he said. "Our connection may be brief and… unusual, but enough for me to be concerned for your welfare. I am here, if you need me. I will come, if you need me to."

She held her breath.

His words felt like a proposition, an invitation to seduction. His touch melted her like a flame melts wax. She felt she would only have to put her arms around his neck and her lips against his and in a moment they would be making love on the settee. God help her, she did need him. She needed to feel him hold her with strong arms, needed to run her hands up his firm chest, to dig her fingers into his hair. She needed to feel him fill her again, as a man fills a woman. She trembled with need.

But she backed away. "I need nothing from you."

He stared at her, a hint of pain in his angry eyes. Her guilt escalated. Obviously he had not shared her carnal thoughts.

He swung away and started walking towards the door. It felt the same as when he had left her before, loneliness engulfing her.

He reached the door and turned back to her. "I will trouble you no further."

As he disappeared into the dark hallway, she collapsed in her chair and placed her hand over where his baby grew.

* * *

Adrian went straight to Madame Bisou's, a gaming hell he knew on Bennet Street. He and Tanner had often spent a night at the tables there, and Adrian had been known to flirt with the pretty girls Madame Bisou employed.

When he walked into the gaming room looking more for a drink than a seat at a table, a voice greeted him. "Pomroy!"

A flaming red-haired young woman wearing a dress of ice blue ran over to him and grabbed his arm.

"Katy Green." He kissed her on the cheek. "But it is not Pomroy. It is Cavanley."

She laughed. "I forgot. Sir Reginald told me about you being called lord now."

She released him and examined him with her elbows akimbo and a line creasing her forehead. "I declare, you look healthy enough. I thought you must be very ill. You have not been here in an age."

He had not been to Madame Bisou's since the previous spring, and it seemed a lot had happened since then. "I've been in France." France was as good an explanation as any.

She grinned at him and winked. "Wait until Madame Bisou hears. You will make her homesick."

The closest the *madame*, born Penny Jones, had come to France had been drinking a bottle of champagne and he and Katy both knew it.

Katy took his arm again and escorted him through the room where the tables were covered with green baize. Three of the walls were lined with faro and hazard tables. Against the fourth wall one of the girls served drinks.

"What are you looking to play tonight?" Katy asked him. "Faro? Hazard?"

He rolled his eyes. "Fool's games." Luck, not skill, made winners in hazard and faro, and luck always favoured the house. "What I really want is a brandy."

"Brandy!" she cried. "Come with me."

He was soon sipping the burning liquid, but it failed to ease the hard rock of emotion inside him.

He'd done his duty by offering to marry Lydia. He ought to be glad he'd escaped marriage. The parson's mousetrap, he and Tanner used to call it, but it nagged at him that she did not think him worthy of marrying. *A libertine*, she had called him. And she wanted nothing to do with him.

It also nagged at him that she'd not actually denied that the child was his. He only knew she did not wish him to be her husband. Why had she not accepted his proposal? He was wealthy. He came from a good family.

Adrian finished the brandy, took another, and answered his own question. She had no wish to be married to a *libertine*.

He could not blame her for that opinion of him. He'd cultivated the reputation of a rake, even if it had never been entirely accurate. He did not trifle with women's hearts. His liaisons with women involved mutual desire, and their partings were mostly amicable.

He finished the second brandy in one gulp and asked for another.

Katy's eyes grew wide. "Oh, ho, you are thirsty tonight."

He extended his glass again for the girl to refill. "Very thirsty. Thirsty enough to get thoroughly drunk."

"Oooh. That must mean a problem with the ladies."

He downed the third glass and thrust his hand out once more. "Have you not heard, Katy Green? Libertines do not have problems with ladies."

At a proper morning hour, Samuel Reed waited in a small parlour off the hall of Lord Levenhorne's townhouse, a place where, undoubtedly, tradesmen and other men who toiled for a living waited for his lordship. Samuel did not resent it. He was only grateful that he had not been summarily ejected.

After at least a quarter of an hour, a footman entered. "Lord Levenhorne will see you now."

Samuel was led to the library, where Lord Levenhorne sat behind an elegant desk with thin carved legs and made of some dark wood—mahogany or oak, perhaps.

"Mr Reed, m'lord," the footman said before bowing and leaving the room.

When Levenhorne looked up, Samuel bowed as well. "Thank you for seeing me, my lord."

"What business do you have with me, Reed? Your card tells me you are from that *New Observer* paper." Lord Levenhorne sounded none too pleased.

But he had agreed to see Samuel, so that gave him courage. "If you read my paper, sir, you will know that I am following the story of Lady Wexin—"

Levenhorne coughed. "I've seen what you wrote."

Samuel nodded. "I wonder, my lord, what you can tell me about the lady. My sources inform me that she is to bear a child—"

"That, unfortunately, appears to be true—" Levenhorne seemed to catch himself. He stopped talking and peered more closely at Samuel. "These are family matters, Reed. Not the stuff for newspapers."

Samuel took the liberty of advancing one step closer. "Ah, but I have a reporter's sense, and I believe there is a story in Lady Wexin." He gave Levenhorne an intent look. "If she produces a son, he will inherit Wexin's property and title, is that not correct?"

"Such as it is," the man murmured just loud enough for Samuel to hear him.

"And you will inherit if she produces a daughter, or if the child is not born in time."

"That is so," Levenhorne said in a careful voice.

"If this child is not Wexin's, however…"

Levenhorne leaned forwards. "What do you know?"

The man was interested. Samuel had him. Levenhorne would tell him what he wanted to know. He spoke carefully. "I am speculating that Lady Wexin's child is not Wexin's."

Levenhorne rubbed his chin. "She certainly did not appear to be a woman in her sixth month."

Samuel almost smiled. He had his verification. Lady Wexin was breeding and the baby was not her husband's.

Levenhorne waved his hand. "It is of no consequence. All she must do is give birth in time and it bloody well doesn't matter who the father is."

Samuel gave Levenhorne an earnest look. "But what if my newspaper can bring pressure on the lady to openly identify the father? Would not there be a chance she'd marry the fellow? If they both acknowledge the baby as that other man's, then the inheritance goes to you."

"Indeed," said Levenhorne in a contemplative voice.

"I will write the story. We have four months to put pressure on her." Four months of building sales of the newspaper. Everyone would want to see what next would happen with the scandalous Lady Wexin. "All I ask is that you support the idea that another man is the father."

"I do support it," said his lordship.

"I am in your debt, then, my lord." Samuel bowed again. "If you hear anything about who the man may be, please send word to me."

Levenhorne stood and extended his hand. "I will do so, indeed, sir."

Chapter Nine

The question remains—who is the father of Lady W—'s child? The time advances quickly that will tell for certain if the baby is the late Lord W—'s heir or another man's child. —*The New Observer*, July 21, 1819

On this warm July day, almost three and a half months after Samuel had first broken the news of Lady W's *interesting condition*, a gentleman walked into *The New Observer* office where Samuel and his brother Phillip sat at their desks. The man's white pantaloons were so tight his legs seemed made of wood. His blue coat fitted so well his forearms barely budged from his sides. With some difficulty he reached up to remove his high-crowned beaver hat. With this in one hand, he struggled to pull a white handkerchief from his pocket to mop his brow.

Samuel cast a glance at his brother, and Phillip clamped his mouth shut, a cough covering laughter.

"I wonder if I might speak to Mr Reed," the fashionable creature said in a voice as soft as the fabric of his pristine neckcloth.

"Which one?" Phillip asked him.

"Is there more than one? Oh, dear." His eyelids fluttered. "I desire to speak to the Mr Reed who writes about Lady Wexin—I beg your pardon—I mean *Lady W*."

"You want Samuel Reed," Phillip said.

"Do I?" He made a slight bow. "Then perhaps you might tell me how I might get hold of him."

Samuel stood. "I am Samuel Reed, sir, and you are?"

The man tittered. "I must beg pardon once more. I ought to have presented myself. I am Lord Chasey, at your service." He bowed again.

"Lord Chasey," Samuel repeated. "What do you wish to speak to me about?"

"About Lady Wexin—I mean, *Lady W*." He tittered again.

"What about her?" Samuel and Phillip asked in unison.

"I am certain that I might be the father of her child."

"You?" Samuel's voice rose an octave. He did not believe this for an instant.

"I do think I am certain of it." Lord Chasey repeated, all seriousness.

"Why do you come here to tell us?" Phillip asked.

From a pocket in his waistcoat Chasey pulled out a quizzing glass and peered at Phillip through it. "And who might you be?"

Phillip rose. "Phillip Reed, the editor of the newspaper."

"Oh!" exclaimed Chasey. "You have the same surname."

"Brothers usually do," responded Phillip.

Chasey's eyebrows rose. "You are brothers?"

"Yes, we are," replied Samuel. "What is it you want of me, my lord?"

"Why, to print my name in your newspaper as being the father of the unborn child. You can call me Viscount C from Yorkshire. That should do it."

Phillip shot Samuel another amused glance. If he was not careful, the two of them would burst out laughing.

"Let me make certain I understand you." Samuel gave him a droll look. "You wish me to report that you take responsibility for Lady Wexin's unborn child?"

"Responsibility?" Lord Chasey squeaked. "Dear me, no. I merely want you to imply that I could possibly be the father."

This man wants his name in the paper. Samuel had encountered many like him before. Who knows? Perhaps Viscount C from Yorkshire thought this would raise him in the esteem of his companions, the way the latest in waistcoats might do.

Samuel rubbed his face. He might as well print the story. The more men who came forwards claiming to be the father, the more newspapers they sold. "Very well, sir."

Chasey beamed.

Samuel could not resist adding, "But you must promise to report back to me every detail of your next meeting with her—all that a gentleman can tell, that is."

"My next meeting—?" Lord Chasey glanced around in distress. He took several quick breaths and mopped his brow again. "I…uh…will certainly report every possible detail of any…uh…future meeting I have with the lady."

Phillip twisted away, covering his mouth. His shoulders shook.

Samuel extended his hand to Lord Chasey. "I shall compose a mention of you for tomorrow's paper."

Chasey stuffed his handkerchief back in his pocket and accepted Samuel's handshake, grinning like an excited schoolboy. "Excellent! That is excellent." He managed to put his hat back on his head. "I will take my leave of you, then."

One more bow and Chasey was gone, the door closing behind him. Phillip let loose, laughing so hard tears came to his eyes. "I'll wager you ten pounds that popinjay has never been within four miles of Lady Wexin."

"No bet." Samuel grinned. "I'll use his name, though. We might as well share the joke with our readers."

Samuel wanted to keep the speculation alive as to whether another man had fathered Lady Wexin's unborn child. To own the truth, Samuel had discovered nothing to suggest that the baby was any man's but Wexin's, but his gut told him there was someone else. Unfortunately, his meetings with Lady Wexin's maid, Mary, had yielded nothing.

No information, that is. Samuel's time with Mary was the best part of his week. They met whenever she could get away, sharing ices at Gunter's or strolling through Hyde Park. The best times were evenings when he waited near the gate for her. He'd stolen no more than kisses, but Mary's kisses were sweeter than another woman's favours.

Lord Levenhorne reported that August 16 was the crucial date. If Lady Wexin's baby was not born at the stroke of midnight, separating August 15 from August 16, it would prove that the father was another man. The story would remain alive at least that long, and Samuel would have reason to keep seeing Mary. She would keep thinking he was Samuel Charles who worked for a printer, but this idyll could not last for ever.

Frowning, Samuel pulled out a sheet of paper and trimmed a quill pen before dipping it into a pot of ink. He scratched out several lines about Lord C, the Irish Viscount who claimed to be the father of Lady W's child.

Ironic that Chasey possessed the same initial as the man Samuel had first suspected to have been Lady Wexin's lover. Beyond the one brief encounter of which Samuel had been a part, Samuel could not discover from Mary or anyone else that Lord Cavanley had ever set foot in Lady Wexin's house. Mary did not seem to know who Cavanley was.

Levenhorne said the betting book in White's did not give Cavanley any odds of being the father. Odds favoured Lord Crayden, who had been known to court Lady Wexin before her betrothal to her murderous husband, but Samuel could not discover that Crayden had called upon the lady either. There were other men who had boasted of being Lady W's secret lover, but none proved more than idle boasting.

The child's paternity remained a mystery. Samuel did not mind using the mystery to keep speculation alive, but the newsman in him pined to beat the other papers to the real story.

He finished the short but tantalising column and poured blotting sand on it, carefully shaking the excess sand back into its container.

Chasey would have to do for the moment, one small step in Samuel's quest to make *The New Observer* number one above *The Morning Post*, *The Morning Chronicle*, *The Times* and all the other papers vying for the position.

Adrian walked into his parents' library. His father was seated behind the desk attending to his correspondence; his mother reclined on a chaise reading.

She closed her book. "Adrian, we were so worried about you!" Her white hair made her look every inch the countess she now was. She'd always been a beautiful woman and remained so in her maturity.

Adrian crossed the room and kissed her on the cheek. "Forgive me. I did not mean to distress you."

His father looked at him over spectacles perched on his nose. "I wrote to you two days ago."

Adrian had received his father's missive, but had stuffed it in his pocket and headed off to Madame Bisou's, where he'd engaged in a marathon of card playing and drinking, something that had become a pattern for him of late. When he'd woken up this morning at Madame Bisou's, he'd had no clear memory of how he'd spent the entire previous day. His father's letter and one from Tanner were still in the pocket of the coat he had slept in.

Adrian answered his father. "I came as soon as I read it." Which was true enough. "I confess, I feared bad news, but you both look the picture of health." Better to shift the attention to their health than to dwell on his own.

"There is nothing amiss with us," his mother said. "Would you like a sherry, love?"

Adrian's stomach roiled. "Later, perhaps."

His father ceremoniously took off his spectacles and folded them, placing them on the desk. "I summoned you because of concern about *you*."

"Me?" Adrian was genuinely surprised.

"This dissipated life you are leading—" his father began.

"—is not healthy for you, dear," his mother finished.

He looked from one to the other. "Dissipated life?"

His father leaned forwards. "This drinking. Spending all your time in gaming hells. Coming home looking as if you slept in your clothes."

Obviously someone from Adrian's household had been reporting on his behaviour. Adrian's bets were on Bilson, the loyal butler. Loyal to Adrian's father, that is.

"Father, my behaviour is not much altered from what it has always been." Except perhaps for the drinking to excess and finding himself in a bed with no memory of how he had arrived there.

"You are drinking entirely too much." His father rose and walked from behind the desk.

His mother cupped her hand against his face. "You will lose your handsome good looks if you drink too much. You'll get a red nose and have blotches on your cheeks."

"Where have you heard such things about me?" Adrian gaped at them.

His father looked chagrined. "Well, people talk, you know."

Former servants obviously did.

Adrian lifted a hand to his forehead. The headache from the previous night's drinking lingered there, no longer a sledgehammer, but a dull thudding. He shook his head. "A few months ago when I asked for something to do, take over one of the estates, perhaps, you all but told me to go drink, gamble and otherwise cavort. Now you are outraged that I am doing what you said I should?"

"I would never have told you to get a red nose, dear," his mother said.

His father huffed. "You wanted to take over one of the estates? How can you expect me to trust you with such a task when you are being so reckless with drink?"

What else was he supposed to do? Adrian wanted to ask.

"I think it is high time Adrian went searching for a wife." His mother nodded decisively. "The Season is over, but he might go to Brighton. There were plenty of eligible young ladies in Brighton when we were there, were there not? It is something to consider."

"I did not mean to put the boy in shackles, Irene," his father retorted.

His mother stiffened. "Marriage is akin to being shackled?"

"I did not say that." His father hastened to his wife's side and put his arm around her. "I merely meant he ought to enjoy life while he can, without duty dictating to him."

His mother pouted. "You implied a man cannot enjoy life if he is married."

"I did not say that," his father murmured.

"You did say it," his mother persisted.

Adrian held up a hand. "Do not argue over this."

His mother pressed her mouth closed, but his father lifted her chin and gave her a light kiss on the lips.

She reluctantly smiled.

His father kissed her again and strode over to a side cupboard, removing a decanter of sherry and three glasses. "Marriage is a great responsibility," he said to Adrian. "I do not encourage you to marry now, while you are engaged in such dissipation. I urge you to show more restraint. Stop the drinking." As he spoke Adrian's father poured sherry into the glasses and handed one to his wife and one to Adrian.

Adrian almost laughed. Only his father could chastise him for drinking at the same moment as handing him a drink.

His mother took her glass. "Well, I do urge you to look about for a wife. There is no hurry for it, I agree, but you might as well discover who will be out next Season."

Adrian set his glass down on the table.

All he could think was that had Lydia accepted his proposal all those months ago, he'd have no reason to become dissipated.

But Lydia had not accepted him.

Adrian picked up the glass of sherry and drained it of its contents.

As soon as he was able, he extricated himself from the insane asylum that was his parents' townhouse and headed back home, vowing to be more discreet in his activities so the details did not get whispered in his father's ear.

Adrian winced at the brightness of the day. The sky was a milky white and hurt his aching eyes if he looked up. He tilted his head just enough to keep his eyes shaded by the brim of his hat. He neared Hill Street, depressing his spirits even more. All of London was depressing him.

Perhaps he should visit Tanner after all. Tanner had written to invite him to Scotland where he and his wife were spending the summer months and awaiting the birth of their first child.

Ha! Not likely he would be welcome there. What was this with having babies? Was every woman bearing a child this summer?

Adrian vowed he would not think of that. Nor of Lydia refusing his proposal.

But Tanner had also offered Adrian another of his estates, Nickerham Priory in Sussex. Adrian had visited Nickerham with Tanner on Tanner's tour of his properties the year before and could agree it would be an excellent place to spend a summer. High on a cliff overlooking the sea and cooled by sea breezes, there would be nothing to do but ride the South Downs or walk along the seashore.

Adrian might very possibly go insane there, left to nothing but his own company and his own thoughts.

Vowing to write Tanner a gracious return letter this very day—or tomorrow—Adrian crossed into Hill Street. He rarely walked through Mayfair without finding himself passing by Lydia's townhouse.

He spied the reporters lounging about her door and became angry on her behalf all over again. The leeches. Why did they not leave the lady in peace? Why could they not content themselves with writing about the thousands of weavers assembling in Carlisle in protest against low wages, the trade crisis in Frankfurt, or an earthquake near Rome? Why devote so much space to speculation about Lydia? He'd read in the papers that the father of her child was anyone from the Prince Regent to a passing gypsy.

Was she in good health? he wondered. Bearing children might be the most natural thing in the world, but many women died from it. Babies died, as well. His mother had borne Adrian a brother and sister, neither of whom had lived longer than a few days.

Staying on the opposite side of the street, Adrian tried not to glance at her house. Another gentleman approached in the opposite direction.

"Good day to you, Cavanley." The gentleman greeted him in clipped, but jovial tones.

"Crayden." Adrian tipped his hat.

Crayden possessed thick black hair that women fancied and a face that always held a smug expression. Adrian was not among Crayden's admirers. Crayden curried any favour that was possible to curry. He insinuated himself into investments lucrative enough to keep his debt-ridden estate from doom's door, but he was equally as likely to drop a friendship if it failed to gain him a profit.

Lord Crayden smiled his ingratiating smile and put his hand on Adrian's shoulder as if he was accustomed to sharing confidences with him. "I suppose I shall have to run the gauntlet, eh? I am calling upon Lady Wexin, you know."

No, Adrian didn't know, and he did not very much like knowing it now. What business did this ferret have with Lydia? Lydia's fortune was modest, Adrian knew for a fact, having been the one to restore it.

"Are you?" Adrian said.

"I am indeed." Crayden clapped Adrian on the shoulder and winked. He crossed the street and ploughed right into the nest of newspaper men, who clamoured after him, waving their hands and asking him questions.

Adrian watched as Lydia's butler answered the door, and Crayden said with a voice loud enough to reach Adrian's ears, "Lord Crayden to see Lady Wexin."

The reporters all pressed forwards, yelling their questions. After Crayden gained entry and the door was closed again, the newspaper men buzzed among themselves for a moment, before turning to look towards Adrian.

Adrian hurried on his way.

Lydia walked to the window of the drawing room and peeked through a gap in the curtain. She thought she'd heard a commotion outside. The newspaper men were still there, all talking about something, but it was not their vile presence that caught her attention, but the figure of a man across the street, looking towards her house.

She'd know Adrian anywhere, even from such a distance, even with his hat shading his face. Had he decided to call upon her again? Even though she'd refused him?

No one called upon her. No one except Lord Levenhorne and he did so merely to check the size of her waistline.

She ought to feel outrage that Adrian would ignore her wishes so blatantly, but instead she felt flushed with excitement. The baby kicked inside her. The baby kicked often now and would be born soon, the physician who attended her said.

She rushed over to the mirror above the fireplace and checked her appearance. Her hair hung undressed in a plait down her back. The gown she wore was an old one Mary had let out so her now larger breasts would not spill over the bodice, and her big tummy would be shrouded by a full skirt. She contemplated changing, but feared nothing else would be ready to wear except nightdresses and robes, and she did not trust herself in such attire around Adrian.

In any event, there was no time, because Dixon entered the room. "There is a Lord Crayden to see you, my lady."

"What?" She thought she had misheard him.

"Lord Crayden, my lady." He held out the gentleman's card.

She stared at it, her spirits plummeting. It was Adrian she wanted to see, wanted to be with even for a little while. She pined to see his eyes filled with concern for her, to feel less alone in his presence.

"But why would this gentleman call upon me?" She handed the card back to Dixon.

She had not even seen Lord Crayden in an age. He had once been a suitor, but never a favoured one. He had no connection to her family or to Wexin's. He certainly was not a friend. His biggest shortcoming, however, was that he was not Adrian.

"I do not want to see him," she said.

Dixon bowed. "Very well, my lady." He turned to leave.

"Wait." She stopped him. "Do you suppose he has been abroad and brings news of my parents?"

It was the only reason she could think of that the gentleman would call. One letter from her parents, dated months ago, had finally reached her from India, but, from its contents, it was apparent that none of Lydia's letters had reached them.

"He did not say so, my lady," Dixon replied.

"Well, send him up, I suppose."

A few minutes later Crayden was announced.

"Lady Wexin." He bowed.

She took a step towards him. "Lord Crayden, do you bring me news?"

"News?" He looked puzzled.

"Of my parents? My brother?" She braced herself.

He blinked. "They are abroad, are they not?"

She released a frustrated breath. "You do not bring news of my family? Why are you here?"

He smiled, showing his white, even teeth. "I call merely to inquire after your health—and to offer my condolences."

She did not believe him. "Condolences? I've been a widow for three-quarters of a year."

His expression turned sympathetic. "I thought it best not to cause comment by calling upon you sooner."

Such as during the brief time after the Queen had died when the newspapers had left her alone? "So you choose now when I am written of daily, with one man after another connected to my name?"

He gave no indication he perceived her barb. "I thought you might need a friend at this difficult time."

When Adrian had offered her friendship she had almost believed him. This man she believed not at all.

"Lord Crayden, I knew you only very briefly during my come-out." And then she'd refused his suit. "It is presumptuous of you to call upon me. Indeed, it makes me very unhappy. You expose me to more gossip I do not deserve."

A wounded look crossed his face. "My lady, my intentions are honourable, I assure you. I have always had a regard for you, as you well know—"

A regard for her dowry, he must mean.

"I have worried over your welfare and could not wait another moment to assure myself that you were in good health."

"Be assured, then, Lord Crayden, to what is none of your concern." Her tone was sharp.

She walked towards the door Dixon had left open. She trusted the butler was nearby.

"I am delighted to know you are well," Crayden continued, undaunted. "I shall rest easier at night."

"That is splendid," she said with great sarcasm, gesturing to the door. "You can have no other business here, then."

He bowed again. "I shall take my leave of you, my dear lady, but I fear you will not be gone from my thoughts."

She laughed drily. "I have become quite used to people thinking of me. Good day, sir."

As he walked past her to the door, he bowed again.

After he left, her biggest regret at his visit was that he'd not been Adrian.

Chapter Ten

All London waits for news of Lady W—. Before midnight calls in the sixteenth day of August, Lady W— must give birth lest the world discover unequivocally that the child is not Lord W—'s progeny. *The New Observer* assures its readers it will keep a vigil up to the very stroke of midnight. In a Special Edition tomorrow morning, *The New Observer* will provide the answer.

—*The New Observer*, August 15, 1819

Samuel waited outside the gate of Lady Wexin's house. The night was warm and the haze that seemed to settle over London in the summer obscured the stars. Candlelight shone from the windows of the houses.

There were only two hours left for Lady Wexin's chance to give birth to a legitimate, and Samuel had planned this assignation with Mary at this hour to discover whether Lady Wexin would make the time limit or not. The house had been quiet all day.

Through an open window he heard the faint chiming of a clock. Ten o'clock. He peered into the darkness to see if he could spy Mary coming. His wait was short. The gate opened and she appeared.

"Mary," he greeted her in a low voice.

"Sam!" She hurried into his arms, warm and delightful.

"Ah, my love," he murmured, wasting no time in bending his face to hers and tasting her eager lips.

Their encounters became more and more passionate each time they met. Their last time together had been spent walking in Hyde Park where Samuel had found a secluded bench and nearly forgot to engage Mary in conversation. Even though pursuing the story of Lady W filled his days, thoughts of Mary consumed his restless nights. He wanted her more desperately than he had ever wanted a woman. What little conscience he still possessed kept him from bedding her.

Her kisses were driving away that fragile resolve. They could so easily walk into the garden to the bench nestled among the fragrant foliage…

He reluctantly broke away from her. "Tell me of your day," he murmured.

"We can sit in the garden," she whispered, taking him by the hand and leading him through the gate to the bench.

He sat her on his lap, her soft derrière so very tantalising and arousing. "Now, tell me how you fare. I want to hear all about your days since I saw you last."

Mary rested her head upon his shoulder. "I have spent the whole day fretting about my lady. She has remained in her bedchamber all day, not talking much, not eating. I know she is so worried and I am worried for her."

"No baby, I take it." He spoke the obvious.

"No baby." She sighed. "She's not even having pains."

"She'll not have the baby tonight, then?" He hoped she would say more.

She squirmed on top of him and he forgot that he wanted

her to answer him. His hands slipped to her waist and he pressed her harder against him.

"Oh, Sam," she groaned, twisting to face him, straddling him.

He kissed her again, his hand cupping one of her pert little breasts. He slipped it under her dress and felt her soft skin, her firm nipple. All he need do was unbutton his trousers and he could couple with her.

"Sam," she murmured into his ear, her tongue tickling the sensitive skin there, "I want to do this with you. I'm sure of it."

He took his hand away from her breast and lifted her off him, feeling like a cad. She was young and fresh and virginal, and he was using her to get his story. How would she feel if he made love to her and then she discovered his real name and purpose?

"No, Mary." She reached for him again, and he moved her arms away. "You are too tempting. I want you, but we cannot do this."

She whimpered. "I know you are right. It is difficult, though."

He laughed softly and brushed her curls from her cheek. "Very difficult."

She took his hand in hers and laid her head against his shoulder. "I wonder if it was like this for my lady."

Samuel jolted back to his purpose. "What do you mean?"

"Well, she must have been with someone. Maybe it was difficult for her, too."

He tried not to sound eager. "Who was she with? Do you know?"

She sighed again. "I cannot think of anyone she could have been with. She's been alone all this time, and it is so sad that her friends have left her. Even when she was going out a little, you know, after the Queen died. I can't remember a time she went out alone." She sat up straight. "Unless…"

His heart pounded. "Unless, what?"

She rested against him again. "It could not be. It is just that she went out once, before the Queen died, but it was on an errand, not to meet anyone."

"It might have been then, though?" he asked, forcing a conversational tone.

"It might have been, but she was going to—" She broke off, as if catching herself in something she ought not to say.

Just the sort of information he wanted to hear.

They had talked of this before, but she was always so careful of what she said, protective of her lady even with the man pretending to court her. Samuel kept hoping that she would say something or remember something that would lead him to the baby's father. Lord Chasey's claim had been a false one, not that Samuel had been surprised. After one of their reporters said Lord Crayden had called upon her, Samuel had checked on Crayden, as well, but there was no evidence he had called upon her before.

Mary rose from the bench. "I should go back to her."

Samuel stood as well, but was not quite as ready to end the conversation. "And you do not suspect anyone in the house." He'd asked her that before, as well.

She shook her head. "I would know if that happened. Besides, our men are not like that and neither is my lady."

He touched her cheek. "Indeed." He spoke as reassuringly as he could. "It is a mystery all London is wondering about, is it not?"

She collapsed into his arms again. "I hate that my lady has to read her name in all those awful newspapers."

"Indeed."

Samuel gave her one more kiss before she walked him back to the gate.

Adrian sat back in his chair at White's. It was past midnight and he'd spent the last three hours in the card room. He'd lost this night, not a great sum, but a loss, nonetheless.

He nursed a brandy, the first of the night. His parents would be proud that he had altered his behaviour of late. His parents' concern and his own alarm had jarred him out of a downward spiral.

Adrian took a sip of brandy and glanced around the room where other gentlemen sat at tables, drinking as he was. None of them seemed to notice he had changed, that his good cheer was forced, that his usual pursuits were boring him.

He closed his eyes, savouring the woody taste of the liquid and the warm feeling spreading in his chest.

Laughter roused him.

Levenhorne, seated at a table in the middle of the room, seemed to find something extremely amusing. A footman stood at his elbow. Levenhorne held a piece of paper in his hand.

"Listen, everyone!" Levenhorne stood and held the paper high in the air. "At midnight tonight the ten months was up! Lady Wexin did not produce an heir. The estate and title are mine."

"Bravo!" shouted one fellow. Others applauded.

Levenhorne bowed with a flourish.

"Dash it," one man said, "I wagered on her having a son."

Levenhorne clapped the man on the back. "You may still have a chance to win that wager. She has not yet given birth."

The other gentleman joined in Levenhorne's laughter.

Adrian's grip on his glass tightened.

Lydia had not had her baby. She'd wanted him to believe the baby was Wexin's, but now there was no chance at all.

Adrian rose and left the room. He retrieved his hat and walked out into the warm summer night.

He knew, had always known. Lydia's baby was his.

Blast her. She must have known it as well.

Adrian walked fast, the idea of his child being born a bastard filling his mind. Before he knew it he was on Lydia's street, in front of her townhouse. He stopped.

The reporters were gone.

They had probably dashed off to write their stories.

Adrian stared at her door for several seconds. It was an unforgivable hour upon which to call, but he suspected the household would still be awake on such a night.

He strode to the door and loudly sounded the knocker.

It did not take long for the door to open. "I told you all to bugger off—" Lydia's butler's fierce expression turned to surprise. "Oh! I—I beg pardon, my lord, I did not know…" The man peered at him. "What do you want, my lord?"

Adrian stuck his foot in the door. "I wish to see Lady Wexin."

The butler's brows rose. "Do you realise the hour, my lord?"

"I am very cognisant of the hour and of what has *not* taken place here this night." Adrian put pressure on the door. "I presume she is not sleeping. Tell Lady Wexin I wish to see her."

The butler still hesitated.

Adrian lowered his voice. "Listen, man. The reporters are gone. No one will know I've come. I beg you, announce me to Lady Wexin."

The butler opened the door and allowed Adrian entry.

Lydia sat in the rocking chair she'd had Dixon purchase for her. She'd hoped to be rocking her baby by this time.

It would be lovely if she could indulge in a fit of tears, yell and scream and pull at her hair, but instead there was only this cold stark terror inside her. By dawn, the world would know she'd become pregnant by another man, a man she'd lain with when her husband, vile man that he was, had been dead only a matter of weeks.

She would have to leave London. Go somewhere where no one knew her, where she could raise her child away from the newspapers and gossip-mongers. Her sister would surely not wish to see her; her parents, if they ever returned, would shun her as well.

How did one sell a house and its contents? Could she afford all the servants? Some would not wish to remain with her, she was certain.

"My lady, do you wish to get ready for bed?"

Mary sounded almost afraid to speak to her. Poor Mary. She had been so faithful, so good about not asking questions. Mary had been the only person who had known for certain this baby was not Wexin's. Now everyone knew.

"In a little while, Mary." Lydia tried to appear composed.

A knock sounded on her bedchamber door. Mary walked over and opened it a crack. "It is Mr Dixon."

Dixon stepped in, looking distressed. "My lady, there is a gentleman to see you."

Someone sent to verify that she had not given birth, she supposed. "Send him away."

"It is Lord Cavanley." Dixon wrung his hands.

Adrian stepped into the room.

"See here—" began Dixon.

Adrian ignored him and walked straight over to her. "Let us speak alone."

Lydia's heart pounded. She glanced from Mary to Dixon, both open-mouthed with shock. "It is all right," she said to them. "I will see him alone."

Dixon needed to take Mary by the arm to escort her out.

When the door closed, Lydia looked up at Adrian, so handsome in the lamplight. She continued to rock back and forth in her chair. "What do you want, Adrian?" she asked.

"Truth." His gaze slipped from her face to the round mound of her abdomen. "Is the baby mine?"

She turned her head away. "I suppose you have surmised that I am not carrying Wexin's child."

"I never thought you were." His voice was deep and angry. "Is the baby mine?"

Lydia glanced into his eyes, which were filled with pain.

"Do you, like the newspapers, think it might be the child of a gypsy or a manservant?"

His gaze remained steady. "Answer my question."

She bowed her head. "The baby is yours, Adrian."

His anger, his pain, his very presence here confused her. She had already released him from any responsibility. Why had he come?

He stepped back. "Why, Lydia? Why keep this from me?"

The cold terror inside her was cracking like thin ice under his gaze. She did not wish to break apart in front of this man, who would be kind to her, as he had been before. His kindness was what had led her to seduce him, but that had been her doing, not his.

"I did not want you to know," she managed to respond.

"You did not wish me to know." He looked so wounded.

She could almost hear the crack-crack-crack of her control. Hot tears stung her eyes and her throat felt tight. She could not speak and so forced a shrug in response.

He swung away for a moment before turning back with a piercing gaze. "I offered you marriage, Lydia. I offered to acknowledge my paternity—"

She waved a dismissive hand and struggled to her feet. "You did your duty."

He came closer to her. "Yes, my duty, but you preferred my child to have a murderer's name."

Her cheeks stung as if he'd struck her. He spoke the truth and hearing it made her ashamed. "I—I did not wish to be married, Adrian." Her voice sounded too fragile, too vulnerable.

"Cut line, Lydia." His eyes flashed. "You did not wish to be married to me."

"I did not want to be married to anyone," she shot back.

He twisted away, making a sound of disgust.

She stepped towards him, placing her hand upon his shoulder. "Adrian, understand me. I thought I had a perfect marriage once. It was all lies, vile, evil lies. Do you really think I would trust any man after that?"

He straightened. "I am not Wexin."

She dropped her hand and wrapped her arms around herself. "Yes. Yes. You are not Wexin, but you are—"

He swung around. "A libertine?"

Lydia turned away, but he circled her so she was forced to look at him.

"You have made it very clear what you think of me, Lydia, and you made your choice, preferring my son or daughter be thought the progeny of a murderer rather than a libertine, but that matters little now, does it not?"

She tried to meet his eyes, but could not bear to see her shame reflected there. "I had a chance to be free of a man's control and I took it."

"You gambled with my son or daughter."

She inhaled a quick breath. She'd gambled and lost.

He took her chin in his fingers and lifted her face so she could not avoid looking at him. His touch, even in this circumstance, even in her condition, gave her a physical awareness of him.

"You cannot pretend my child is Wexin's now. What were you planning to do?" A muscle in his cheek flexed and he bent closer to her.

She shuddered. "I do not know."

He released her and stepped back from her.

She shook her head in confusion. "I expect nothing from you, Adrian. You are free. I take full responsibility."

He stood straight and tall in front of her. "The blood that flows through that child is mine. That makes the child my duty. My responsibility."

She rushed forwards, grabbing the front of his coat. "I will not allow you to take my child from me," she cried, feeling her emotions rise to hysteria. "I will deny you are the baby's father! You cannot have my child!"

His eyes widened briefly. He did not speak.

Lydia let go of his coat.

Finally, he spoke in a low and rumbling voice. "You misunderstand me, madam. My duty is to marry you, acknowledge the child and take responsibility for you both."

And then what? she wanted to add.

"I am waiting for your answer." He looked down at her.

She glanced up at him. "That was a proposal? You wish me to marry you and give you control of me and my child? To have your secrets kept from me? How can I put this plainer, Adrian? I have no wish to be married at all, let alone be married to a man such as you."

His eyes shot sparks. "Do not be so foolish, Lydia. This has nothing to do with what you want. Or what I want, for that matter. We must think of the child. If we marry in time, your son would be an earl some day. Your daughter would possess not only name, but fortune. No matter what you think of me, I offer a life of comfort, of advantage to our child."

Her heart pounded. "No, Adrian. Forget me. I will leave London and you will never hear of me again."

He stepped closer and seized her arms, leaning so close only inches separated their lips. "What of our child then, Lydia?" His eyes were like daggers. "You offer the child no name, no advantages, no protection, only the disgrace of being a bastard." His gaze did not waver and did not soften. "You must marry me."

She still could not speak.

He shook her. "For God's sake, Lydia. You must marry me."

She gasped and admitted her greatest fear. "You will be able to take my child away from me."

He released her. "Yes, as your husband I will have that right. I do not expect you to believe me, a mere rake, if I tell you I would never be so cruel to you."

"I cannot believe you, Adrian."

He recoiled. "Then I will not waste time trying to convince you of my character. Make your decision."

She sank back into the rocking chair and tried to soothe herself, rocking back and forth. He stepped away from her and stood, arms folded over his chest, waiting.

His words offered so much. Comfort, safety, respectability. For her and their child.

Their child.

Would the child have his smiling mouth? The cowlick in his hair? His amber-coloured eyes?

She had no choice.

She took a deep breath. "Very well, Adrian. I accept," she whispered. "I will marry you."

It seemed a long time before he nodded. "I will go to Lambeth Palace today and procure the special licence. If I can snag a clergyman I will return here and we will be married right away."

As easy as all that, it would be done, and her life and the life of her precious child would be his to dictate. She felt as if she was giving up everything.

He had not professed love, as Wexin had done. He'd not professed devotion. He'd promised to do his duty to their child. Theirs would be a marriage of convenience—of necessity, rather.

She shivered.

He stared at her, so distant, so filled with an anger she could not begrudge him. All the fault in this situation was hers and hers alone.

"Have we come to an understanding, then, Lydia?" His voice actually shook.

She was not the only one overcome with emotion.

She extended her hand. "We have an agreement, sir."

He walked back to her, a masculine stride of grace and power. "An agreement, madam."

He grasped her hand. His hand was warm, his grasp strong, and, at his touch, her body again tingled with awareness of him. She wished she could be immune to this carnal yearning for him. It made matters worse.

He released her. "I will call upon you later today. May I suggest that your staff be prepared to allow me entry at your garden gate?"

To avoid the reporters who were certain to return. "I will have the gate attended after noon."

"After noon, then." He bowed.

He continued to gaze at her, but finally turned and walked towards the door.

"Adrian, wait!" She pushed herself to her feet.

He turned to her. The anger and pain remained in his face.

She took a deep breath. "May we—may we leave here? Leave London? I have no wish to give birth while reporters watch." The scandal was about to become so much worse.

She might have imagined a slight softening of his stiff posture. He nodded, almost imperceptibly. "I will arrange it."

A moment later he was gone.

Lydia buried her head in her hands and released the tension in a flood of tears.

Mary hurried back in the room. "My lady!" Mary rushed to her side, her questions unspoken.

Her maid and all the servants would wonder who was this Lord Cavanley to call upon her this night of all nights.

Lydia raised her head and, with her bare fingers, wiped the streaming tears from her cheeks. "Wish me happy, Mary." She stifled a sob. "I am to be married."

Chapter Eleven

Special Edition. Midnight arrived. Midnight passed. Lady W—'s interesting condition remains interesting. The child she wished the world to believe fathered by the late Lord W— was not born by the deadline, proving she carries some other man's child. But who is the father? —*The New Observer*, August 16, 1819

Samuel stood at the back of the newspaper offices, where the two pressmen continued to run off copies of the Special Edition, hanging the sheets over lines for the ink to dry. They'd sold out once and hoped to sell another two hundred copies.

Samuel checked the pages that had hung the longest. "These are ready. Let's get them out to the streets."

The men carefully pulled papers from the line and carried them to the back door where hawkers waited to take them to the streets. Only one story was printed in this edition—Lady Wexin's failure to give birth within ten months. The columns were filled with a rehashing of all the speculation that had come before.

The rhythmic din of the printing press went silent, and the only sounds to be heard now were the shouts of the men outside. Samuel said a silent prayer that the hawkers would sell out and the pressmen would go to work again. Perhaps he and his brother might soon afford the steam-powered press that gave papers like *The Times* an edge.

Samuel intended to keep this story alive until some new scandal captured the public's attention. Then he would keep that scandal alive as well. His brother had been right. Scandal sold papers.

Today Samuel planned to call upon Lord Levenhorne. Levenhorne must have something to say about Lady Wexin's failure to produce Wexin's progeny. Samuel still hoped he could discover the truth about the child's paternity.

Through the curtain separating the press room from the office, he heard the front door open.

"Excuse me, sir." The voice was feminine. And familiar. *Mary!*

"I am searching for a print shop," Samuel heard her say. "Can you give me the proper direction? I have walked up and down this street and I cannot find a print shop anywhere."

His brother, who had been working in the office, answered her. "We are the only printers on this street."

"There must be another," she insisted.

Samuel started to edge his way towards the back door, but his escape was blocked by the pressmen.

"My friend Samuel Charles works for a printer on this street," he heard Mary say.

Send her on her way, Samuel silently pleaded. *Do not say another word.*

"Samuel? You must mean my brother, Samuel Reed." *Damned Phillip.*

"He is in the back. I'll fetch him." Phillip walked to the doorway and shouted through the curtain, "Samuel! Someone to see you."

"You are mistaken—" Mary protested.

Samuel's shoulders slumped. He crossed the room and slid the curtain aside.

"Samuel!" Mary cried, shock written on her face. "But—but—"

"I know, Mary." Samuel's voice filled with gloom. "You did not expect a newspaper office."

"This—this is *that* paper! The one that writes such nasty things about my lady." She blinked in confusion.

"I'll leave you two alone." Phillip sidled to the doorway and disappeared into the back.

Mary's huge luminous eyes fixed on Samuel. "I do not understand this."

He averted his gaze. "This is where I work, Mary." He inclined his head towards the curtain. "My brother and I own this newspaper."

"You *own* it?" Her eyes grew even wider.

He nodded.

"But—"

He shrugged, reasoning he might as well tell her the whole. "I wrote the stories about Lady Wexin."

"You?" Her voice squeaked.

"They sold newspapers, Mary."

She turned away from him. When she turned back, her eyes were filled with tears. "Did—did you befriend me to find out about my lady?"

Samuel nodded.

"And—and you p-pretended to be my sweetheart?" she stuttered.

Not all of it had been pretending. "Mary—"

She backed away from him. "Oh, no. Do not answer that! I will not believe you, whatever you say. You made me betray my lady."

"Mary, you never betrayed her." Mary had never told

Samuel much of anything, but that had not kept him from wanting to see her again and again.

She shook her head. "You asked me a lot of questions, always. And I told you things. I thought you were interested in me, but you weren't." She shivered. "You just wanted me to talk about my lady!"

"Mary. Please. Listen to me." Although he was uncertain what he could say to her.

"No!" She clamped her hands over her ears. "I am going away. I came to tell you I am going away, but that is all I'm going to tell you."

He walked towards her. "Away? Where? Why, Mary?"

She reached the door and had her hand on the knob. "You only want to know because of Lady Wexin, but I won't tell you. Not another thing." She fixed her eyes, full of anguish and betrayal, on him. "Goodbye, Samuel."

She rushed out of the door, not even closing it. Samuel hurried after her, but she ran down the street and climbed into a hackney coach.

He watched the coach drive away and turn out of sight.

His worst nightmare had come true.

Mary had discovered exactly what a cad he really was.

Adrian arrived in a carriage at the side gate of Lydia's property promptly at one o'clock in the afternoon. He brought with him a special licence, a clergyman and a ring.

Lydia's footman waited to open the gate. This time when Adrian entered the house there were plenty of witnesses. The cook, a scullery maid and a housemaid all watched from the kitchen doorway. The butler led Adrian and the clergyman to the stairs, delivering them finally to the drawing room on the first floor.

"I will fetch m'lady." The butler bowed to Adrian.

While the reverend rocked on his heels, Adrian walked

over to the window and peeked out. Several reporters stood outside, talking among themselves, looking bored, but showing no indication that they realised visitors had arrived. One man, unnoticed by the others, stared at the house. Adrian recognised Reed, the reporter who had accosted Lydia all those months ago and set into motion the events that had led Adrian here this day.

Lydia walked in the room and Adrian turned away from the window. Her maid and butler entered behind her.

She wore a pale pink dress with a high lace collar and matching lace cape. Its skirt was wide, but not too voluminous to conceal that she was big with child.

The reverend tossed Adrian a knowing look that made Adrian want to pitch him across the room.

Instead he stepped forwards to take Lydia's hand. "Our agreement stands?" he asked her in a quiet voice.

"It stands," she whispered back to him.

The clergyman approached her.

"May I present Reverend Keats to you, ma'am," Adrian said.

"Lady Wexin." The reverend bowed.

"Reverend." Her voice was barely audible.

She looked very pale, and Adrian wondered if she was ill, but, somehow, her health seemed too private a matter to discuss in front of the clergyman.

"Shall we begin?" Adrian said instead.

She cleared her throat. "Yes."

Reverend Keats glanced around. "But what of your witnesses?"

Lydia turned to her butler and maid. "Mr Dixon and Miss Shaw are my witnesses."

Keats looked down his nose at them and Adrian had a second wish to throttle him.

"I have no objection to these witnesses," Adrian told the reverend.

"Well, let us begin, then." Reverend Keats pulled out his prayer book from a pocket in his coat.

Adrian and Lydia faced him.

The reverend opened the book and read speedily, "Dearly Beloved, we are gathered together in the sight of God…"

The words barely made sense to Adrian. He felt as if he were watching from a great distance, seeing himself standing shoulder to shoulder with Lydia, noticing the tables and chairs in the room and the colours of blue and gold that predominated.

Reverend Keats asked, "Wilt thou take this woman…?" and Adrian heard himself answer, "I will." The reverend said, "Wilt thou take this man…?" and Lydia said, "I will."

Keats joined Adrian's right hand to Lydia's. Her skin felt smooth and warm in his palm. Her hand trembled. He glanced at her. She looked flushed and frightened and unhappy.

It plunged him into gloom. He'd never imagined marrying a woman who did not want him. Nor wishing so much that this woman felt differently.

"Repeat after me…" Reverend Keats said.

Adrian repeated, "I, Adrian Purdie—"

Her eyes darted to him when he spoke his middle name. Her mouthed twitched.

"My great-grandfather's name," he whispered to her.

"Take thee—" Keats raised his voice.

Her eyes momentarily filled with mirth and Adrian's spirits suddenly rose.

"Take thee, Lydia Elizabeth." He gazed at her when he said the next words, "To be my wedded wife—"

His depression returned. He wanted a marriage like Tanner's, like his parents', a marriage begun in joy. He wanted this marriage to begin in joy.

At Keats's signal Adrian released her hand and reached in his pocket and took out the ring he had purchased that morning from Mr Gray, the jeweller. He had also purchased all of the jewellery Lydia had sold to Mr Gray nine months ago.

He placed it on her finger. "With this ring, I thee wed…"

She gasped. The ring, with clusters of twenty-two diamonds, caught the light and shot it back like so many sparks against flint. Adrian nodded in satisfaction. At least the ring pleased her, if not the groom.

When Reverend Keats said, "I pronounce that they be Man and Wife together…" the words echoed through Adrian's brain. Man and wife. Man and wife. Keats rushed through the final prayers, reading so fast Adrian would not have caught the words even if he had been able to pay attention.

Man and wife.

The reverend grew silent. Lydia lifted her gaze to Adrian. Like that first day when he'd gazed upon her, she stole his breath away. He leaned down and touched his lips to hers very lightly, dutifully. She remained still, eyes still gazing into his.

It was done.

Her maid had tears streaming down her face. Her butler appeared as worried as a disapproving father.

Adrian took the Reverend Keats aside and placed a purse in the man's hand. "Thank you, sir." He gave the man a warning glance. "I have paid you very well to keep this wedding a secret. If I hear news of it before my announcement, I shall hold you responsible. I hope I am being quite clear."

The man nodded and cast an understanding glance towards the new Lady Cavanley. "I quite comprehend, Lord Cavanley. I have given you my solemn oath before God—"

Adrian could no longer even look at the man.

The footman appeared at the door, flanked by the cook and the two maids. He carried in a tray of champagne and three glasses. Before the man poured, Adrian asked that he fetch enough glasses for all the servants, which seemed to please Lydia.

When they each held a glass of champagne, the maids tittering as they took theirs, Adrian raised his glass in a toast.

"To happiness," he said.

Not more than an hour had gone by before Lydia and Mary were assisted into the Cavanley carriage that pulled up to the garden gate. First stop, the coachman deposited Reverend Keats at his church, where he would record the marriage in the registry. After the reverend left, Lydia and Mary were alone in the carriage, while Adrian rode beside the carriage on his horse.

Lydia leaned back against the soft red cloth that upholstered the carriage's seats. In what seemed the wink of an eye, her life had been totally altered. Again.

They were destined for an estate in Sussex near Eastbourne, Adrian had told her, but that was all Lydia knew of it. She shifted her awkward body, trying to find a comfortable position. The baby kicked wildly inside her, as if resenting being jostled about.

"Is anything amiss, my lady?" Mary asked, still looking as if she might burst into tears at any moment.

"Nothing amiss," she assured the maid. "I was just getting comfortable." Or trying to get comfortable.

Mary nodded and quickly averted her face, blinking rapidly.

Lydia glanced away, confused. She'd offered for Mary to stay in London to be near the young man she sneaked out to see in the evenings. Mary had refused.

The girl had gone out that morning to tell her sweetheart she would be leaving town. Lydia had not had a chance to discover if Mary had found him. She glanced back. "Were you able to get word to your young man about coming with me?"

Mary wiped her eyes and nodded and turned her head back to the window.

Her misery made Lydia's heart ache. "Are you certain you wish to make this journey?"

Mary nodded. "I am certain, m'lady."

"We could send you back to London, if you wish it. It is not too late."

Mary shook her head. "I do not wish it."

Lydia shifted her position and again the baby kicked in protest. Mary had brought several pillows along, and Lydia tried to position them to give her more comfort. "I would understand if you wished to stay with your young man."

Mary's head whipped around and her eyes were steady. "I wish to attend you, my lady."

Lydia sighed inwardly. She feared the girl had accompanied her out of loyalty, sacrificing her budding romance. Still, she was so very glad to have Mary with her.

Horse hooves sounded louder outside the carriage. Lydia glanced out of the window. Adrian—her *husband*—came alongside and leaned down on his horse so that his face was level with the window.

"We will stop soon," he told them. "We must change horses."

Lydia squirmed into another new position. "Thank you for telling us."

He nodded and spurred his horse forwards again.

Lydia watched him, his muscular thighs grasping the sides of the horse, his back straight and tall. She felt her skin flush.

She quickly leaned back in her seat. She must not lose her heart to this man who had married her out of duty.

The thought made tears come to her eyes, but she feared that if she started weeping, both she and Mary would never stop.

They would spend the night at an inn tonight, travelling no more than four hours today and at least as many hours tomorrow. Lydia doubted Adrian would share a bedchamber with her. There would, of course, be no consummating of their marriage, not with her so grotesquely huge, but she thought it would be lovely to fall asleep with his arms around her.

She shook away the foolish thought.

* * *

Lydia's back ached and her ankles were swollen by the time they pulled into the Old Crown Inn at Edenbridge.

Adrian appeared at the door to help her alight. "We will stay here for the night."

The sky was still light, but Lydia was glad they would not travel any farther. Adrian took her hand as she manoeuvred herself out of the door, her belly preceding her. He then assisted Mary.

"I rode ahead and arranged a parlour and a meal." He gave her his arm and walked with her across the yard to the inn's door on the street.

Before they entered, she said, "I should like to walk a little, if you do not mind." Her legs felt restless and she was certain the ache in her back would disappear if only she could move around.

Mary had already gone in a back door with Lydia's portmanteau.

Lydia glanced around. The street led to the bridge over the river. "I will only walk to the bridge and back."

Adrian frowned. "I will accompany you."

They walked in silence, their progress slow, because Lydia could not move fast these days. Still, moving felt much better than being cramped inside the carriage. Walking eased the ache in her back, as she had hoped. The air was fresh, and the village pretty with its mix of white Tudor, red brick and brownstone buildings.

They reached the bridge and leaned on its wall to watch the river flow under it.

Lydia's legs shook, but she was uncertain if that was due to being confined or because he had not spoken to her.

She took a breath. "Tell me about this house where we will be staying."

"Nickerham Priory?" He shrugged. "It was once the home

of Augustinian monks until Henry VIII had the lands seized."
He glanced down at the water flowing under the bridge. "Almost
all the monks died of the plague, it is told, but at night when the
wind is just right, you can hear their ghostly voices chanting."

She turned to him. "You are jesting with me."

There was a twinkle in his eye. "Perhaps. Perhaps not."

She inhaled a deep breath of fresh air and felt heartened by
his good humour. "Has the property been in your family since
Henry VIII?"

He shook his head. "Not at all." He paused. "It has been in
Tanner's family that long, however."

She gasped. "Do you mean Lord Tannerton's family?"

"Yes. It is Tanner's property. He offered me the use of it
for the summer."

"Oh, how awful," she groaned.

"Not awful." He sounded defensive. "It is quite a fine place."

"But I cannot impose on Lord Tannerton," she said. "Not
after…" She almost said her former husband's name, a name
she hoped never to speak aloud again.

He fixed his gaze on her. "Tanner does not hold you responsible for what Wexin did."

"He cannot consider me innocent." she said. "Surely his
wife cannot."

He made a dismissive gesture. "Nickerham is a pleasant
place, and no one will find us there. Tanner offered the
house to me for the summer and even he knows nothing of
our—connection."

She glanced away. Her wishes in this matter were, of
course, of no account. She might never believe Lord and Lady
Tannerton would welcome her anywhere, but the vow she had
taken earlier meant she must obey her husband.

She stepped away from the bridge's wall. "I'm ready to go
back to the inn."

Chapter Twelve

⌒⌒⌒

Lady W— has disappeared. Her servants claim they do not know her destination. Her natural child must be ready to be born any day. Has her mysterious lover whisked her away?   —*The New Observer*, August 17, 1819

They were about an hour away from Nickerham Priory when the coachman stopped at a coaching inn for another change of horses. Adrian, dusty from the road, walked up to the carriage to assist Lydia.

This day's trip had not been as easy as the previous day. Lydia's face was pale and pinched and she had dark circles under her eyes as if she'd not slept at all the night before.

Adrian did not know if she'd slept or not, but she had been so exhausted when they'd stopped at the inn, he'd arranged a separate room for her and the maid. He had had their meal sent up to the room, as well. He spent his wedding night alone.

He worried she was ill. When he'd asked her, though, she vowed she was well. When they stopped this time, however, she looked even more fatigued.

He escorted her to the necessary, during which time they

spoke the merest civilities to each other. He waited for her, gazing up at the blue sky.

At least the weather was fair.

Her maid approached him, not looking sullen for a change, but worried. "M'lord." She spoke in a quiet voice, her eyes downcast. "Do we have far yet to travel?"

"About an hour," he responded.

She bit her lip.

"Why do you ask?" Adrian supposed the maid was tired of the carriage, too.

She hesitated. "I—I think m'lady is having pains."

"Pains?"

The maid nodded. "She tells me 'tis nothing, but I think the pains come very regular."

He did not understand. "Regular?"

She gave him an exasperated look. "I believe m'lady is having birthing pains, my lord."

"Good God." He stared at the door of the necessary for a moment before striding up to it. "Lydia! Are you in distress in there?"

There was a pause before he heard a muffled, "No."

He considered pulling the door open to see for himself.

"I am coming out." She opened the door. "What is it, Adrian?"

He met her with hands on his hips. "Why did you not tell me you were having pains?" His voice came out sharper than he intended.

"Because…" She paused, wincing for a moment. "I thought it a mere trifle."

"A trifle?" He supported her with his arm around her. "Your maid says the baby is coming." With Mary on his heels he started to assist his wife back to the carriage, but stopped abruptly. "Maybe we should stay at the inn. Send for a midwife."

"No," Lydia protested. "The pains are bearable. We are close, are we not?"

He started for the carriage again. "An hour away. Less, if we make haste." If they abandoned the easy pace he'd set for them because of her condition.

The maid ran and climbed in the carriage ahead of her.

Adrian helped Lydia inside. "Are you certain you want to try to reach Nickerham?"

She positioned herself among the pillows. "Very—" A spasm seemed to seize her.

He reached for her. "That is it. We stay here."

She clasped his hand, but did not let him pull her out of the carriage. "No, Adrian. I do not want my baby born in an inn. We shall be forced to stay here for days, and someone is bound to discover who we are."

He stared at her, uncertain of what to do.

"Please, Adrian," she begged.

He shook his head. "Think of how it would be if you gave birth on the side of the road—"

She squeezed his hand. "If we have only an hour until we reach Nickerham, I can make it, but let us leave now."

He looked into her eyes, which pleaded with him. "As you wish, Lydia."

He released her and closed the door and ran to the front of the carriage. "We need to leave immediately," he said to the coachman. "Push the horses as fast as you are able."

"For what reason, m'lord?" The coachman was another of his father's old faithful servants who tended to look upon Adrian as the boy he'd once been.

Adrian levelled his gaze at the man. "The lady is in labour."

The man's eyes widened and he immediately turned to the men hitching the new team. "Hurry up, lads! We need to be off!"

Adrian swung his leg over the saddle of his horse and called to the coachman, "I'm going to ride ahead. Alert the household."

He ought to have sent advance word of their arrival, but in the haste of his marriage, he'd not thought of it. His visit was expected, but the servants knew not when, and not that he'd bring with him a wife in labour.

The coachman waved him on and climbed up on the box.

Adrian pushed his horse as much as he dared.

How ironic it was. If Lydia had gone into labour a mere two days earlier, she might have avoided marriage to him altogether.

It took Adrian only three-quarters of an hour to reach Nickerham. He galloped through the stone arch of the gatehouse and pulled his horse to a halt at the house. Bounding up to the door, he sounded the knocker. "Quinn. Answer the door!"

The butler, a burly man almost as tall as Adrian, opened the door a crack, surprised to see him. He swung the door wide. "Mr Pomroy— I mean, Lord Cavanley—we were not expecting you—"

Adrian entered the hall. "Surely Tannerton wrote to you?"

The man bowed in apology. "Forgive me, sir. Indeed the Marquess wrote to us. I meant we were not informed of what day you would arrive."

Adrian had no time for this. "Never mind that, Quinn. My wife will arrive in a moment—"

"Wife?" Quinn cried.

"My wife," he repeated. "You must immediately send for a midwife. She is in labour."

"Labour!" The man's eyes nearly popped out of his head. His hands fluttered in the air. "But—"

"Send for a midwife and alert Mrs Quinn." Mrs Quinn was the housekeeper. "Have her ready a bedchamber with all the— the—things a midwife needs."

Quinn rushed off, yelling his wife's name. Adrian hurried back outside to take his horse to the stables. By the time he'd finished handing the animal to the grooms, he heard the carriage in the distance. He ran to meet it as it arrived at the front of the house, the horses huffing and blowing from the hard ride.

Adrian opened the carriage door even before it came to a full stop. He lifted Lydia from the carriage. "Can you walk?"

"Yes," she replied in a breathless voice, but she doubled over in pain when he set her on her feet.

Feeling helpless, Adrian held on to her arm while she endured the pain, which seemed like several minutes but must have lasted only a few seconds.

She gave him a quick glance after it passed. "I'm all right. I can walk."

A bustling Mrs Quinn rushed from the house and before Adrian knew it, she, a housemaid and Lydia's maid took charge of Lydia, whisking her away. Adrian followed them into the hall and up the stairway to a bedchamber. Lydia glanced back at him right before the door closed and he was left standing alone in the hallway.

The midwife arrived about two hours after they'd arrived at Nickerham Priory. She was immediately admitted to the bedchamber from which Adrian could hear female voices and occasional moans. He'd been escorted to a parlour down the hall from the bedchamber, but he spent most of the next few hours pacing the hallway, staring at the closed door.

His wife was giving birth to *his* child in there. His wife. His child. Facing a battle of life and death. That's what childbirth was, Adrian thought, a battle of life and death.

Quinn or one of the footmen came from time to time to ask if he needed anything. He needed the waiting to be over.

Waiting alone in the parlour was too reminiscent of when he'd been ten years old and home on school holiday. His mother had been behind a bedroom door then, making sounds very much like Lydia's. The sounds became very loud, frightening, even to a lad who considered himself game for anything. Eventually someone remembered to come tell ten-year-old terrified Adrian that he had a little sister.

He remembered his feeling of wonder and pride when he'd been briefly allowed in his mother's room to see his sister, all small and pink and prunish. He'd touched her tiny little hand with his finger and she had stared up at him with blue eyes.

Adrian had gone from his mother's room to the old nursery, where he pulled out old toys from the cupboards, searching for a wooden rattle he remembered was there.

The next day, one of the servants came to tell him the baby had died. Adrian had only seen her once, touched her once. Adrian's mother had been ill a long time after that, and Adrian had feared she would die as well.

"Please, God, do not let this mother and child die," he prayed. "Not Lydia. Not this child." He felt like one of those friends who only appear on your doorstep when they need something. "Not for me, God," he added hastily. "Do it for Lydia and the baby. Not for me."

After several hours, the sounds coming from the room worsened, and it was like Adrian was ten years old again, frantic and frightened.

Lydia let out so loud a shriek Adrian rushed to the door.

He tugged it open. "What happened?" he cried. "Is she all right?"

He saw her lying on her back on the bed, her maid and Mrs Quinn flanking her.

Another maid hurried over to the door. "'Tis all right, my lord. She's doing well." She closed him out again.

Lydia's shrieks commingled with the raised voices of the other women. Adrian kept his hand on the door handle as the sounds intensified, Lydia's pain searing into him as if happening to himself, as if history was repeating itself.

He'd not expected to feel this helpless desperation, this terror of losing them, *his* wife, *his* child. He thought again and

again that he was responsible for this. He'd impregnated her.
He'd planted the seed from which the baby grew. If she died,
if the baby died, he was responsible. "Please, God…"

Suddenly there was a cry of a different sort, and the
women's voices turned joyful. Adrian opened the door.

The baby was in the midwife's hands, the cord still
attached. Lydia was half-sitting and reaching for the baby. The
maid ran to the door again and blocked his view.

"Congratulations, m'lord," the maid said. "You have a
fine-looking son."

Lydia gazed with wonder at the wrinkled, squalling face
of her son. Mrs Quinn wiped the child with a towel, and
Mary cooed, "He looks lovely."

Lydia was speechless. She could not even compose a
mental prayer of thanks for this truly wonderful gift, but her
heart soared with gratitude.

A son. Alive and healthy.

"Put the babe to your breast, dear," the midwife told her.

The baby searched around, limbs trembling until his lips
closed over her nipple and he began to suckle.

"Helps with the afterbirth," the midwife added.

Lydia wanted to laugh with joy. He was so clever to reason
it all out so soon. The sensation of nursing him was a surprise
and a delight.

The afterbirth was delivered without mishap, and Lydia
was hardly aware of the cutting of the cord. She had the
illusion that nothing could hurt her as long as she could gaze
at her lovely, handsome baby.

Soon she was all cleaned up, and the baby dressed as
well. Before she knew it she was reclining on clean, dry
sheets, in a clean, dry nightdress, holding her now-sleeping
baby in her arms.

"My lady," Mrs Quinn said, "your husband is right outside the door. Do you wish to see him?"

Lydia was surprised he was not abed. The hour must be close to dawn. "Of course. Tell him to come in."

At his appearance the other women quietly left the room. He stood some distance from her. "How do you fare?"

She lifted her eyes to him and wondered if she, perhaps, fared better than he. He was in shirtsleeves, his waistcoat unbuttoned, his hair dishevelled, his eyes red.

"I feel remarkably well," she responded.

"And the child?" he rasped.

She smiled. "He is a son, Adrian, and he seems the very picture of health."

One of his hands shot out to brace himself on a nearby chair.

"Would you like to see him?" she asked warily, confused by the change in him.

He approached closer, close enough for her to be aware of his scent, familiar from their long-ago lovemaking, among all the new scents of baby.

He looked down at the child and was silent for a long time. "He's so small." His voice caught.

It felt like a criticism. "The midwife assured me he was big enough."

Still he stared at the baby. "I had forgotten new babies were so small."

"I think he is lovely," she said in defence.

She noticed then that the baby's lips were formed in that same shape as his. She glanced up at him to be sure. It pleased her that her child would have a perpetual smile, like his father.

He stepped back and rubbed his face. "And do you feel well?"

He had asked before. "Yes. I do."

He nodded and averted his gaze. "Is there something I can fetch for you or some service I can perform?"

"I cannot think of anything." She peered at him. "Did you not sleep, Adrian?"

"No." He looked down at the baby again.

"You should sleep," she said.

Adrian's behaviour unsettled her. He looked sad, even with his smiling lips. Sad and something more.

Perhaps he'd suddenly realised he was saddled with a wife and child.

"You look very tired," she added.

"I'll leave you, then." His voice did sound weary. He backed away, pausing by the bedchamber door. "I am glad you are well," he said before he walked out.

The weeks of confinement were a hardship for Lydia. By even the day after her child was born, she'd felt like dancing around the room—and did dance around the room with the baby in her arms when no one was checking on her. She loved the time with her baby, loved nursing him, even loved changing his nappies, but the midwife had left strict orders for her to stay in bed. It was an order she could not help but disobey.

The bedchamber seemed too small to contain her happiness. When the infant was asleep, Lydia pined to walk outside in the fresh sea air that she inhaled in big gulps until Mrs Quinn came in and chastised her for opening the windows.

Sometimes from the window she saw Adrian gallop across the grassy land to the cliffs. She could spy the water in the distance, beyond where the land dropped off.

The smell of salty air reminded her of summers at Brighton. She, her sister and their governess had walked along the rocky beach or played at the water's edge, finding sea shells, and letting the water dampen their skirts as the waves washed in.

She would take her son to Brighton some day, she thought, and play at the water's edge with him.

Adrian visited her and the baby once a day. A duty visit, she thought of it. He never remained too long, but always asked after her health and the health of the baby. The baby stared at him when he spoke in his deep voice.

There was so much she avoided discussing with him, though. Naming the baby, for one. He never brought up the topic, and it was getting harder and harder for her not to attach a name to her darling baby. She called him her angel, her darling, her miracle, but those were not names.

There was also the whole problem of christening the baby. Finding godparents when you were hidden away and shunned by society would be difficult. She certainly knew of no one who would perform such a role for her.

Still, she loved the freedom of being away from anyone who knew her or anyone who wished to invade her home or sell her private matters to the newspapers and caricaturists.

Mary acted as baby nurse as well as lady's maid, although Lydia was rarely in need of another person caring for the baby. Poor Mary. She had once been so happy, but even Mary's melancholy could not put a tarnish on Lydia's joy.

Adrian had arranged for a physician to attend her and the man pronounced her and the baby the healthiest he'd seen in years. Lydia secretly thought it was due to her open windows and dancing around the room, the outward expression of her happiness.

As the weeks sped by Lydia tried very hard not to think about her marriage or her future, because she had no idea how she and Adrian would eventually get on together. Or how she could possibly endure it when her baby left for school and she would be alone again.

In the mere blink of a eye it was October and days consisted of crisp breezes; nights of frost. On one October day when the sun shone bright and the sky was blue, the physician came to call and pronounced her recuperation period to be at an end. The physician even approved travelling with the baby. After he left her bedchamber, Lydia felt like a prisoner released from Newgate. Leaving the baby under Mary's watchful eye, Lydia sought out Adrian in parts of the house she had never seen.

She found him in the library writing letters. She, too, had written letters during her recovery. To her parents to tell them of her marriage and baby, but she no longer felt optimistic that the letters would reach them. Worrying over the fate of her parents and brother was something she avoided, lest it spoil her happiness.

"Adrian?" She stepped inside the room.

"Lydia." He set down his pen and stood.

"The physician was here."

"I know," he said. "He spoke with me."

"Oh." She had not realised that the physician reported to her husband. "What did he say to you?"

He paused, as if deciding what to tell her. "He said your time of recovery is done. You can be up and about."

She nodded, uncertain why he spoke so hesitantly about something mundane. "He told me the baby and I could travel."

His expression stiffened. "Is there some place you wish to go?"

"Me?" She had not expected him to give her a choice. "I suppose if there were somewhere I need not impose on Lord Tannerton…"

He ran a hand through his hair. "I have assured you—"

"I know. I know." She held up a hand to stop him from assuring her one more time. "But you asked what I wished."

He nodded and seemed to wait for her to speak.

He never made it easy for her to talk to him, always so stiff and formal around her. She could hardly believe this was the same man who had charmed her when she'd been at her lowest point, who had shown her kindness and good humour.

And passion.

She flushed with the memory of making love with him.

But after all she had done, calling him a libertine, trying to pass off his child as another man's, *marrying him*, she no longer expected him to desire to make love with her.

Somehow the loss of lovemaking was worse for her knowing how splendid it could be.

She bowed her head. "Forgive me, Adrian. I disturbed you. Do sit and go about writing your letter. Forget my churlish remark. I—I've been so very tired of my bedchamber. I took my foul mood out on you."

She expected him to sit, but instead he walked out from behind the desk.

"Have you seen the house?" he asked.

She was taken aback. "Only what rooms I encountered before finding you."

"I could take you for a tour, if you like." He came closer. "Is the babe asleep?"

She nodded. "I just nursed him. He should sleep for a couple of hours."

"Then it is a good time to show you the house." He was close enough to touch now.

She looked up into his eyes and felt that jolt of awareness of him. Was she never to be near this man without thinking of bedding him? "I—I had thought to take a walk. I have yearned to be out of doors."

The day was sunny and warm and it would be soothing to feel the sea breeze upon her face.

"I will show you the garden, then," he said.

She blinked. "I had thought to walk to the sea."

"The sea, then," he said.

She hesitated. "Give me a moment to fetch my hat."

A few minutes later, Adrian watched Lydia descend the stairs looking as beautiful as when dressed in a ballgown and all men's eyes, including his, instantly turned to her.

Her dress was a simple one, pale blue and flowing loosely around her, but its bodice strained against her full bosom. The effect was erotic, as erotic as when he'd once come to visit her bedchamber and spied her nursing the baby. She'd been sitting on the bed that day, one leg exposed, her nightdress gaping open and the baby's tiny hand pressing into her breast as he suckled. Adrian had turned away and waited until the fire in his blood cooled before returning later to make his daily visit.

"We can walk through the garden," he said as she reached him and took his arm.

"That would be lovely." Her voice was breathless and her face tinged with colour as if she'd already spent an hour in the fresh air.

He escorted her through the small formal garden, and pointed out the stable and some outer buildings they passed.

She glanced towards where the sky met grass. "Is this the way to the sea?"

"It is." He had been walking at a slow pace for her sake. "It is some distance. Do you feel up to it?"

"Oh, yes!" She smiled.

She suddenly looked as if she could walk a dozen miles and show no more than a sparkle in her eyes.

"I have not walked so far in an age," she exclaimed, talking almost as if they were friends.

"Will you be able to do it?" The cliffs were a good quarter of a mile away. "We shall be gone an hour at least."

Her countenance darkened and she bowed her head. "Forgive me, Adrian. Will I keep you from something?"

He gave a sarcastic laugh. "Believe me, you will not."

This stay at Nickerham had been the very epitome of nothing to do. If he thought his life devoid of any meaningful employment previous to this, he had not appreciated the utter uselessness of fatherhood. He was needed for nothing here and had none of his usual distractions to help him forget it.

She became more subdued and he found his own mood depressed again. They walked in silence.

"It is not far now," he said finally.

The sound of waves heralded the sea, and the wind added an extra flourish, billowing Lydia's skirt and tugging at her hat. She paid no heed to it, broke away from him and ran to the edge of the cliff.

She stretched out her arms. "It is beautiful!"

"Indeed." His eyes were riveted on her as she twirled around and again faced the water.

The physician had made a point of telling him marital relations could be resumed. Before that moment, Adrian could at least pretend lovemaking would harm her when he left her sitting in her bed or seated in a chair in the dishabille of her thin nightdress. It had been easy to keep his distance when he told himself she needed to stay in her room and care for the baby.

Now she was silhouetted against the sky, the shape of her body revealed by the sun and wind. Most of all, her smile, her joy was an elixir, one he was uncertain he could resist. How the devil was he going to go on, filled with desire for a wife who'd not wanted him?

She joined him for dinner that evening for the first time, sitting adjacent to him, so close he could smell the lilac in her hair and the sweet scent of baby's milk. The meal was a simple one of poached cod, roasted potatoes and buttered parsnips, so there was no need for Quinn to attend the table. Adrian was left very much alone again with his wife.

"This is a pretty room," Lydia commented as they started to eat.

He'd never managed to show her the house. As soon as they had returned from their walk to the sea, the baby's wails could he heard echoing through the house. She had run up the stairs to tend to his needs.

"I hope the food is to your liking," he said. Perhaps they could get through the meal spouting polite platitudes.

"It is very nice."

He took a long sip of wine.

They fell into silence again, and the clinking of their cutlery against the porcelain plates seemed to reverberate in the room. Adrian had never been at a loss for words where women were concerned. Flattery and flirtation, so easy for him otherwise, seemed to utterly fail him now.

Lydia put down her fork and faced him. "I would like to select a name for the baby."

He nodded. At least she spoke, even if it was about a topic he had no idea how to discuss. "What name have you selected?"

She looked surprised. "I have not selected any name. I thought I must consult you."

Adrian had no idea how to name a child. "You must have names."

"I do not." She glanced away. "I suppose we could name him after my father, but it is not a very pretty name."

"I do not believe I've ever heard your father's given name." He took another sip of wine.

"Xenos."

He nearly sprayed the wine from his mouth. He coughed instead.

She rolled her eyes. "You may laugh. Everyone does."

"How the devil did he come by a name like that?" he asked.

"My grandfather apparently fancied himself a Greek scholar. Our estate is filled with antiquities."

He frowned. "I know you have sent letters to your father." He'd posted the letters himself in the village.

"I wrote to tell them of our—our marriage and the baby." She blinked. "I have had only one letter in a year. I do not know if my letters reach them."

"I'd heard they were abroad."

"A grand tour to India with my brother." She lowered her head. "But the letter I received was months ago. I fear something has happened to them."

Adrian took another sip of wine, vowing to send a man in search of her parents. He could at least discover their fate for her.

"Well." She seemed to compose herself. "I think you can agree Xenos is not a suitable name for our son."

Our son, she'd said. It cheered him to hear her include him.

He poured himself some more wine. "The name passed down in our family is Purdie."

She laughed, then covered her mouth. "I am sorry. I fear I almost laughed when hearing the name for the first time as well."

At their wedding, he thought.

She looked at him in alarm. "Do you wish to name our son Purdie?"

He could not help teasing her. "Perhaps."

"Well," she sputtered. "I suppose—if you insist."

He enjoyed her obvious dismay. "In that case, another family name must be added."

"What name is that?" Her eyes narrowed warily.

"Peterkin."

"Peterkin?" She winced.

"Peterkin." He made himself face her soberly. "How does Purdie Peterkin Pomroy sound?"

Her face paled. "Adrian…must we?"

A grin escaped. "No, indeed. I was thinking of, perhaps, Percival or Peregrine. Or perhaps, Parker."

She peered at him. "You are jesting, are you not?"

His grin widened. "Do you not like my choices? How about Piper or, even better, Pip?"

She laughed. "You *are* jesting! Can you think of any names that do not begin with the letter P?"

He sipped his wine and winked, enjoying this interplay with her. "Perhaps."

She placed a piece of parsnip in her mouth and, after swallowing it, slowly licked the butter from her lips.

Dear God.

He drained the contents of his wine glass.

"Seriously," she said, but still smiled, "we must choose a name."

He gazed at her. "Choose what suits you."

A wrinkle formed between her eyes. "I thought perhaps there was someone you would wish to name a son after."

"My father's name is Edmund."

She sobered. "Would he wish this child named after him?"

Adrian hoped his father would accept this son and eventual heir, but he truly did not know.

He poured more wine and lifted the glass to his lips. "We could name him Adam after Tannerton."

She blanched. "Oh, Adrian, please, no. I cannot name him after Lord Tannerton. Please."

"Why not?" At least he knew Tanner would be genuinely flattered by the choice.

She leaned towards him, the edge of the table pressing into her breasts so that it looked as if they would burst free of the confining dress. "It would be a cruelty to Lord Tannerton, would it not? To name *my* son after him."

He averted his gaze. She would likely think of her former husband every time she spoke her son's name. Adrian had no wish for that.

"Tell me." He met her gaze again. "If you had delivered the baby a few days before you did, would you have named him after Wexin, to make everyone believe he was Wexin's son?"

Her hands flew to her cheeks. "Never!" She shook her head. "Never! I am glad my baby has nothing of Wexin in him!"

Her vehemence gratified Adrian.

He tapped on his glass. "My grandfather's name was Ethan. We could name the boy Ethan Purdie Pomroy. That should solidify his place in the family."

She averted her gaze. "Ethan." Her eyes, looking dreamy, slid back and caught his. "Ethan." She reached for Adrian's hand and clasped it. "Ethan is perfect, Adrian. Perfect."

It seemed as if the air rushed out of his lungs. She was that breathtakingly beautiful.

Quinn entered the room to remove the dishes. "Some brandy, m'lord?"

It broke the moment.

"Very well, Quinn," Adrian said, somewhat sadly.

Another evening alone. Even drinking brandy gave no pleasure when alone.

Lydia glanced at Adrian through lowered lashes. "Perhaps—perhaps you might drink your brandy upstairs with me? We can continue our discussion there while I take my tea."

It was an invitation Adrian could not refuse.

Chapter Thirteen

Over two months have passed and still no news of the notorious Lady W— or her fatherless child. No one has seen
her. No one has heard from her. But one man must know.
The mysterious man who whisked her away. Her secret
lover, perhaps?—*The New Observer*, October 20, 1819

Lydia's heart beat wildly as she ascended the stairs, Adrian
following her, carrying the decanter of brandy and a glass.
The day had been full of pleasure, first walking to the sea,
then sharing dinner. Even more gratifying, Adrian had
actually talked with her about their son. It almost felt like a
normal conversation between husband and wife. It had emboldened her to invite him to tea in her bedchamber.

Just to continue their conversation, she told herself.

She laughed nervously when she opened the bedchamber
door.

Mary rose from the rocking chair, holding the baby. "He
is starting to fuss, my lady."

Lydia hurried over and took the baby from Mary's arms.
"Did you change him?"

"I did, my lady. I believe he is hungry."

Lydia stared down into the face of her son, who was squeaking and squirming. "Ethan," she whispered. She looked up at Mary, who had noticed Adrian's presence. "Thank you, Mary." Lydia smiled at her. "You must get your dinner. I will not need you."

Mary darted a glance at Adrian as she curtsied. She picked up the baby's soiled linen and hurried out of the room.

"Perhaps this is not a good time for tea and brandy." Adrian remained just inside the doorway.

Lydia swayed with little Ethan, who had quieted for only a moment at his father's voice. "Please stay. He needs nursing in a little while, but you can stay. I can nurse him very discreetly."

A small line formed between her husband's eyes. "Are you certain?"

She gestured to a cushioned settee near the rocking chair. He walked over to it, but remained standing, his bottle of brandy and glass still in hand.

"I'll be only a moment." Holding the baby, she grabbed the shawl that she'd worn on their walk. Mary had folded it and placed it on a chest near the bed.

As Lydia returned to the rocking chair, Mrs Quinn brought in the tea and placed it on the table nearby.

"How is the little lamb today, m'lady?" Mrs Quinn smiled at Adrian as well. Unlike Mary, the housekeeper saw nothing unusual in a husband and new father sharing after-dinner tea with his wife in her bedchamber.

"He is splendid, Mrs Quinn." She held the baby out so the older woman could see for herself.

The housekeeper tickled the fussing baby with her finger, but he only fussed the more. "He is a lusty boy, he is. And a hungry one." She chuckled.

Mrs Quinn left the room, closing the door behind her. Lydia settled in the rocking chair, draping the shawl around her before unfastening the bodice of her dress, all while holding the baby. "Ethan." She smiled at knowing his name at last.

Adrian sat and poured a glass of brandy. "Shall I pour your tea?" His voice was unusually low.

"In a little while, perhaps."

Little Ethan squirmed as she lifted him under the shawl and put him to her bare breast. They were both very skilled at this routine now, and she was free to transfer her attention to the man sitting across from her.

He took a sip of brandy and averted his eyes.

"Do I make you uncomfortable, Adrian?" she asked.

He glanced back at her. "I've not often been in the presence of a nursing mother." One corner of his mouth turned up. "Never before, in fact."

"Never?" She raised one brow. "A rake such as yourself?"

His smile disappeared and he took another sip of brandy. "Do you think I have left a long trail of bastards, Lydia?"

"Forgive me," she murmured. "It was a poor attempt at a joke."

He shrugged. "You would be surprised, then, that a *rake* such as I has always been careful about not fathering a child." He glanced at the lump under her shawl. "Except once."

She felt her cheeks go hot. She was indeed surprised to know this. "I am sorry, Adrian."

He poured himself more brandy.

She watched him. Even in this simple task he moved like a man. Or, at least, the way he sat, the way he held his glass, the way he put it to his mouth made her think about him being a man. The baby suckling at her breast made her equally aware of being a woman.

She wanted him to touch her, to feel his hand sliding along her bare skin, to feel his lips upon her breast.

She took a quick breath. There could not possibly be a

woman more wanton than she. It had been her wantonness that had trapped this man into marriage with her.

She positioned her shawl so she could gaze down at little Ethan. Her wantonness had also brought her this precious gift, a gift she would never regret.

She glanced back at Adrian, who seemed lost in his own thoughts. Desire surged through her again. What harm could it do to be wanton with him now? He was her husband, after all. He was a man as well, and men, everyone knew, enjoyed indulging in such needs. Perhaps Adrian, her husband, would not mind so very much coupling with her again.

She'd intended to sip tea and talk with him about the problem of having the baby christened, but any thoughts of church flew out of her mind. The baby pulled away from her nipple and, when she moved him to the other breast, she neglected to be certain the shawl covered her.

When he finally looked at her again, she let the shawl slip even further. "We do not know each other very well at all, do we, Adrian?" she murmured. "But we are married."

His expression was still hard. "You have married a rake, Lydia, but—" he glanced at Ethan "—you had little choice."

She blinked. "I am prepared to be a wife to you."

He gave a dry laugh and drained his glass. "Generous of you, Lydia."

She must close this distance between them, the distance she'd created.

"It is not so terribly generous of me, Adrian. You, more than anyone else, should know how—how selfish I am to indulge my own desire." She took another breath for courage. "You know that is my weakness."

He stared at her a long time. "Are you trying to seduce me, Lydia?"

She forced herself to look into his eyes. "Yes."

* * *

Adrian knew his brain was fuzzy with the amount of wine
and brandy he'd consumed, more than he'd consumed since
that long-ago episode at Madame Bisou's. Perhaps he would
deduce on the morrow that he ought to have considered her
frank invitation more carefully. But, what the devil, she was
beautiful, desirable and willing.

And she was his wife. They'd already experienced the most
profound consequence of indulging their desires. What more
could happen?

The yearning in her eyes was as compelling this time as it
had been that first time, except no longer did their lovely
sapphire colour reflect pain and loneliness and confusion.
Gone was the desperation of so many months ago. He'd eased
all her problems. Why not reap some reward?

He reached across the table between them and pulled her
shawl away. She gasped, but not with shame. With excitement.

Her chest was bare, her breasts swollen with motherhood. His
son—his *son*—suckled at one, tiny fingers clutching her skin.

Adrian leaned back and watched. Lydia's breathing accelerated and her skin flushed pink. She gazed at him through
lowered lashes, arousing him with her own growing excitement, deeply moving him with her devotion to the baby.

He watched in wonder as his son's lips slipped off the
nipple, continuing to move as if suckling still.

Lydia looked up at him and smiled. "I'll put him in the cradle."

She rose, the shawl slipping from her shoulders, the bodice
of her dress still open, exposing her breasts. She held the
baby against her shoulder for a few moments, patting his back
until a surprisingly loud belch escaped his lips.

Adrian followed her to the cradle. "How long does he sleep?"

The baby turned his head towards Adrian.

"He likes your voice, I think." Lydia smiled. "Would you
like to hold him?"

"Me?" Adrian took a step back.

She held the baby out to him. "Here. Hold him. He won't break." She carefully placed him in Adrian's arms. "Ethan, meet your father."

Adrian stared down into his son's face, the wide, blue baby eyes gazing up at him. A pain seized his heart like he'd never felt before. His limbs grew weak and he feared he might drop this most precious of objects.

"Hello, Ethan," he managed.

His son's eyes remained fixed on his face, as if Adrian was the most important sight the infant had ever seen. A wave of protectiveness washed over Adrian, as well as a feeling of profound helplessness. His eyes blurred. What if Ethan fell ill? What if some accident befell him? What if Adrian could not keep him safe from every harm?

He glanced up at Lydia. "Is he healthy, do you think? Is he strong?"

Her expression was nearly as full of wonder as her son's. "He is healthy and strong."

He felt only a modicum of relief.

Lydia stepped closer and put her hand on Adrian's arm as she, too, gazed at this wonder they had created.

"He looks like you." She touched her finger to the baby's lips and the baby made more sucking movements. "He has your mouth."

Adrian glanced up at her and back to his son. "He does?"

She touched Adrian's lips in the same gentle manner. "Yes, he does."

Adrian grinned. He had a son, a son who looked like him. *Nothing bad will happen to you, my son,* Adrian said silently. *Not if your father can prevent it.*

All of a sudden, the baby's mouth opened and he uttered a cry. His arms and legs shuddered. Adrian looked up at Lydia in alarm.

"He is tired, I think," she said.

"Shh, shh," Adrian murmured, rocking the baby. "Do not cry."

In no time at all, Ethan's eyes closed and he became still except for a twitching of his lips, lips that looked like Adrian's.

"Put him in the cradle," Lydia whispered.

Adrian bent down to do as she said, but he did not know how to get the baby out of his hands without dropping him. He gave Lydia a pleading look. "You do it."

Smiling, Lydia took the baby from Adrian's arms. With ease she gently placed him in the cradle and covered him with a blanket.

There was a tapping at the door. Lydia crossed the room, grabbing her shawl again and wrapping it around her. She opened the door a crack, spoke to her maid a moment, and closed it again. She returned to Adrian.

"I told her we would require nothing until morning." She had some difficulty meeting his gaze.

He glanced back at his son, who slept so peacefully Adrian felt his heart twisting again.

He was shaken by the emotions that had burst forth in him when he held his son. He suddenly wondered if his father had felt the same when first holding him, and his grandfather, when first holding his father. Adrian had felt his father's love for him his whole life. Had it begun at such a moment like this?

Adrian stared down at his son again and knew his love for this child would never waver.

After a long moment, he glanced up at Lydia.

There was disappointment in her eyes. "You have changed your mind, I think." She assumed a brave look. "It is all right. Truly, it is."

It suddenly became important to share with her what had just happened to him. She was a part of these new emotions, after all.

He met her gaze. "I once drove my phaeton in a race from London to Richmond, flying over roads so fast I nearly lost my seat a dozen times. At the end of it, I barely knew my name, the scenery flew by me so fast." His mouth widened into a smile. "That seems tame after holding my son."

She stared back at him. "Did you win the race?"

He laughed. "No. Tanner won and looked as if he'd just come from a leisurely turn around Hyde Park."

She grasped the bedpost and leaned her cheek against it. "If you think that was exhilarating, try knowing he came from inside your body." She took a breath. "You see? I do understand, Adrian, why the moment has passed for you. I do understand."

He stepped closer to her, so close only the bedpost was between them. He swept her cheek with the back of his hand. "If we created that life together, I suspect we can do anything. Even recreate a moment that has passed."

He pressed his lips to hers, a gentle kiss, not unlike the one he had given her after their wedding vows had been spoken. That kiss had been intended to reassure her that he would always do right by her. This one held the hope for some happiness together.

She deepened the kiss as if in confirmation of that hope.

His body caught up swiftly, flaring into arousal made all the more powerful by the knowledge he and this woman had created his son.

She moved away and climbed on the bed, kneeling so her face was even with his. "Do you wish to race with me, Adrian?"

He leaned towards her so that his lips were within an inch of hers. "That depends," he murmured. "Do I ride you, or do you ride me?"

She laughed, the sound lusty, her breath hot against his face. "Both," she rasped.

He seized her, crushing his lips against hers. She moved closer to him and buried her fingers in his hair. While parrying tongues with her, he peeled off his coat and waistcoat and tossed them on the floor. She broke away and hurriedly unfastened her bodice and pulled the dress over her head. Her hair came loose, raining pins as it tumbled to her shoulders like a flaxen waterfall. He kicked off his shoes and tossed away his shirt.

"I need help with my corset." She turned her back to him, holding up her glorious hair.

Adrian made quick work of the corset's laces. The garment was gone. That left only her shift and his trousers. He vaulted onto the bed while she lay back, welcoming him on top of her. He kissed her again, trailing his lips down her neck. She writhed beneath him, groping to unbutton his trousers.

He was already hard and wanting her urgently. It felt much like a race, each of them rushing as fast as they could for the pleasure they had only once shared together.

He slid off her only long enough to remove his trousers. At the same time she pulled off her shift. If this were a race, they remained neck and neck, both naked at once. This time she climbed on top of him, straddling him. Both as eager as quivering racers at the gate, he guided his length inside her.

He had forgotten this bliss, this feeling of connection to her. She felt like heaven, writhing on top of him, her head falling backwards, her eyes half-closed.

Let the flag drop. Let the race begin.

He set the pace, moving her, his hands grasping her waist. She gazed down at him, a smile of pleasure on her face as she caught the cadence of their contest.

"Faster?" he asked.

She laughed, and he was gone, lost to the race, sprinting to the finish, glorying in the fact that she kept up with him, that she wanted to win the race as much as he did.

The sensation built and thought failed him. There was nothing but the race and the woman who filled all his senses.

He felt her pulsate around him, an urgent moan of pleasure escaping her lips. His climax came a scant second later, his voice melding with hers. When the pleasure ebbed, she collapsed on top of him.

"Mmm." She rested her head against his heart.

His breathing and heartbeat slowly came back to normal.

"Ahhh," he said.

She slipped off and nestled against him. "I won."

He turned on his side so their faces were an inch apart. "I think it was a draw."

She rose up on one elbow. "You are mistaken. I won."

He pulled her down again, turning to taste the tender skin at the nape of her neck. "There is only one thing to do, then," he murmured in her ear.

She squirmed beneath his lips. "What is that?"

He rose over her. "I demand a rematch."

Adrian jolted awake to the baby's shrill cry.

Lydia, illuminated by moonlight pouring in the window, held the baby in her arms.

"What is wrong?" Adrian sat up, his heart pounding.

She turned and smiled. "Nothing is wrong. He is hungry again."

Adrian frowned. "Should he be hungry again?"

She carried the baby to the bed and climbed up next to him. "Oh, yes. He may even wake again before dawn comes."

Adrian manoeuvred himself behind her and pulled her against him. With his arms around her he rested his chin on her shoulder and watched his nursing son. Lydia relaxed against him while the babe buried his nose in her breast and suckled energetically.

Adrian watched his son and a lump formed in his throat. With Lydia he'd finally accomplished something worthwhile.

When the baby finished nursing and Lydia returned him to

the cradle, Adrian waited to embrace her again, to taste the sweetness of her lips, to experience the intense pleasure of making love to her.

He smiled as she approached him.

Marrying her might be his finest accomplishment, marrying her and giving his son his name. Perhaps this was just the beginning of wonderful things from their marriage, the beginning of meaning to his life.

It was something to hope for.

Samuel handed his brother the story he'd copied nearly word for word from the North Shields newspaper.

On Friday se'night an inquest was held at the George Tavern, Docwray Square, on the body of Joseph Cleckson, the unfortunate person who was killed upon the New Quay, during the riot—

"You ought to allow me to travel to North Shields, Phillip."

To Samuel these episodes of rioting, the sheer anger and discontent of the people, were the most important news events of recent times. There was unrest everywhere, and the gentlemen in the Lords and the Commons ought to be finding ways to put a stop to them. It had been their Corn Laws, after all, that had driven up the cost of bread, creating a hungry and angry populous.

Samuel went on, "I should like to interview some of the people affected."

"Don't be daft." Phillip skimmed Samuel's copy. "The North Shield's paper does the job for us." He handed the copy back to Samuel. "Send this on to the typesetters."

Samuel snatched the copy out of his brother's hand. "You are not heeding me."

Phillip shook his head. "We've been over this before, Sam.

Travel is expensive. Let us merely continue to copy what the out-of-town papers write." All the newspapers copied each other's stories, that was nothing new.

"Then let me take up the story here in London," Samuel persisted. "Let me discover what unrest is brewing here."

Phillip crossed his arms over his chest. "You are going to upset the royals with that nonsense. I thought we agreed not to do that."

Samuel leaned towards his brother. "It doesn't have to upset the royals."

Phillip turned back to the pile of papers in front of him. He lifted one to read. "We decided this long ago, Samuel. We'd stick to gossip and scandal, anything sensational. Leave the risky reporting to the other papers." He looked up at Samuel. "That reminds me, what ever happened to the Wexin widow?"

"She disappeared." Samuel felt a shaft of pain near his heart. He felt the pain every time he thought about Lady Wexin—and Mary.

"No progress discovering where they have gone?"

Samuel shook his head. "No one knows, it seems. Not even her servants." Nor had Lord Levenhorne known anything when he had called on him, heavy-hearted, after Mary had left town with Lady Wexin.

Phillip picked up another newspaper and buried his nose in it. "Then dig into some other *ton* scandal. Some earl or somebody must be sleeping with his brother's wife or his wife's sister. Everybody likes to read about that sort of thing."

Samuel had got wind of a wealthy widow who was plainly smitten with a much younger, impoverished gentleman. He supposed he could sensationalise their "accidental" encounters.

Somehow it did not excite him.

Samuel pictured how Mary's eyes would probably sparkle in joy at the older lady and her young gentleman falling in love, but she would cluck her tongue at reporting it in a newspaper.

He pressed his fingers against his forehead. It was pointless to think of Mary. Mary was gone. Disappeared with Lady Wexin, and Samuel would never see her again. He wagered they had fled to the Continent, where all notorious members of the *ton* fled to escape the consequences of their foolish actions.

He glanced at his brother. Would Phillip fund him the money to search for Mary—and Lady Wexin—in France? If he travelled to France, he had a chance of finding them. God knows he could not find them in Great Britain.

He blew out a disgusted breath. Phillip would never advance the funds for a trip to France. He'd just refused money for a jaunt to North Shields.

Samuel scraped his chair away from his desk and rose to deliver his copy to the typesetters, already busy at work on the next edition.

Chapter Fourteen

…the mob set no bounds to their rage. "Manchester
over again!" "Blood for blood!" were vociferated inces-
santly. The window frames of the two lower storeys of
the house were completely demolished…
                    —*The New Observer*, October 21, 1819

"The London papers, m'lord." Quinn set them next to
Adrian's plate. He glanced at the dates. Some of the papers
were at least a week old.

Lydia and he were breakfasting in a sunny parlour with
huge windows overlooking the garden. While these newspapers were making their way to Nickerham Priory this past,
glorious week, Adrian had come to Lydia at night, and during
the day she'd stolen more and more time away from baby
Ethan to be with him. They took walks on the cliffs overlooking the ocean. They made quick trips into the village. They
ate dinner together and made love all night. This was the first
time they had shared breakfast together.

"You receive the London papers?" Lydia shivered. She
would be happy to never see another newspaper again.

Adrian glanced up. "Did you wish to see them?" He handed one to her before she could answer.

"I do not." She pushed it back to him.

He opened one of the papers and was soon engrossed in it.

Lydia reached for her teacup. "What do you read?"

His eyes narrowed in concentration. "There was a disturbance in New Shields involving the keelmen. One man was killed."

She gasped. "How dreadful."

He made a sound of disgust. "There is a great deal of rioting lately."

Over the Corn Laws, she knew. The Corn Laws were intended to protect the profits of wealthy land owners by keeping grain prices high and restricting foreign imports. Unfortunately, they also made it very difficult for the poor to buy bread.

"At least writing of riots and such is the sort of news one ought to read in the newspapers. Not stories of me."

"There is nothing of you in the papers today." He smiled. "Thus far."

She took a sip of tea. "That relieves me."

"Your name rarely appears now," he assured her in a more serious tone.

"Rarely? That must mean there was much written at first."

"Well, there was," he admitted, looking back at the paper.

Her curiosity got the better of her. "What did they say of me, then?"

He lowered the paper. "That you had disappeared and were assumed to have fled to the Continent. There was a good deal of speculation about who accompanied you, however."

She groaned. "Those poor men, to have their names attached to mine."

He shook his head. "Spare them no pity. It was considered somewhat of a coup among the male set to be connected to you." He averted his gaze for a moment, as if thinking. "Perhaps I should feel insulted that my name was missing."

"Stop jesting about it," she cried, although he'd almost made her laugh. "It is horrible to be the object of such lurid speculation."

His gaze softened. He reached over and clasped her hand. "Do not credit what is written. It is not worth such worry."

She could almost believe him when he touched her so tenderly. "It is such a relief to be away from it all."

"I am certain it is, but you cannot stay away for ever." He spoke in a very matter-of-fact tone and turned back to the newspaper.

It was not a trivial matter to Lydia. "I see no reason for me to return to London."

He lowered the newspaper again. "Nonsense. You must return to London."

"It is not nonsense." Her heart pounded painfully at the thought. "Why can I not live in the country?"

"I have no place for you to live in the country, for one thing, and, as you have said before, we cannot impose on Tanner's generosity for ever." He stared at her. Disapprovingly, she thought. "Even without all that, we have obligations in London."

"*I* have no obligations in London," she retorted.

"You have a townhouse and servants to see to."

"You can see to them for me. You are my husband. They are your property now." A wife's property became her husband's upon marriage, unless special agreements were made beforehand. She had made no such agreements upon her marriage to Adrian.

He leaned forwards. "We must announce our marriage and see Ethan christened. We cannot do that in a place where we are unknown."

She did feel an obligation to have Ethan christened, but a christening in London would be fraught with problems. Who would be godparents? Who would come? Even her sister would consider her too scandalous to attend.

"I do not want to return to London." Her spirits plummeted.

Adrian gave her a level look. "We must, Lydia."

She turned her head away. Her throat constricted, and it became painful to breathe. She could not even think of returning to the unhappiness she'd endured in London. She felt near panic at the prospect.

She dug her fingernails into her skin, trying to be strong about this. Adrian was still buried in his newspaper and took no notice of her distress.

She tried again. "Adrian, you have no idea what awaits us if we return to town. Everyone will know of—of Ethan's birth. The newspapers…"

He placed the newspaper on the table. "Best to brazen it out. Face them all, and tell them to go to the devil. We have married and that should satisfy everyone."

Her insides twisted. "You cannot know what it is like, Adrian. There is no brazening it out."

"Ignore the papers, Lydia," he said firmly. "They will tire of you. We'll pay no heed to them."

Ignore them? Impossible.

He lifted the horrid newspaper again, placing it like a barrier between them.

"I do not want to return to London," she murmured again, but he was not listening.

"Good God!" He rose from his chair.

She jumped.

"Our decision is made for us." He pointed to the paper. "We must travel to London as soon as possible."

"No, Adrian—"

He held the paper out to her. "You do not understand. Your parents—"

Were dead? She just knew he would say her parents were

dead. She stopped breathing. She wanted to cover her ears. Those hateful newspapers—they even brought her news that her parents were dead.

"Lydia, your parents, your brother, have returned to England. They are in London."

Alive? She felt like weeping with relief.

"We must pack up. Leave today, if we can," he said.

Her brief moment of relief vanished. "No!"

He gaped at her. "You must see your parents. Explain to them what has happened to you."

"We can write them a letter." She would much prefer writing them a letter.

It must take a few days for the newspapers to arrive from London and a few days more for her parents to send an announcement of their return. By this time her parents would have heard about Wexin. Someone was bound to have informed them. They would know about the baby, about him being conceived out of wedlock, and they would know she'd tried to pass him off as Wexin's.

They would know the whole sordid mess.

"My parents will not want to see me, Adrian." Not her father, who was a stickler for proper behaviour. Not her mother, who put appearances before everything else.

"Of course they will want to see you." He looked at her as if she'd just sprouted horns.

She stood. "You do not know them! They will hate me now, like everyone else!" Her voice quavered as her panic rose. "Everyone hates me in London. They think I made Wexin kill his friend! They know I conceived a child who was not Wexin's. You know that! You cannot make me go back."

He grabbed her by the shoulders. "Lydia! Cease this immediately!"

She could not stop herself. She'd held it all in for so many months. It was like a dam breaking. "You cannot make me go back! The newspapers will write about me again. Tell lies about me. They will tear into every part of me. I cannot take that! I cannot take all those people reading about me, laughing at the pictures drawn of me…" She tried to pull away from him.

He held her shoulders firmly. "It will not be that way. You are married. Ethan is legitimate. Your parents will understand—"

She laughed like a maniac. "Do you think they will like my marriage to you? They will hate it. My father would never have allowed you to court me." She glared into his eyes. "Ours is a scandalous marriage. Wait until the newspapers get hold of it. I can see it—the scandalous widow marries the *ton*'s most notorious rake. Wait until you see your picture in a print-shop window! Wait until they write about you! You will regret this marriage as much as I do!"

He released her. "You regret this marriage?"

She turned her face away. She was breathing hard. All she wanted to do was return to her bed and weep into her pillow. "No. It makes Ethan legitimate, but it will make you and me miserable." She looked at him again, this time through a veil of tears. "Give me Ethan and let us live in the country. A cottage. A hovel. I do not care."

He seemed to have become very tall, very broad-shouldered suddenly. She felt dwarfed by him.

"We will leave for London today." His voice was as hard as granite. "You, me and Ethan. You will see your parents. You will attend social events. What you feel in private is your own affair, but, for Ethan's sake, we will present ourselves without apology. Do you understand?"

"You dictate to me?" She barely suppressed her outrage.

"I do dictate it. It is the only way." He gave her a firm nod and brushed past her out of the door.

She wished she were glass. She'd be shattered on the floor, then, and this pain and panic would be done with. As it was, she now had to endure the fact that she'd just told her husband he made her miserable and that she would rather live in a hovel than with him.

They left for London that day, as her husband had dictated, and the day after that Lydia stood in the bedchamber of Adrian's London townhouse holding Ethan while Mary unpacked her trunk. There was a connecting door leading to Adrian's room, she imagined, although she doubted he would wish to use it.

This room must have once been Adrian's mother's. It had expensive painted wallpaper, French-style furnishings, satin bed coverings and curtains. At least the colours favoured Lydia, all pale blues and whites and golds.

Lydia would have so much preferred staying at her own townhouse among the servants who meant so much to her, but she had not dared to make that request of Adrian. They had hardly spoken since her outburst.

She felt an ache that had settled inside her ever since she'd shouted at Adrian. She'd said horrid things to him, things that tore through the fragile fabric of their marriage. The previous night in her lonely bed in the inn, Lydia had missed him terribly, and the enormity of what she'd said to him washed over her.

By morning, however, she'd regained some of the fortitude that had seen her through the past difficult year. Things were not nearly as desperate as they once had been. She had food. Shelter.

A baby.

The baby made it all worthwhile.

Mary tripped while carrying clothing to the bureau, and the pile of folded clothes tumbled to the floor in a jumble. "Oh, no!" Mary cried as if she'd broken a piece of priceless Chinese porcelain.

"No harm done, Mary," Lydia assured her.

"I beg your pardon, my lady." Mary scooped up the clothing and set about folding it again. "I am so very clumsy."

"You are not at all clumsy." Lydia peered at her. "Do not look so upset."

Mary hung her head. "Beg pardon, my lady."

Lydia could not bear for them both to be in the dismals. She tried to cheer Mary up. "Perhaps you will see that young man again now that we are in London, the one who courted you. That would be nice, would it not?"

Mary's head whipped up. "I do not even think of him any more!"

Lydia drew back. "Very well, Mary."

Lydia had Mary's misery on her conscience as well as her own. Mary had never returned to her once-cheerful self while they'd been at Nickerham. Lydia had thought it was because she missed her suitor. She still thought so, no matter Mary's protests.

The maid loved caring for Ethan, at least. Mary had begged to be Ethan's nurse rather than continue as Lydia's lady's maid. It made no sense to Lydia for the girl to wish to lower her status in the household, but Lydia could not refuse her. It meant searching for another lady's maid, one who did not object to waiting upon a lady of scandal.

Ethan began fussing, and Lydia walked the room with him against her shoulder. "He is all at sixes and sevens, I think, from the carriage ride."

Lydia wandered to the window and looked out onto Curzon Street. Adrian had gone out almost immediately after they'd arrived, delaying only long enough to present his stunned servants to her.

He told Lydia he would call upon his parents. They'd known he had spent the last few months in Sussex; now they would learn the real reason why. Lydia was grateful Adrian had not compelled her to accompany him. Think what a reception she would be given.

She'd had a note delivered to her parents asking permission to call upon them. Better to warn them than to turn up on their doorstep. When it came to writing the note, Lydia could not think of what to tell them. She'd scribbled something hurriedly, and Adrian had dispatched a footman to deliver it and await a reply. The footman had not yet returned from the errand.

Lydia was convinced of what Adrian had yet to discover. Neither of their families would be happy about their marriage.

He would soon learn how it felt to be besmirched on the pages of newspapers as well. Eventually the newspapers would learn of her marriage and her return to London. Perhaps the reporters would appear on the doorstep by tomorrow. After enduring some of that harassment, perhaps Adrian would agree to send her and Ethan away. Far away.

Mary finished emptying the trunk, and Ethan finally fell asleep. Mary took him from Lydia's arms to carry him to the nursery, which seemed a great distance away, even though it was up only one flight of stairs.

And now Lydia had nothing to do except wait.

"You did what?" shrieked Adrian's mother. "Say it is not so."

"I will say it again." Adrian stood before both his parents in their drawing room. It was not the most convenient time to call upon them as they were bound for a dinner party. "I am married to Lady Wexin."

"Of all the foolish, addle-brained—" His father, dressed in formal attire, sputtered. "But she was to have some bastard child."

"My child," Adrian said in even tones. "My son."

"A son!" his father bellowed.

"My son," Adrian repeated, adding, "your grandson."

"But I am too young to be a grandmother!" his mother wailed.

His father gaped at him. "Do you mean it was you she had the affair with?" His expression turned indignant. "And you did not tell me of it?"

Adrian gave his father a withering glance. It was completely lost on his father, however.

His father laughed. "I'll be damned. It was my son who bedded her."

"This is all wrong, Adrian." His mother sniffed and dabbed at her eyes with her handkerchief. "I wanted to attend a wedding and a wedding breakfast and have all my friends present."

What might it have been like to marry Lydia in a church with family and friends around? Perhaps matters would be different between them.

Still, he could not regret that night of lovemaking, or assisting her later, or even their hasty marriage. They'd been briefly happy at Nickerham Priory. When he showed Lydia that the *ton* would accept them and the newspapers tire of them, perhaps they could grasp that happiness again.

His father crossed the room to give his wife a reassuring pat on the hand. "It is a damnable way to start a marriage."

To that statement, Adrian feared he could agree.

"Do not use vulgar language, Edmund," his mother chided.

"Mother." Adrian softened his voice "Will you call upon my wife? If you accept her, the *ton* will be hard pressed to cut her entirely."

She dabbed at her eyes again. "I shall be the laughingstock of all my friends."

"Please, Mother," he persisted.

She released a long, deep sigh. "Oh, very well. I will call upon her. We must put the best face on this that we can."

His father squeezed his wife's hand. "You are everything that is good."

Adrian walked over to her. "I agree." He leaned down and kissed her on the forehead.

His father clapped him on the back. "We shall do our duty by her, I assure you."

There could be no firmer commitment from his father.

Adrian embraced him, his tears stinging. "I must take my leave. I have barely shaken the dust off from our journey."

After kissing his mother again, Adrian turned towards the door.

His father put his hand on Adrian's shoulder. "I'll walk you to the hall."

When they stepped out of the drawing room, the butler and footman, obviously listening, jumped to the side.

In the hall, while they waited for the butler to fetch Adrian's hat, his father leaned close to his ear. "Tell me, son, how did you accomplish it?"

Adrian gave him a puzzled look. "Accomplish what?"

"You know." His father smiled sheepishly. "How did you make the conquest of her when others did not? Your name was not even in White's book."

Adrian pulled away. "It is a private matter, sir."

His father went on as if he had no idea how outrageous it was for him to inquire about it. "Well, I confess I pine to know it. I know many a gentleman had the thought—"

Adrian gave him a direct look. "You are speaking of my wife, Father."

His father's face fell in disappointment. "Well, I merely wanted to know. You are my son—"

The butler appeared with the hat. Adrian took it. "Good day, Father."

His father opened his mouth to speak again, but seemed to think better of it. He smiled at Adrian and waved him off.

Stepping back onto the pavement, Adrian felt a surge of optimism. The interview with his parents had gone much better than he had expected.

Would it reassure Lydia?

He wanted desperately to reassure her all would be well in time. He'd badly mismanaged the whole episode between them when she'd gone into a panic over returning to London.

He ought to have convinced her that she had done nothing to be ashamed of, that her one lapse—making love with him—had been at a desperate time for her.

Many *ton* marriages were hasty ones. He could have named some for her. Adrian had seen it over and over. When those couples spoke their vows, they were welcomed back like sheep to the fold. He'd be damned if he'd allow it to be any different for their marriage.

Adrian had one more stop to make before returning to his house, a stop he had not mentioned to Lydia. The newspapers had also reported that the Marquess of Tannerton was in town. Adrian intended to enlist his friend's assistance.

Tanner and his wife were intimately connected to the scandal that had brought such unwanted attention to Lydia— if they accepted her marriage to Adrian, who else would dare shun them?

Chapter Fifteen

It has been learned that the notorious Lady W—'s parents, Lord and Lady S—, who lately arrived from a lengthy tour abroad, learned about their daughter's murderous husband while in Bombay, India. The newspaper that found its way to the exotic land of the Maharajas was none other than *The New Observer*, newspaper to the world. —*The New Observer*, October 23, 1819

"It is so good to see you." Tanner gave Adrian an enthusiastic hug.

"Good to see you, too." Adrian had missed Tanner.

"Come see my son!" Tanner gestured for Adrian to follow as he bounded up the marble stairway.

They entered a pretty nursery with bright windows and a watchful nurse seated in a chair. Tanner pulled Adrian over to an ornately carved mahogany cradle that looked like it had served generations of marquesses.

"My son, William," Tanner whispered, looking down at a peacefully sleeping infant, who looked of a size with Ethan, but was as dark haired as Ethan was blond.

"Fine fellow," Adrian responded.

As they tiptoed out of the room again, Tanner boasted of little William's lusty wails and strong grip. "He's a game one." Tanner grinned.

Would Tanner's grin fade when Adrian told him about his own son?

They made their way to the drawing room, about twice the size of his parents', but looking as if unchanged for two decades.

Lady Tannerton walked in behind them. "I've ordered tea."

"Tea!" cried Tanner. "I'd say we need some port first." He opened a cabinet and took out a decanter and two glasses. He gestured to his wife with a third glass, but she shook her head.

She turned to Adrian and extended her hand. "It is good to see you, Lord Cavanley."

"And to see you, ma'am." He accepted her confident handshake.

Tanner poured the port and handed a glass to Adrian. "Now tell me—what the devil were you doing at Nickerham Priory all this time?"

Adrian gave him a grave look. "That is what I must discuss with you."

Lady Tannerton broke in. "Would you prefer I leave you, then?"

Adrian stopped her. "Please remain, ma'am. I wish you to know about this as well."

Tanner and his wife exchanged questioning looks.

Adrian took a gulp of port and was about to plunge right in when the tea arrived. He waited until the footman had set the tea tray on a table and left the room. Lady Tannerton sat in one of the nearby chairs and poured a cup of tea for herself.

Adrian glanced at each of them in turn. "I am married."

Tanner and his wife exchanged looks again.

"I will explain."

Adrian began the story with his rescue of Lydia from the reporter, merely implying the events of which his father had been so curious. He skipped over Lydia's desperate financial situation and his secret assistance to her and spoke instead of the effect on her of all the newspaper stories and gossip. He told of how he learned of her pregnancy, and of how he married her. His voice trembled with emotion when he talked about the birth of his son at Nickerham Priory.

Tanner gazed at the floor much of the time or quietly sipped his drink. Lady Tannerton regarded him with a sympathetic expression. At least Adrian hoped it was sympathetic. He desperately wanted his boyhood friend to understand his choices and also for them both to understand the difficulties Lydia had endured.

Adrian stared into his port as he brought the story to an end with the reason for their return to London.

No one spoke.

He finally looked up, and Tanner broke into a smile. He crossed the room and clapped Adrian on the shoulder. "But this is splendid! Our sons will grow up together as we did!"

Lady Tannerton also smiled. "Why did you not bring Lady Wexin—I mean, Lady Cavanley—with you?"

Tanner held up his hands. "Wait a moment. You two are driving me mad with this 'Lady' this and 'Lord' that. By God, we are all friends."

Lady Tannerton laughed and looked up at Adrian. "Do call me Marlena."

He bowed. "Then I am Adrian to you."

"What do we call your wife?" Tanner said.

Adrian liked the natural way Tanner said *your wife*. "She is Lydia."

Marlena smiled. "What of Lydia? Why did you not bring her?"

He slid Tanner a glance. "I needed to be certain of your feelings first."

"Pom." Tanner addressed Adrian as he'd done all their

years together. He would probably be the only one who would ever do so. "We have always been sympathetic to her. That cursed Wexin left her in a terrible position."

"You must tell her of our feelings," Marlena insisted.

"I have," he assured her. "But she blames herself for Wexin's actions."

"Fustian," Tanner responded.

Adrian shrugged. "You must understand, she has endured so much ill treatment, she is reluctant to believe anyone would feel sympathetic towards her. She fears her own parents will shun her. She is to see them tomorrow."

"Surely they will understand!" Marlena glanced aside. "It must have been so difficult for her, being alone. And then to wait for her baby to be born…"

"Indeed," Adrian felt suddenly as if a weight was off his shoulders. He had not realised how worried he'd been about Tanner's reaction. "Our marriage should put everything to rights. I'm convinced the newspapers and the *ton* will tire of the gossip if we re-enter society and ignore everything they write."

Tanner raised a finger. "You need an entrée. I believe you need a marquess making a show of welcoming her."

Adrian's response was restrained. "I had hoped to beg you for that."

"No need to beg, Adrian," Marlena said. "Of course we will welcome her."

He decided not to mince words. "Would you be willing to be our son's godparents?"

His friend smiled wider. "We would be honoured."

"In fact," Marlena added, "Tanner and I intended to ask if you would be our son's godfather, but now your wife can be godmother as well."

This was more than Adrian could have desired. "Are you certain of this?"

"Of course we are." Tanner lifted his glass to Adrian.

"We should arrange to christen them together," Marlena mused. "As soon as possible, I think. With a dinner afterwards." She turned to Tanner. "Do you think the Duke of Clarence would attend if you asked him to?"

The Duke of Clarence was the Prince Regent's younger brother and, since the death of Princess Charlotte, third in line to the throne.

"Brilliant idea!" Tanner slapped his hand on the table. "I am certain His Royal Highness and his princess would attend. He may even agree for them to be godparents to both boys. No reason why our sons cannot have more than one set of godparents. It would start things off splendidly."

Adrian stared at him. "If you are able to contrive that, Tanner, you will earn my eternal gratitude."

Tanner laughed. "You always say that when I get you out of a scrape." He added, "Leave it all to me. I will arrange it for the next Sunday, if at all possible."

"I will call upon Lydia tomorrow," Marlena said. "To welcome her back to town."

When Adrian took his leave a short time later, Tanner walked him to the door. "How do you fare, Pom?" he asked as they crossed the hall. "This marriage cannot be a comfortable one, not with the way it came about."

Adrian did not answer right away. There was too much to say and no time to say it. Indeed, he was not yet certain how much he ought to confide in his friend.

He might have told Tanner that he'd briefly thought his marriage might turn into something quite special. Since his quarrel with Lydia, Adrian did not know if he could ever scale the breach between them.

"I am determined to do my best by her," he finally answered.

"I would expect no less from you." Tanner briefly gripped his shoulder.

Adrian said goodbye and stepped outside. The hour was later than he thought and the sky was already dark. Turning up his collar against the evening chill, he set a brisk pace down South Audley Street. Soon Adrian would show Lydia that the gossip would cease. Soon she would be able to return to the life she'd been born to.

When he reached his townhouse the butler attended the door.

"Lady Cavanley received an answer to her letter," Bilson told him when he crossed the threshold.

From her parents. Adrian's brows rose. "And?"

Bilson frowned and shook his head.

"Thank you, Bilson," Adrian said.

Adrian found Lydia in her bedchamber, seated in a chair facing the window, the letter in her hand.

"You received word." It was not a question.

She turned and stared at him with blank eyes. She handed him the letter.

He read:

Dear Daughter,

Your father and I are pleased to find you in excellent health; however, the scandal and notoriety in which you have embroiled yourself during our absence prevents us from receiving your call on the morrow. The accounts of your behaviour, of which we have now been fully apprised by unimpeachable sources, are not the sort our family can condone.

Yours, etc.,

Catherine Strathfield

He threw the letter down. *Those damned heartless idiots.*

"Lydia." His voice came out harsher than he intended.

She did not even glance at him. "I told you they would not want to see me."

"They will change their minds."

Her gaze slid to him, but her eyes still showed no emotion. "Now it will be written that my parents refuse to see me."

And she blamed him for it.

This battle might be harder won than he thought. "Your parents will come around."

She turned her face away. "I suppose your parents greeted the news of our marriage with great joy."

"They were quite reasonable," he told her. "My mother will call upon you."

She gave a mirthless laugh. "Such enthusiasm."

"I made another call, Lydia." She still did not look at him. "I called upon Tanner. He and his wife have agreed to be Ethan's godparents, and I accepted that we would be godparents to their son."

Her eyes widened.

"They will arrange a double christening to take place in St George's in Hanover Square as soon as possible."

"Why did you not discuss this with me beforehand?" she rasped.

"I took the father's prerogative of arranging the christening, nothing more," he countered.

She glared at him. "How dare you put me in this position, Adrian? How can I be a godparent to Lord and Lady Tannerton's child? How can I? And how can I ask them to be Ethan's godparents?"

"Who better?" Adrian's patience was fraying. "Who else, for that matter? Tanner remains my friend whether you are easy with it or not, and I do not know who else we might have asked. It is more than generous of him to do this for us." He moved closer to her and leaned into her face. "I'll brook no argument on this matter, Lydia. We will have the christening. Tanner and his wife will host a dinner party afterwards, and no one will dare refuse an invitation."

"That is splendid, Adrian." Her voice dripped with sarcasm. "Force people to associate with me. That will be so pleasant for everyone." She whipped her face away.

He straightened and walked out of her room before this discussion eroded into the shouting match they'd had in Nickerham, and before they again said things to each other that were better left unspoken.

The next morning when Adrian sat down to a breakfast of muffins, butter and potted beef, Bilson informed him that Lydia had requested her meal in her room.

"Thank you, Bilson." He schooled his expression to look bland.

He tried to convince himself that she merely needed time to accustom herself to all the changes in her life. Eventually they would have to find a way to deal comfortably with each other. They could not avoid one another for ever.

At least she would not ask him what he meant to do today. He'd rather not quarrel with her over the tasks he intended to accomplish as soon as the hour permitted it.

He wiled away the time reading the newspapers. *The New Observer* was the only paper that wrote about Lydia. The paper reported that her parents were so shocked at reports of her behaviour that they intended to banish her from the family.

Adrian stuffed the paper in his pocket. No need for Lydia to read that drivel.

Ironically, one of his errands was to send an announcement to a newspaper, telling London of his marriage and of Ethan.

The other was a more difficult task.

When Adrian finally went out, the weather was crisp as befitted the autumn day. He walked several hundred yards to a row of houses that faced Hyde Park. Lord and Lady Strathfield's townhouse. Lydia's parents.

He sounded the knocker and was admitted.

"Lord Cavanley to speak to Lord Strathfield. Lady Strathfield, too, if she wishes." He handed his card to the butler.

In a sonorous voice the man asked, "May I inform my lord and lady as to the purpose of this call?"

"Tell them I wish to speak to them about their daughter."

The butler's brows rose. He bowed. "Allow me to escort you to the drawing room."

Adrian cooled his heels in the drawing room, which was adorned by Indian statues and silks undoubtedly purchased on their lengthy tour.

Lord and Lady Strathfield soon entered.

"Cavanley?" Lord Strathfield said by way of greeting. "I expected your father." Both he and Lady Strathfield looked on guard.

Adrian bowed. "Good morning, to you, Lord Strathfield. Lady Strathfield. My father is Earl of Varcourt now."

"Old Varcourt died?" Strathfield coughed.

"He'd been ill a long time," Adrian said hurriedly.

"I cannot fathom why you should call," Lady Strathfield said.

"It is about your daughter." Adrian pulled their letter to Lydia from his pocket. "This letter states that you refuse to see her."

"Why do you possess that letter?" Lord Strathfield's tone was sharp.

"She gave it to me." Adrian looked directly into their eyes. "I urge you to reconsider your decision to cut her. Not only is it cruel, but it is completely foolish—"

"Now see here—" Strathfield broke in.

Adrian talked above him. "Listen to me."

"Reconsider?" cried Lady Strathfield. "After she has dragged our good name through the newspapers? Married to a murderer, for heaven's sake. Parading lovers in and out of her house? Trying to foist her bastard off as—"

"There were no lovers." He tried to remain calm. "The

newspapers printed falsehoods. She deserves your pity for all she has been through."

"Bearing a bastard does not deserve my pity," Lady Strathfield said hotly. "I am mortified at her complete moral lapse." She lifted her gaze heavenwards. "My husband called upon Levenhorne and learned of her little scheme, to pass the baby off as Wexin's."

"My dear, I do not think it wise to discuss our private affairs so openly," Strathfield broke in. He turned back to Adrian. "You, young man, are a fine one to moralise. Your reputation is well known, I assure you."

His wife gave a tight, false smile. "I suppose you were one of her many men. You are an acknowledged rake, are you not? Is she in your keeping? Is that why you have the letter?"

"She is not in my keeping." Adrian's voice turned low.

Strathfield seized the floor again. "Then why are you here, sir? Whether we acknowledge our daughter or not can be no affair of yours."

Adrian looked from one to the other. "As her husband, it most certainly is my affair."

"Husband?" the Strathfields cried in unison.

"Husband," he repeated. He narrowed his eyes. "Did she not explain that in her letter?"

"She most certainly did not!" her father retorted.

He nodded, supposing he ought to have expected that. Perhaps she thought announcing her marriage to a rake would not gain her entrée to her parents' house.

"The child is mine as well." He fixed a steady gaze on Lady Strathfield. "And he is no bastard."

Lydia had watched her husband leave the townhouse that morning, just as she settled down to nurse Ethan.

Her emotions had been in a turmoil since knowing she

must come to London. How nice it would be to be back at Nickerham Priory walking along the cliffs with Adrian.

She must not think of that brief happy time between them. It would be impossible to regain it in London.

She dreaded the christening. Dreaded it. The *ton* would not welcome her. Her own parents refused to see her.

Would it have made any difference to her parents if she'd told them she was married? She'd only scribbled a quick request to call upon them, giving no details at all.

No matter what she had told Adrian, she had truly believed her parents would see her and had harboured a secret hope they would understand all she'd been through.

Lydia shook her head. How foolish of her.

Her throat tightened. Soon the newspapers would learn of her presence in Mayfair and of her marriage to Adrian. The reporters would return.

Ethan finally fell asleep, and Lydia rose from the chair to carry him to the nursery. When she entered, Mary was there folding a basket of baby linen that had been laundered upon their arrival the previous day.

"He is sleeping," she told the maid. "And I am at liberty to watch him today." Because she would not be calling upon her parents, of course. "You could visit your mother, if you like."

She'd hoped Mary would smile at this prospect. The maid had not seen her mother since June.

The girl merely nodded. "As you wish, my lady. I am certain my mother would like that very well."

"Go, then," Lydia told her.

Mary curtsied and left her. Lydia fetched her sewing from her bedchamber and brought it back to the nursery. She wandered about the room. It had been a guest bedroom turned into a nursery when the cradle and rocking chair were brought down from the attic the day before. She sat in the rocking chair and picked up a piece of white dimity with which she was sewing a new shirt for Ethan. He'd already outgrown his other clothes.

A few minutes later the butler came to the door, sounding out of breath. "M'lady." He stopped for a moment. "The Marchioness of Heronvale and the Marchioness of Tannerton have called."

She rose, dropping her sewing on the chair. "They have called? To see Lord Cavanley?" Why would those ladies call upon Adrian?

The butler shook his head. "To see you, my lady. They are waiting for you in the drawing room. I took the liberty of ordering tea."

"Thank you, Bilson." He'd ordered tea. She could not refuse the visit if he'd already ordered tea.

Lydia looked down at herself, still in an old morning dress stained from her milk and Ethan's lusty burps. She was an appalling sight.

She collected her wits. "Send one of the maids to help me dress and another to watch over the baby. He'll sleep."

Bilson bowed and rushed out of the room.

Lydia managed to be half-dressed by the time the maid came to assist her. She pinned up her hair while the maid did her laces, and within ten minutes she was hurrying down the stairs to the drawing room.

This must be about the christening, she thought. It made some sense that Lady Tannerton would wish to speak to her about the christening. Perhaps to ask her not to appear at the ceremony. Sometimes mothers did not attend christenings.

But why would Lady Heronvale come? Lydia had no more than a nodding acquaintance with that lady.

She took a breath and walked into the drawing room. "My ladies. Forgive me for keeping you waiting." She curtsied to each of them. "Lady Heronvale. Lady Tannerton."

"Why, you look lovely!" exclaimed Lady Heronvale.

What did she expect? That she would be scarred from the scandal?

Lydia remembered that Lord Heronvale was Levenhorne's brother-in-law. Perhaps Lady Heronvale had been sent to spy on her.

Lady Heronvale smiled. "Let me present you to Lady Tannerton."

Lydia curtsied again. She dimly remembered Lady Tannerton from her first Season, before her first marriage.

Lady Tannerton extended her hand. "I am so very glad to have the pleasure of knowing you at last." She shook Lydia's hand warmly.

"We came to welcome you back to town." Lady Heronvale spoke as if this were the most normal thing in the world.

"And to talk to you about the christening," added Lady Tannerton. "Serena has very kindly agreed to assist with the guest list. I probably know less than you about who we ought to invite."

Lydia did not know of anyone who would want to come.

The tea arrived.

"Won't you have tea? I will pour." Lydia gestured for them to sit.

Lady Heronvale smiled prettily. "Oh, before we have tea, may I be so presumptuous as to ask to see the baby?"

"Oh, yes!" agreed Lady Tannerton. "May we see the baby?"

Lydia had no choice.

She led them up the flight of stairs to the nursery. The maid attending Ethan stood and curtsied and moved into a remote corner of the room.

The ladies peered into the cradle. Ethan's little pink mouth moved as it often did when he slept. Lydia always supposed he was dreaming of nursing. He clutched his blanket with one hand. The other hand rested on the lace of his cap.

"Oh, he is precious!" exclaimed Lady Heronvale. "He is so fair!"

What had she expected? Was she searching for clues to the baby's paternity?

Lady Tannerton gently stroked the baby's forehead with her finger. "I believe he is every bit as big as my son." She glanced up at Lydia. "My son is about one month older."

"And I have a daughter the same age." Lady Heronvale laughed. "Your boys will be rivals over her!"

Lydia remained guarded. This affability could not be genuine, especially from Lady Tannerton who had suffered so much because of Lydia.

Lady Tannerton gazed back at Ethan. "No one seeing this boy will dare question his paternity. Not with that little mouth." She gave Lydia a steady look. "He is the very picture of your husband."

Lydia stiffened. "Did you come to discover if my baby was indeed my husband's?"

"Oh, no!" exclaimed Lady Heronvale.

Lady Tannerton did not waver. "We came here to offer our friendship and our help. I assure you, I have experienced too much of life to ever judge another woman's difficulties."

"And I assure you, there are secrets in our family as well," Lady Heronvale added. She gazed down at the baby and her voice turned dreamy. "But when you look upon something so precious as a little baby—this dear little one—what does anything else matter?"

Lydia looked from one lady to the other. "I do not believe this."

Lady Tannerton put a hand on her arm and looked her directly in the eyes. "Believe us."

Lady Heronvale tore herself away from gazing upon the baby. "Yes, and there is much to do. We have a christening to plan! We shall not leave so important a task to the fathers."

She linked arms with the other two ladies. "Do you know who Marlena says we must invite?"

"Who?" asked Lydia suspiciously.

"The Duke of Clarence!" Lady Heronvale laughed again. "He may even agree to be your son's godparent!"

Lydia's jaw dropped.

"It is true," Lady Tannerton said. "He is another friend of my husband's, and Tanner intends to ask him if he and Her Royal Highness, Princess Adelaide, would be our sons' godparents. Tanner said the Duke has always been fond of your Adrian, so he is confident the answer will be yes."

Lydia felt as if she'd run a great distance. "The Duke of Clarence?" she whispered.

Chapter Sixteen

Marriage Announcement. Viscount Cavanley to The Lady Wexin, formerly Lady Lydia Strathfield, August 16, in Mayfair... Birth Announcement. August. The Viscountess Cavanley, a son and heir.
—*The Morning Post*, November 1, 1819

"This is an outrage!" Phillip Reed shot to his feet, sending the chair to his desk clattering to the floor.

Samuel nearly suffered an apoplexy. "What is it?"

Phillip held up a newspaper. "It is *The Morning Post*, that is what it is! An announcement. Two announcements!" His face turned an alarming shade of red. "They've stolen the story right from under us, and I want to know why the deuce we did not know this first."

Samuel walked over to him. "What? What story?"

"Lady Wexin!"

Samuel froze.

Phillip thrust *The Morning Post* into Samuel's hands.

Samuel read for himself. "Lord Cavanley?" The one man Samuel knew the lady had seen.

He'd found no indication of any other encounter between

Cavanley and Lady Wexin. Cavanley had spent more time at Madame Bisou's gaming house than anywhere else. He'd given up on the man. Prematurely, it seemed.

Phillip picked up the chair and threw it down again. "Why did you not discover this? You were following the story. What the deuce have you been doing?"

Samuel had been looking into the presence of unrest in the various guilds in the city to gauge if the level of discontent would spawn an assembly the size of Peterloo or a riot like that at North Shields, but he'd best not admit that to Phillip.

"I have been out and about, with my ear to the ground for any news of the lady. I've been speaking to her parents' servants regularly. I have heard nothing." Of course, he had not checked for a couple days.

"Well, *The Morning Post* certainly heard," Phillip huffed.

Samuel glared at his brother. "Do not plague me with this! Those were announcements! Someone brought them to the *Post*."

Phillip put his fists on his hips. "Blast it, you should have known before the announcement was made! It is your story, Sam, the best story we've ever had. What happened to your source inside her house? Could you not worm the information out of that servant?"

"How dare you question my skills at reporting? All you do is sit here and select what to steal from other newspapers." Samuel grabbed his hat. "I'll endure no more of this." He stormed out of the office.

Samuel strode down the street, not really heeding where he was headed, angry at Phillip for ringing a peal over his head, angry at himself for slacking off on the story and missing out.

Phillip was right. He should have known that Lady Wexin had returned to town as soon as her feet alighted from the carriage. He should have sensed it in the air.

Because Mary would be with her.

Samuel reached the line of idle hackney coaches and grabbed the first one.

"To Mayfair," he said to the jarvey.

Samuel had the hack stop at Hill Street, alighting in front of the Wexins' townhouse. A reporter from another paper was just stepping away from the door.

The man shook his head at Samuel. "You've seen the *Post*, then, have you? Some surprise, eh?" All the reporters knew this was Samuel's story. "She's not here, though. I'm off to Cavanley's place."

Samuel walked with the reporter to the Cavanley house, where others had already gathered. The reporters engaged in some good-natured ribbing at Samuel's expense about *The Morning Post* breaking his story.

"What do we know?" he asked.

"She's in there," one of the men said. "She's married to him. One of the neighbour's servants said the Marchionesses of Heronvale and Tannerton called on her yesterday. Her mother-in-law, Lady Varcourt, came today."

Lady Tannerton had called upon Lady Cavanley? That was interesting, Samuel thought, but, more importantly, had Mary come to London with her?

"Cavanley's been out, but not her," another man said.

Samuel nodded. He hung around with the others for a while, but, as soon as he could contrive to do so, he slipped away and walked around to the garden gate, peering through its cracks at the back of the house. He saw no one.

His spirits plummeted, but what had he expected? Even if he could see Mary, she would not speak to him. And there was nothing he could say to her that would make any difference at all.

Still, he just wanted to see her, to glimpse her trim figure, her pretty round face, her huge, expressive eyes. He just wanted to see her.

He made his way back to the front of the house. His colleagues were all abuzz.

"What happened?" he asked.

"Wouldn't you like to know?" one of them muttered. The others drifted away.

Samuel paced back and forth, thinking Phillip would kill him if he did not discover what this latest piece of information was. He sidled up to one of the younger lads, there to run errands for his newspaper's reporter.

"Interesting news, eh?" he said.

The young fellow nodded. "You can never guess with the Quality, can you?" Then he peered at Samuel. "I thought you didn't know."

Samuel shrugged. "I knew about it yesterday."

"Go on," he said. "You couldn't have."

Samuel rocked back and forth on his heels. "I did." He gave the fellow a sideways glance. "In fact, I know more than you do."

"Y're bamming me."

"I'm not," Samuel said. "I'll make a wager with you. If I don't know more than you, I'll give you a shilling."

The lad grinned. "A shilling?"

Samuel pulled a shilling from his pocket and held it up. "You must convince me you know what I just heard, however."

The lad stared at the shilling. "That the Cavanley baby and the Tannerton baby are to be christened together at St George's in Hanover Square, do you mean?"

Samuel handed the shilling to the fellow and walked off.

The christening took place one week later on Sunday, 7 November, with the Duke of Clarence and his new wife, Princess Adelaide, standing up as godparents to both infants. The sunny, cool day, as well as the presence of the Royal Duke and perhaps sheer curiosity, resulted in a full church. Only a very few invitations had been regrets.

Lydia had hastily commissioned her old modiste to make a new gown for the event. After a tearful reunion with the dear woman, which surprised Lydia almost as much as the welcome from Ladies Heronvale and Tannerton, the modiste outdid herself in creating a stunning gown. The design was elegant and the fabric a perfect complement to Lydia's colouring, pale yellow muslin with threads of gold running through it so that it caught the light and shimmered. Lydia's hat was a matching confection woven with strands of gold, and decorated with ribbons and flowers and lace. The ensemble cost a fortune.

Perhaps Adrian would object to the cost of keeping her in London.

At least the dress gave Lydia a small measure of confidence. She knew she looked the part of a tasteful and wealthy wife and mother. Adrian had said nothing when he saw her in the gown, and Lydia had been unable to interpret the intense expression on his face.

She'd done well, she thought, greeting people who could not quite meet her eye, pretending not to notice whispers behind gloved hands. She made herself focus on Ethan, her son, remembering that this was *his* day, not the day the notorious Lady W—now the notorious Lady C—came out of seclusion.

Lydia had attended St George's Church in Hanover Square many times, but, after a year's absence, it felt unfamiliar to her. The parents and godparents were gathered around the baptismal font. Lydia held the Tannerton infant, named William after the Duke of Clarence, and Lady Tannerton held Ethan. When the water was poured over little Ethan's head, he gurgled with pleasure, as if he'd known he must charm everyone to assist in improving his mother's reputation. William, the son of the Marquess, wailed in outraged protest.

When the ceremony ended, Lydia handed baby William to his nurse and soon found herself walking down the aisle next to the Duke of Clarence.

She took the opportunity to speak to him. "I wish to thank Your Royal Highness for the extreme honour you have done my son. I hope it has not caused you or Her Royal Highness any distress."

To her surprise he grasped her hand and squeezed it fondly. "My dear lady, I know something of being the object of gossip and a great deal of falling in love. And I know, too, that we are devoted to our children no matter how they begin life."

The Duke of Clarence had lived for many years with a woman he could not marry, the actress Mrs Jordan, and they had several children together. Even though the Duke and Mrs Jordan had been estranged in later years, it was said the Duke grieved deeply at news of her death only three years ago.

"Thank you, Your Royal Highness." Lydia curtsied.

The Duke smiled at her. "I wish you every happiness in your marriage, my dear."

A wish Lydia feared had already become impossible. "I wish the very same to you and more," she told him.

The Duke of Clarence had lately married a German princess half his age, young enough to bear him legitimate children. When the Regent's only child, the Princess Charlotte, had died in childbirth two years ago, all the unmarried royal dukes rushed to marry and breed, to secure the succession. Although the royals' illegitimate progeny were numerous, the only legitimate child had been born to the Duke of Kent the previous May, Her Royal Highness Princess Victoria.

The Duke spied his young wife. "I must go to her," he said, patting Lydia's hand.

Lydia emerged from the church and stood alone among its columns until Adrian appeared at her side. The large group formed itself into a procession of sorts to walk to the Tanner-ton townhouse. The Duke's attendants led, followed by the Duke and Duchess. Tanner and Marlena walked behind the Duke, and Lydia and Adrian behind them. Mary and the other

nurse followed with the babies. The air was cool, the sky free
of clouds, and the walk was rather pleasant after being inside
the church.

Once within the house, the ladies took each other's babies
again, and, with their husbands and the Royal Duke and his
Duchess, they stood in a reception line. Marlena, as the Marchioness of Tannerton insisted Lydia call her, stood on one
side of her and Adrian on the other. Any unkind remarks or
behaviour would be witnessed by the Marquess and his friend,
the Duke. No one dared. If anyone tried to escape the receiving line, Lady Heronvale—Serena—pulled them over to
admire the babies.

"Look!" she would say each time she brought someone up
to see Ethan. "Does he not favour his father?" She made it
seem the most natural thing in the world to do, and Lydia was
still not certain why she was doing it.

Lydia glanced down the line and inhaled a quick breath.
Her family approached. Adrian stepped a bit closer to her,
brushing against her. She glanced at him. She had forgotten
how handsome he looked in formal attire. Women's heads
turned to admire him.

Serena walked up to Lydia's parents at the crucial moment.
"Is he not the finest baby?"

"Oh, yes, indeed." Lydia's mother spoke with a little too
much expression in her voice.

A moment later her mother was suddenly in front of Lydia.

"Lydia, darling." Her mother made as if to press her cheek
against Lydia's, but did not quite make the contact. "How
good to see you."

Adrian brushed against her again.

"Mother," she managed.

Her father nodded at her. "Lydia."

Her sister murmured, "Lovely baby," but did not look her
in the eye. Her brother-in-law merely shook hands, and her

brother gave her a bored look, muttering something about events such as this being tedious. It was an odd reunion of people she had not seen in over a year, but Lydia breathed a sigh of relief when they had passed.

Adrian leaned into her ear. "My parents now."

She glanced at Lord and Lady Varcourt as they chatted with Tanner. Adrian's father was nearly as tall and straight-backed as his son, but his hair, though still abundant, was fading into grey.

Adrian's mother had called upon Lydia, an interview that had been tense and uncomfortable, but blessedly short. Lydia did appreciate her gesture, and Lady Varcourt had genuinely oohed and aahed over Ethan. Lydia had forgotten how stunning Adrian's mother was, with hair so white it looked as if she'd powdered it, a clear complexion free of lines, and, most surprising of all, the same smiling mouth her son and grandson possessed.

In the reception line Lady Varcourt took Ethan out of Marlena's arms, rocking him and talking nonsense to him and showing him to her husband. Lydia noticed Adrian gazing proudly at her.

After Lady Varcourt gave the baby back, she and Lord Varcourt turned to Lydia.

"How are you, dear?" Lady Varcourt said loudly, embracing Lydia with exaggerated affection. "So good to see you again. And what a lovely party this is!"

"Ma'am," Lydia responded.

Adrian's father looked at her with a gleam in his eye that made her feel uncomfortable rather than welcome. "Well, well, well."

Adrian addressed them. "I am delighted you could attend, Father. Mother." His mother presented her cheek for him to kiss.

"But of course we would attend!" cried his mother loud enough for others in the room to hear.

After Adrian's parents passed through, the crush of people waned a bit. Lydia spied a man in a dark brown suit standing near gentlemen all dressed in black.

She gasped. "Adrian." She forgot they were barely speaking. "That reporter is here."

He looked to where she indicated. "Reed." He left the line to speak to Tanner.

When he returned to her, he leaned down to her ear. "Tanner invited one representative from each of the newspapers. Better to have them report the truth than make up stories of the event, he said."

Rather like letting the fox in among the chickens, Lydia thought. Reed wandered through the crowd. He glanced in her direction, caught her eye, and immediately looked away.

Two gentlemen worked their way down the receiving line. One was a man whom she did not know. His neckcloth and collar were so high he could not turn his head. His coat so perfectly fitted his body that he could barely lift his arms.

He was soon in front of her.

Adrian turned towards her. "Let me present Lord Chasey."

"Charmed, m'lady." His eyelids fluttered and his gaze seemed aimed at the space between her and Adrian. "Charmed."

He passed Lydia and shook Adrian's hand, or rather he allowed Adrian to grasp his limp fingers before he quickly moved away.

"I cannot think he was invited," Adrian murmured.

The second gentleman moved down the line.

Lord Crayden, her one-time suitor and the man who had called upon her when she was pregnant and the newspapers wrote about her daily.

"He was not invited," she whispered.

Adrian surprised her by responding, "I dare say not."

As Crayden passed Marlena and stepped towards Lydia, she saw Tanner and Marlena exchange questioning looks.

"My dear lady," Crayden said, gazing into Lydia's eyes.

"Lord Crayden," she responded in a flat voice. "You were not expected here."

He gave her a wide smile that only pretended to be charming. "I confess, I could not stay away." He leaned closer, nearly smothering the Tannerton baby in her arms. "The chance to see you again—"

Baby William started to cry, and Lydia glared at Crayden. "Now see what you have done."

Little Ethan, who had been so good through this whole evening, sputtered into a wail as well.

"Oh, dear!" Marlena said to Lydia. "I think we had better retire for a moment."

Lydia followed her up an elegant marble stairway into a large nursery. Mary and the other nurse took the babies and changed their linen while the ladies collapsed into chairs.

"My feet are so sore." Marlena groaned. "I wish I had worn my half-boots."

Lydia smiled, still feeling uncomfortable around this woman. "I think the babies did well."

Marlena laughed. "Ethan was a real champion; our William, I fear, did not do nearly as well."

"He did not like the water."

They nursed the babies and chatted about the party as if they were friends, but to Lydia it still felt unreal, as if she was play-acting. Afterwards, they left the babies in the care of Mary and the other nurse and returned to the party.

Marlena was soon pulled from Lydia's side, and Lydia found herself alone. She tried to glance around the room in a serene, not frantic, manner and spied Adrian in a far corner surrounded by both gentlemen and ladies. Serena and Heron-vale chatted with Lord and Lady Levenhorne, and Lydia certainly did not wish to approach them.

She decided to seek out her parents or sister, who could

be depended upon to continue their familial show of affection, at least while the *ton* watched. To her dismay, Lord Crayden stepped in her path.

"My dear lady, what service might I perform for you?" He had the affront to thread her arm through his.

She pulled it away. "I can think of nothing." This man's attentions were mystifying.

He pursed his lips in disappointment. "I should like nothing more than to be in your company a little longer." He darted a glance to where Adrian stood. "I see your new husband does not need you. He is among friends."

Lydia noticed interested looks in her direction. She would have to tread a thin line with this gentleman, neither looking impolite nor friendly. "I am certain my husband has many friends with whom he wishes to speak."

Lord Crayden laughed and leaned into her ear. "Many lady friends," he whispered. Straightening, he added, "But you knew that, surely. I take it he plans to continue his friendships, then." He cocked his head towards Adrian again.

Lady Denson, a pretty young widow whose elderly husband had died several years ago, gazed up at Adrian and laughed at something he said.

Lydia turned away.

"I confess," the loathsome Crayden went on, "I am surprised she was invited."

Lydia met his eyes. "Perhaps she entered without an invitation, as you did." She walked away from him and did not look back.

Her family had disappeared from where they had been standing, so Lydia was forced to make her way through the room, the eyes of the guests upon her. She crossed into another room to look for them. The Tannerton townhouse was elegantly decorated, if not in the most modern style, very tastefully done. Huge *jardinières* of flowers everywhere enhanced the beauty.

As Lydia walked through the rooms, some guests smiled at her and some felt free to cut her now that they were away from the watchful eyes of a marquess and a royal duke.

She was about to give up her search when she nearly collided with her sister.

"Oh," her sister exclaimed. "It is you."

They were alone. "I am glad we have this moment, Joanna."

Her sister's eyes darted to and fro, as if to be certain they were indeed alone.

"I have long wanted to thank you," Lydia told her. "I do not know how you accomplished it, but I cannot be more grateful to you for coming to my rescue when—when things were so bad for me." Her throat constricted with emotion. "I do not know what I would have done without your assistance."

Her sister stared blankly. "What are you talking about?"

"The money," Lydia explained, shaking her head in confusion. "Paying my debts. Restoring my portion."

Joanna looked shocked. "I did no such thing. My husband forbade me to assist you and, I assure you, even if he had not, I would not have done so."

"But—"

Her sister bustled away before Lydia could say another word. *Who had helped her, then?*

It took a moment for her to catch her breath. She did not know what to think. Someone else had paid that enormous sum, but who?

When she could fill her lungs with air again, she glanced up and saw Mr Reed, the reporter, staring at her. She straightened and bravely met his gaze. He bowed to her and walked away.

Lydia forced herself to return to the drawing room, where Adrian still stood tête-à-tête with Lady Denson. She felt her cheeks flame. She turned in another direction but was stopped by Lady Varcourt, Adrian's mother.

"I was looking for you." Lady Varcourt's expression turned

distressed. "Oh, dear. What do I call you?" Her gloved fingers fluttered at her chest.

Lydia understood the dilemma. What, indeed, ought she to call her mother-in-law?

"Call me Lydia," she answered her.

Lady Varcourt formed a smile. "Lydia." She gave Lydia a serious look. "Dear, I saw you talking to Crayden and I thought I should warn you about him." Lady Varcourt glanced over to where Crayden stood conversing with another gentleman. "I could never like him. His smiles are so false—"

On that they could agree. At least Lady Varcourt's smile seemed…dutiful.

Adrian's mother went on, "Crayden has been toadying up to anyone who might lend him money. Do beware of him, would you, please?"

"I will do so, ma'am," Lydia replied.

Lady Varcourt went on, "In any event, do tell me, *Lydia*—" she put extra emphasis on the name "—when did you and my son—how shall I put it?—get together? To make this—this child of yours, I mean." She added with a happy sigh, "My grandson."

Lydia could not believe her ears. "I beg your pardon, ma'am?"

Lady Varcourt continued as if she'd not spoken. "I merely wondered, because Adrian gave us no inkling of it. My husband told me Adrian's name was not even in the betting book at White's—"

"The betting book?" Lydia gasped.

"I see you are getting acquainted, Mother." Adrian came to Lydia's side.

She turned to him, her voice tight. "Your mother was telling me of the betting book at White's."

"Tell me you were not." Adrian's eyes flashed back to his mother.

"Not at all," Lady Varcourt responded. "I was asking her how you—er—met…"

* * *

From his spot in the doorway Samuel watched the exchange between Lady Varcourt, her son and Lady Cavanley. Something the Countess had said shocked Lady Cavanley and outraged her son. Samuel ought to burn with curiosity as to what had been said, but instead he felt like a veritable Peeping Tom.

Heronvale had instructed that the reporters must merely observe. No speaking to the guests, and, above all, no approaching Lady Cavanley. Samuel followed the Marquess's rules, but he did watch Lady Cavanley most of the time. He'd seen all manner of things about her—the pain in her eyes when someone cut her, the surprise at whatever her sister said to her, and now this horror at whatever her mother-in-law told her.

To Samuel, Lady Cavanley had always seemed like one of the caricatures drawn of her, the kind displayed in print-shop windows. In one she was drawn as a fool, in another, a strumpet, another, a spendthrift—but always mere line and ink. In person, though, she was a living, breathing, feeling woman. In person she was rather as Mary always described her.

Mary.

Samuel's heart had almost stopped when he had seen Mary in St George's Church. With the baby in her arms, he thought she had never looked so pretty.

The butler walked to the doorway and announced, "Dinner is served."

The most top-lofty of the guests headed towards the dining room, where they would join the Marquess and the Royal Duke. Lesser folk went to sit at tables that footmen were now setting up in other rooms.

Samuel had been told there were fifty invited guests, but there were more than fifty people strolling through these rooms. This was the time those uninvited guests would slip out before anyone noticed there were no seats for them at the tables. Reporters were supposed to leave now, as well.

Samuel waited for all the guests to be seated, then made his way to a servants' staircase at the back of the house. He climbed one flight of stairs and emerged into a hallway. Listening carefully for voices, he stealthily made his way down the hall.

Lady Tannerton and Lady Cavanley had come to this floor with their crying babies earlier in the evening. The nursery ought to be on this floor, and if Mary was caring for the Cavanley baby, she would be on this floor.

He listened at closed doors until behind one he heard female voices. Holding his breath, he rapped on the door.

A maid answered. "What do y'want, sir?"

He tried to peek in the room. "I would like to see Mary for a moment, if that is possible."

She disappeared, closing the door, but he could just make out her saying, "Someone t'see you."

The door opened again and through its gap he saw Mary.

Her large eyes grew huge. "Samuel!" She glanced behind her and quickly stepped out into the hall, closing the door. "You shouldn't be here, Samuel."

"I had to see you." His heart pounded in his chest.

Her expression turned to outrage. "What are you doing here? Are you spying on my lady?"

"No, I—"

She did not allow him to finish. "I don't want them to find you talking to me. I'll be dismissed."

He reached for her, but she stepped back. "I was invited, Mary," he tried to explain. "The Marquess invited reporters."

Her eyes flashed. "Then he's a daft one. He ought to know better, seeing all the lies you write. How you hurt my lady." She turned her head away and wiped tears from her eyes. "I don't know what she'd have done if it hadn't been for his lordship." She clamped her mouth shut and refused to look at him. "There you go again. Tricking me into talking to you. Well, I won't say another word, so go away, Samuel."

"Please, Mary," he begged. "Listen to me. I miss you. I care about you more than anything. Meet me. Let me make amends. Meet me next Saturday at one o'clock. At Gunter's Tea Shop. One o'clock."

She shook her head as if she could not bear hearing his words. She opened the door and stepped back into the room.

"One o'clock," he cried as she closed the door and disappeared from his view.

Chapter Seventeen

His Royal Highness, The Duke of C—, and Her Royal Highness, The Duchess of C—, stood as godparents to both infants, the son of the Marquess of T— and the son of Viscount C—. The dinner party hosted by the Marquess was an elegant affair, with the finest of the *beau monde* attending. Curiosity was rampant for the new Lady C—, who was resplendent in yellow and attended by one former suitor, while her new husband doted upon the lovely widow, Lady D—

—*The New Observer*, November 9, 1819

Samuel pulled one of the sheets of paper from its drying line and skimmed the copy.

"What?" He read again and stormed into the office.

His brother Phillip sat with his feet on his desk, reading another of the newly printed pages by the light of a lamp. It was not yet dawn, but they wanted to be first to get the paper out that morning.

Samuel slammed his copy on the desk. "This is not the story I wrote."

Phillip looked up idly. "I edited it a bit."

"Edited it? You put in information that I did not give you. What is going on, Phillip?" Samuel snatched up the copy again and pointed to the story. "See? This part about a suitor and Lady Denson—"

"Is it not true?" Phillip asked.

Samuel sputtered. "Yes—yes. In its way it is true, but—"

Phillip shrugged his shoulders. "There you are, then. Nothing to fret about."

Samuel jabbed his finger at the paper again. "I did not write this. Everyone knows this is my story, but I did not write this. They will think I did."

Phillip placed his feet back on the floor. "Before you fly into a pet, tell me this…" He leaned his elbows on his desk and gave Samuel a direct look. "Were you in attendance at that party? Because I could have written the drivel you handed me if all I possessed was a copy of the guest list. Where were you while all this intrigue was taking place?"

Samuel stiffened. He had seen Crayden approach Lady Cavanley, and he had seen Lady Denson corner Lord Cavanley. He'd also seen Lady Cavanley extricate herself from Crayden as soon as she was able, and Lord Cavanley casting gazes out into the crowd as if he were searching for his wife.

Samuel glared at his brother. "I wrote a respectful piece about a social event involving a royal duke and a marquess."

Phillip slapped his palm on the desk. "Exactly. And the story was tedious in the extreme."

Samuel secretly agreed, but he still protested. "It was respectful of the Royal Duke."

His brother waved a dismissive hand. "Everyone knows the Duke of Clarence is off to Hanover any day now. Can't afford to live in England, poor fellow." He laughed. "And as far as the Marquess is concerned, you could have made more of the connection between him and Lady Cavanley's first husband."

Yes, Samuel could have reminded the readers of the sordid

events that bound the Marquess, his wife and Lord Wexin, but it seemed churlish to do so on what was supposed to be a happy occasion.

He'd be damned if he'd admit that to his brother, though. "So, from where did you steal your information about the party? There cannot possibly be anything printed before our edition."

Phillip grinned. "I have a source."

"A source?" Samuel blinked in surprise. "Who?"

His brother put his feet upon the desk again. "I will tell you once I am certain he is worth the money I pay him."

"Why not tell me now?" Samuel's voice rose.

One of the pressmen stuck his head through the curtain on the doorway. "The ink is dry."

Phillip stood up. "Excellent! You have made excellent time." He followed the man into the back.

Samuel lowered himself into a chair and buried his face in his hands. How was he to make amends to Mary now?

Adrian came out of the dining room, looking for Bilson. He found the butler below stairs taking inventory of the wine cellar.

"M'lord." Bilson looked surprised to see him.

"Where are the newspapers, Bilson?" He was used to reading the papers at breakfast.

Bilson stared at him. "Lady Cavanley took them, sir."

Lydia? Blast it. He'd wanted to read what was written about the christening before she did.

"Thank you, Bilson." He climbed the stairs again and entered the hall.

He'd been proud of her at the christening two days ago and he'd told her so in their brief carriage ride home afterwards. She'd done everything well. Not only had she been the most beautiful woman present, but she also had held herself proudly, even when some of the guests had behaved badly.

Yesterday had been a reprieve. The party had broken up too late for the morning papers and there was only a brief mention in the afternoon ones. It had not been a pleasant reprieve, however.

Lydia remained in her room or in the nursery and had begged off dinner. Rather than spend the evening staring at four walls, Adrian had gone off to White's, where he played cards until the wee hours, with some winnings, but no enjoyment.

Adrian rubbed his eyes as he passed the table in the hall. On the table were a stack of invitations.

He smiled.

They'd done it! They'd faced society and won. One appearance together had been all it took. He bounded up the stairs to tell Lydia.

He knocked on her bedchamber door.

"Who is it?" he heard her say.

"Adrian."

The door burst open and she stood in the threshold, thrusting a newspaper at him. "I told you it would be this way!"

He had no choice but to take the paper. "What is it?"

She swung away and walked towards the window. "Read it."

Adrian glanced at the masthead. *The New Observer.*

He read:

Curiosity was rampant for the new Lady C—, who was resplendent in yellow and attended by one former suitor, while her new husband doted upon the lovely widow, Lady D—.

He had not *doted* upon Lady Denson. His brow wrinkled. Who was Lydia's former suitor? He greatly disliked the idea of another man paying addresses to his wife.

"It has started," she said, pointing to the window. "They are out there already."

He looked up. "The reporters have been around since the marriage announcement appeared."

She whirled on him again. "Well, they have not disappeared, have they?"

It may have been premature of him to think matters resolved. He took a breath. "What of the other papers?"

She began pacing. "They are less blatant, but have patience. They will soon try to outdo the *Observer*."

Adrian glanced back at the story. "This is Reed's paper."

"Whom your friend, Tanner, *invited*," she reminded him.

He looked back at the article and frowned. "Former suitor—who did he mean?"

She threw up her hands. "He could mean anyone!"

"You must have some notion," he insisted. He'd like to call the man out, although he somehow doubted he could fight a duel merely because a man courted her.

She glared at him. "I assure you I do not, but I suspect you know precisely who he meant by *Lady D*."

"Lady Denson, I presume." He tried not to sound defensive.

"You *presume*?" She laughed, then narrowed her eyes. "You really must be much more circumspect in your flirtations, Adrian, if you wish to avoid gossip."

"It was not a flirtation," he protested. Too loudly.

She turned away.

He came after her and touched her arm.

She flinched, but turned her head to look at him over her shoulder. "If you insist on continuing this foolish charade, you must at least pretend to be the devoted husband."

"Lydia!" His voice rose, but he clamped his mouth shut. Self-rightous protests would not help the situation, especially since her point was well taken. He ought never to have left her side.

"I will remember that," he said quietly.

She faced him, eyes wide with surprise.

He tried to smile at her. "I must learn to be a husband and not a rake, must I not?"

Her brow creased as if confused.

He wanted to reach for her, to comfort her by holding her close, but she took a step back and crossed her arms over her chest.

He looked down at the newspaper again. "I am sorry for this, Lydia, but it changes nothing. We are making progress. There are a stack of invitations that have arrived. Let us discuss which to accept. Perhaps you will join me in the library in an hour and we will attend to it."

She just stared at him.

He tried to think of more to say. "You looked splendid the other night. Do you have more new gowns coming? You must order as many as you need."

She looked down at the old, rather shabby morning dress she wore, then lifted her chin. "I have ordered new gowns."

"That is good," he murmured.

They stood just a few feet apart in this room that was unchanged since his mother had lived here. It was all he could do not to take Lydia in his arms. He yearned to rekindle the passion they had so briefly shared together, but she was still so angry at him he dared not make any attempt.

Finally Adrian said, "In an hour, madam."

Lydia's stomach was in knots when Adrian walked out of the bedroom. She felt worse than after she'd read *The New Observer*. She'd expected him to rage at her as she'd raged at him, but he'd been reasonable, and now she was no longer certain he had been indulging in a flirtation with Lady Denson, as it appeared. Perhaps he meant what he said about learning to be a husband instead of a rake.

She pressed a hand against her stomach. She was afraid to believe in him, afraid to believe in anything except that the reporters would seize upon whatever she did and make something sordid out of it.

That was no excuse for her to behave badly towards Adrian, though. It was wrong of her to blame him for what the reporters wrote and for how the fine members of the *beau monde* acted towards her—some of them, at least. It was wrong of her to blame Adrian for her own confused emotions.

Lord and Lady Tannerton ought to despise her the most and yet they professed to offer friendship and support. Lady Heronvale's efforts to be helpful were equally as mystifying. Other people had treated her kindly, as well. Even Adrian's parents were trying to be nice to her.

Yet Lydia's own parents could barely look at her, and her sister openly rejected her and denied ever helping her.

Who had given her the money?

And had Adrian—her husband—truly been flirting with Lady Denson?

Lydia's new lady's maid rapped on the door and entered. "Pardon, my lady. Your new gowns have arrived."

The new woman was an experienced lady's maid who preferred the formality of being addressed by her last name, Pratt. Luckily for Lydia, Pratt had been too desperate for employment to refuse working for a lady embroiled in scandal. It did not mean the woman felt compelled to be friendly towards Lydia.

"Thank you, Pratt."

The woman crossed into Lydia's dressing room to put away the rainbow of muslin, lace and silk draped over her arms.

Lydia followed her. "I believe I will change. Is there a new day dress for me to wear?"

"There is indeed, my lady."

Lydia would at least appear presentable when she answered Adrian's directive to meet him in the library.

When she entered at the appointed hour, Adrian had a stack

of invitations in his hand. They sat in adjacent chairs and considered the invitations, one by one.

Lydia tried to remain civil to Adrian while they discussed each invitation. One was for that very evening, to attend the theatre with Lord and Lady Tannerton. Tannerton had secured a box in the Theatre Royal, a distance away in Richmond. A comedy was to be performed, its title ironic to Lydia: *Man and Wife; or, More Secrets Than One.*

It would mean a long carriage ride each way, confined with Tanner and Marlena, the two people who were almost killed because of her. But she would not readdress that issue with Adrian.

It would also mean being away from Ethan for several hours and that thought made her ache inside. Ethan regularly slept during the hours they would be gone, but what if their carriage overturned? What if he became ill? Neither of those matters were very likely, not likely enough to refuse the invitation.

She suspected few people who knew her would travel as far as Richmond for a play. For that reason alone, it seemed the best invitation to accept.

That evening Lydia took care in her appearance, choosing one of her new gowns in an ice-blue silk. Pratt threaded matching blue ribbons through her hair. The paisley shawl she carried was an old one, but it matched beautifully.

When the Tannerton carriage came to pick them up, Lydia soon learned that the Levenhornes would be part of their party, travelling with Lord and Lady Heronvale, who also would share the theatre box. She wondered if Adrian had known that all along.

The carriage ride was not as dreadful as she had imagined it would be. Tanner and Adrian entertained her and Marlena with stories of their schoolboy antics. Lydia learned her husband was the more reckless of the two, the instigator of wild schemes, such as releasing a flock of chickens in the headmaster's room or sneaking out at night to watch the older boys kissing tavern girls at the local pub.

Adrian did not mention whether he had also kissed tavern girls when he became the older boy.

The time passed quickly. When they arrived at the theatre, Adrian helped Lydia down from the carriage, taking her hand and looking directly into her eyes. He held her arm as they entered the theatre and climbed the stairs to Tanner's box.

Lord and Lady Heronvale and Lord and Lady Levenhorne were already there.

Lady Heronvale greeted Lydia as if they were bosom bows. "Lydia! How wonderful to see you!" She grasped Lydia's hands and surveyed her. "You look stunning. I defy anyone to say otherwise. Now, do tell how little Ethan is doing."

Lady Levenhorne smiled at her. "Your dear little baby is such a darling!"

The same baby who, had he been born two days earlier, would have stolen her husband's inheritance, Lydia thought, but she answered the ladies' questions politely and asked politely after their children.

She glanced at Adrian, standing with the other gentlemen. He looked over at her, raising his brows as if to ask if all was well. She nodded to him. It reminded her a little of the silent communication she'd witnessed between Tanner and Marlena, the sort of communication married couples ought to have.

"I have champagne." Tanner lifted up a bottle from a table that had been set up with wine bottles and glasses. Champagne was an extravagant choice.

"Come, let us sit. Tanner will pour for us." Marlena gestured to the chairs in front.

Serena sat next to her. "I was curious to know how you thought the christening went."

"It was a beautiful ceremony," Lydia replied. "And a lovely dinner."

Serena made a face. "That is not what I meant. I meant for you. How did you think it went for you?"

Lydia fixed a smile on her face. "I had a lovely time."

Marlena broke in. "Well, I thought you did splendidly, Lydia. Most people want to wish you well, you know, and the others you handled with exceptional grace."

It was one of those moments that made it seem as if these two ladies offered genuine support, but why would they? Why would anyone wish her well? And she certainly did not feel she had *handled* anyone. It was more a matter of maintaining her composure. Like tonight.

"Thank you, Marlena," she said.

She glanced out into the theatre and was surprised by how small it was compared to King's Theatre or Covent Garden, which she'd attended last.

Over a year ago.

The theatre was lit with candles and had only two tiers of boxes. King's Theatre had five. This theatre could not seat many more than two hundred. Lydia was stunned to see that there were probably that many people in attendance tonight, and far too many people she recognised.

"I cannot believe it, but this has suddenly become the event of the evening. It looks as if all Mayfair is here," Lady Levenhorne said. "My husband told me only yesterday that no one he spoke to was planning to attend. I suspect he was wrong."

People had turned towards their box, pointing and laughing and whispering to each other.

"Did your husband say I would be among your party?" Lydia asked her.

Lady Levenhorne blinked. "Why, I believe he did."

It became quite obvious the people in the other boxes were staring at Lydia. She shrank back in her chair, but it did no good. Tanner had chosen a box with a prime view of the stage and that meant the whole house had a prime view of Lydia.

Marlena put a steadying hand on Lydia's arm. "Pay them no heed, Lydia."

Lydia spied her parents in a box on the right, her sister and brother-in-law sitting with them. Her mother stared directly at Lydia and whispered something in her sister's ear.

Adrian brought her a glass of champagne. She glanced into his eyes, and he must have seen her distress. His gaze swept the house and he bent down to her ear, so close she felt the warmth of his breath. "You look beautiful, Lydia. Who would not stare at you?"

She glanced into his eyes again and felt the same jolt of attraction that had first occurred so long ago. It greatly surprised her. She thought she had killed off her own attraction when she so thoroughly killed off his with her rash and cruel statements.

He returned to his friend Tanner. As the other ladies chatted around her, Marlena kept her hand on Lydia's arm. Lydia drank her champagne faster than was typical of her.

Soon the announcement came that the performance was ready to begin. The Irish melodist, Mr Webb, was the star performer in the comedy this night, but it mattered little who performed. Lydia was the main attraction.

Someone sat in the seat behind her, and Lydia knew without turning around it was Adrian. Her senses were heightened to him, as if he'd chipped a hole in a dam and now all the water had broken through.

Someone else noisily took the chair next to Adrian. "Good God," she heard Tanner say, "I hope this is less tedious than that blasted *Don Giovanni*. I endured that opera twice."

The music started, the curtain opened and Mr Webb came

out on stage. Lydia tried very hard to concentrate on the comedy and on Mr Webb, whose voice was pleasant and who delivered his lines in a humorous manner. Lydia might not have laughed out loud, but the play made her smile a few times.

Too soon it was over and the audience clapped and cheered. An intermission was announced and it seemed as if everyone instantly got up to go somewhere else.

"That was lovely, was it not?" exclaimed Serena. "I enjoyed it very much."

Lydia had, too, she realised.

Adrian put his hands on the back of Lydia's chair as he rose, his fingers brushing the nape of her neck. She felt the touch as acutely as if he'd branded her with a hot iron.

"Ned," Lady Levenhorne called to Lord Heronvale, her brother, "I see Helen in one of the boxes. We must make her a visit." She looked over to Lydia. "Helen is our sister. Lady Rosselly."

Lydia knew that. She'd only been estranged from the *ton* for a year. Everyone knew everyone else.

"I suppose we must," said Lord Heronvale.

"Yes, I suppose we must," grumbled Levenhorne.

"Shall we stretch our legs as well?" Tanner asked his wife. Marlena stood. "I would like that."

Adrian glanced at Lydia, who rather hoped to hide away. Her breasts were full of milk and they ached, making her wish she'd stayed in the nursery with Ethan.

"Come, Lydia," cried Tanner. "Come with us. Don't let them keep you confined."

All the curious onlookers, he meant. She glanced at Adrian.

"It is up to you," Adrian said.

"Do come, Lydia," Marlena chimed in. "We shall walk together and show them all we are great friends."

When they stepped out of the box, the hall was a *mélange* of people all in a hurry. Lydia took hold of Adrian's arm, but

Tanner and Marlena were soon separated from them, and Lydia could no longer see them in the crowd.

"This is ridiculous," Adrian said after they had pushed their way through throngs of people. "We should return to the box."

"Yes," Lydia agreed. "Please." She was enduring far too many ill-mannered stares from young men staggering from too much to drink.

With difficulty, they reversed direction.

A woman's voice called out, "Cavanley!"

Adrian turned quickly to see who it was, and Lydia's grip on his arm loosened. At that same moment a young buck seized her other arm and pulled her away.

"The notorious Lady W!" he cried. "I recognise you!"

"Release me!" Lydia tried to pry his fingers loose from his vicelike grip.

"Not yet." He grinned insipidly, and she smelled drink on his breath. "Must show the fellows I'm with the notorious Lady W! The Wanton Widow! What else d'they call you?"

"Lady Cavanley," she said in a firm and haughty voice. "Release me before my husband finds you."

The young man laughed. "Oh, he's over there. He's occupied well enough."

Through the crowd she spied Adrian's back. He was with Lady Denson, who had seized him by the arm as well.

"C'mon." The young gentleman pulled at Lydia.

She saw her parents approaching. "Father!" she cried, but he turned his head away.

Her mother gave her a scathing look. "Scandalous!"

They passed her by.

It was too much. Lydia ceased resisting her inebriated captor and rushed at him instead. He let go of her in surprise, and she shoved him so hard he fell against the wall. The people around her gasped, but she pushed through them and headed back to the theatre box.

Someone else touched her arm and she whirled on the man.

It was Lord Crayden. "Lady Cavanley, I came to offer you assistance."

"I need nothing," she cried, hurrying to Tanner's box.

Crayden stayed with her and was next to her when she put her hand on the doorknob. At that same moment, Adrian and Lady Denson walked up.

"Lydia!" Adrian sounded alarmed.

Lydia supposed it was because he saw her with Lord Crayden.

Lady Denson laughed. "He was worried about you, but I told him you would come to no harm." She glanced at Crayden, amusement in her eyes. "I think we have interrupted something private, Cavanley. You'll just have to come with me."

Lydia could not even look at this woman taking possession of her husband, but opened the door of the box and went in, slamming it behind her. Her heart still beat so fast that she thought it would spin right out of her throat. She retreated to the wine table at the back of the box and grabbed an open bottle of champagne. She poured herself a glass and downed it in one gulp.

She felt something cool and damp on her chest and looked down at herself. The front of her gown was stained with milk. She almost laughed. She'd been abandoned by her husband and her parents, accosted by a stranger, and now even her own body was betraying her. She quickly wrapped her shawl around her to cover up the soaked front of her gown.

She closed her eyes to compose herself, but all she could see was Lady Denson on Adrian's arm.

Adrian pried Lady Denson's fingers away. "That was badly done, Viola."

She grabbed on to him again. "I was only making a jest!" She glanced at Crayden, who stood with a smirk on his face. "Was it not a mere jest, Crayden?"

"I took it as such," Crayden said.

Adrian pried her fingers away again. "Stop this. I must attend to her at once."

He reached the doorknob before she could re-attach herself to him and opened the door and went inside. She followed him.

He turned on her. "Go, Viola."

She made a helpless gesture. "I cannot. I have no escort."

He strode to the door and opened it, but Crayden, who would have made an adequate escort, had gone.

"You may take her back, Adrian," Lydia said from the recesses of the box. "I do not need you."

He walked up to her. "I suddenly lost you."

She stepped away from him. "Yes, well. No harm was done."

Lady Denson came to Adrian's side. "Do forgive me, Lady Cavanley," she said in a sweet voice. "I truly was making a jest. I assure you—" she gave Adrian a meaningful glance "—as soon as your husband lost you, he was quite distressed. I was at a loss as to how to comfort him. We came searching for you at once."

Adrian waved her away. "I could not see. What happened to you?"

"Nothing happened to me," Lydia said. "When we were separated, I merely came back to the box when Crayden approached me."

The alert sounded for the audience to return to their seats.

"I must go back now, I'm afraid," Lady Denson said.

"Take her," said Lydia.

Adrian felt he had no choice. He strode to the door and Lady Denson skipped after him.

When they were out in the hall, walking towards her box, Adrian spoke to her. "You kept me from pursuing her, Viola. You put her at risk and made a jest of it."

When Lydia had slipped from his arm, Adrian had turned

to go after her, but Viola had stopped him, delaying him, and he'd lost sight of Lydia completely.

Viola drew him aside. "I am sorry, Cavanley." She sounded quite sincere. "You know how I enjoy seeing you. I quite forgot everything else."

He glared at her. "I do not want your regard. Do you understand? I am married—"

She broke in. "But you had to get married. Everyone knows that. She accused you of being the father of her baby!"

He shot back, "I am the father of her baby."

She gave a sad smile. "Oh, that is dear of you to be so noble, but you deserve happiness, Cavanley, and I can give it to you." She threw her arms around him and kissed him.

He had to pry her away. "Where is your box?" He pulled her along by the arm.

"We have passed it," she said.

He retraced their steps. "You had better tell me which it is or I will leave you right now."

She told him.

When they reached the box, he released her and stormed away, not even waiting to see if she entered safely.

Out of the corner of his eye he saw Crayden.

When Adrian returned to Tanner's box, he wanted only to explain to Lydia how it had happened that he'd lost her. He wanted to assure her that Viola was a nuisance to him, nothing more.

As luck would have it, the whole party had returned, and Lydia was again seated with the other ladies. She did not even look over when he entered.

"Where the devil were you?" asked Tanner.

"On a blasted errand," Adrian replied.

Tanner's brows rose.

"It is a long story." Adrian took his seat behind Lydia.

He watched the farce, *The Sleeping Draught*, although he

paid no attention to it. He was attuned to his wife, who sat
with her hands folded in her lap and did not move a muscle.
He, on the other hand, had a strong urge to fidget.

When the performance ended and goodbyes said to the
Heronvales and Levenhornes, Lydia behaved with perfect
cordiality. In the carriage, she answered anyone who spoke
to her, but said as little as possible. Adrian doubted she wanted
to say anything to him.

Eventually Marlena fell asleep on Tanner's shoulder while
Lydia gazed out of the carriage window into the darkness.
Although the inside of the carriage was only dimly illumi-
nated by the carriage lamps on the outside, Adrian could see
Tanner's worried expression.

"I'm going to be at White's tomorrow at around three,"
Tanner said. "Will I see you there?"

It was an invitation to tell him what was going on.
"Perhaps," Adrian responded, glancing towards his wife.

Chapter Eighteen

Can anyone expect more from marriage between a rake and a wanton woman? In their first appearance in society they continue their dissolute ways.
—*The New Observer*, November 9, 1819

Adrian and Lydia no sooner stepped into the hall than Lydia ran up the stairs. Adrian quickly gave the attending footman his hat and gloves and went after her.

She was not in her bedchamber.

He heard the baby crying and he bounded up another flight to the nursery.

Lydia was unfastening the front of her dress and Mary was holding the baby in one arm and assisting Lydia at the same time. They both looked over when he entered.

Lydia quickly looked away, turning her back to him. "I need to nurse Ethan." She took the baby from Mary and sat in the rocking chair, wrapping her shawl around her exposed skin and concealing the nursing baby.

Adrian turned to Mary. "Leave us."

Mary paused a second, looking uncertain before curtsying and walking out of the door.

"This is not a good time for a discussion, Adrian," Lydia said. "Not while I am nursing Ethan."

He stood over her. "I will not rest until I speak to you."

She looked up and he saw far too much in her eyes—pain, anger, distrust, humiliation and, worst of all, resignation. He felt responsible for it all.

She lowered her head. "When I am finished, I will speak with you."

"In my bedchamber," he said.

Her gaze flew back to him. "If you insist."

"I insist."

Adrian left her with their son and felt as estranged from both of them as he'd felt the day of Ethan's birth.

He guessed she would have preferred a discussion in a sitting room or the library, but he wanted a place more private. When he walked into the bedchamber, dominated by the large four-poster bed, he realised she might fear he had something else in mind.

Good God. She could not think he would impose his marital rights on her if she were unwilling?

His valet awaited him, and it was easier to allow the man to ready him for bed than it was to explain that he wanted a moment with his wife first. So Hammond set about the routine of assisting Adrian out of his coat, standing aside as Adrian removed his other clothes, holding up Adrian's old figured silk banyan until he slipped his arms into its wide sleeves and wrapped it around himself. Hammond gathered Adrian's shirt and underclothes to launder, his coat and breeches to brush, and his boots to polish. He headed for the door.

"Bring me a bottle of sherry, would you, Hammond?" Adrian asked him. "And two glasses."

"Very good, sir," Hammond said in a tone that sounded more like approval than agreement.

Adrian lit every lamp so that it looked less as if he was arranging a seduction, even if he wore a robe and nothing else. He pulled two comfortable chairs and a small table away from the bed and arranged them in a cosy seating area. When Hammond delivered the sherry, Adrian placed the bottle and glasses on the table he'd set between the chairs.

He surveyed the room.

It still was dominated by the large four-poster bed, and, worse, it still looked like a room belonging to his father. Sitting in one of the chairs, he poured himself a sherry and decided that some money ought to be spent on redecorating the house. Perhaps Lydia would enjoy the project.

A few more long minutes passed. Adrian was in the midst of taking a sip of sherry when Lydia knocked on the connecting door between their rooms. She opened it before he could tell her to come in.

"You are dressed for bed." Her voice was tight.

He placed the glass on the table and stood. "You are not," he replied.

She still wore her blue gown and was wrapped in her shawl.

He gestured for her to sit. "Hammond was waiting to assist me. It seemed easiest to just let him proceed." It was the sort of excuse he might have come up with if he had been bent on seduction.

She eyed him suspiciously as she walked to the chair.

"Some sherry?" he asked as she sat.

She glanced at him. "This is not a social call, Adrian. It is a summons."

He poured her a glass and set it in front of her. "It was a request, Lydia. Not a summons. A request to talk to you, nothing more."

"It was a summons," she repeated, but more to herself than to him.

She reached for her sherry and the shawl slipped off her

shoulders, exposing the bodice of her gown, which had two dark spots staining the fabric over her breasts.

"What happened to your gown?" He gestured to the stains.

She looked down at herself. "My milk came while we were at the theatre."

His brows rose. "It did? Such a thing can happen?"

She gave a dry laugh. "Well, it did happen, so the answer is, yes."

He took his seat. "Is that why you rushed away from me in the theatre?"

Her eyes flashed. "I did not rush away from you. An inebriated young man pulled me away and tried to drag me off to show to his friends."

"No." Adrian half-rose. "Did—did he injure you?"

"It is more likely I injured him." She lifted the glass to her lips and sipped. "But not until my parents walked past me. You were busily occupied with Lady Denson, and even Crayden stayed back until I had freed myself."

He sat down again, averting his gaze. "I ought never to have let her detain me."

"Indeed." Lydia spoke as if she was holding in a great deal of emotion. "But you made the choice."

The wrong choice.

He leaned forwards. "Are you certain you are unharmed?"

She lifted her glass again. "There are no visible marks."

He bowed his head. Just invisible ones.

His head shot up again. "Your *parents* walked past?"

She pressed her lips together tightly before answering. "They saw what they wished to see. 'Scandalous', my mother said."

"Curse them. And Crayden as well. Why did he not assist you?" He looked at her again with regret. "Forgive me, Lydia. It was I who ought to have assisted you."

She avoided looking at him. "I suppose if the young man had not recognised me, nothing would have happened. I would have remained at your side and Lady Denson would have been disappointed."

"He recognised you?" Adrian leaned forwards again. "Is he known to you?" *Give me a name*, Adrian thought, *and I will call him out*.

"He was not known to me," she snapped. "He recognised me. From the prints of me or from being pointed out in the theatre box, I do not know which, but he called me the notorious Lady W and the Wanton Widow, so he knew who I was."

Adrian's grip tightened on the arm chair.

She added, "He knew me from the gossip about me, nothing more."

He closed his eyes and saw the people in the pit and the theatre boxes all pointing at her. She'd endured it with admirable fortitude. Then he'd taken her out into the theatre's hallway, oblivious to the danger that awaited her. He'd allowed another woman to distract him and he'd turned away from his wife. He had abandoned her to the rowdy crowd.

She interrupted his self-recrimination. "I thought there was something important you wished to discuss." This time her voice trembled with emotion. "If not, may I leave now?"

He opened his eyes. "Lydia," he whispered, "do not leave."

She averted her gaze.

He did not know what to say to her. Being sorry he had failed her was not enough.

Silence loomed between them, and all Adrian could think was that his father was right about him. Perhaps all he was fit for was to have a good time, to play games, with cards, with women. He professed to accept responsibility for a wife, but he shirked it at the first opportunity.

She broke the silence. "Well, if you are not going to speak, perhaps you will answer my question?"

"Of course," he said, his gaze meeting hers again. "What is it?"

Her eyes narrowed. "I want you to answer truthfully. Do not mince words with me."

"I will answer truthfully." He could at least speak the truth.

She took a breath as if gathering courage, then kept her gaze steady. "Do you wish to pursue a liaison with Lady Denson?"

It was not the topic he expected. *"What?"*

She went on. "We have been out in society together a mere twice, and both times you have attached yourself to Lady Denson. You told me this morning that you were not engaged in a flirtation with her, but men sometimes say one thing and mean another." She glanced away and back again. "I do wish you would tell me the truth now." She blinked and shook her head. "Because if you do wish for a liaison with her, I cannot prevent you. I would simply ask that you allow me to live somewhere where I need not see it or read about it."

Ah, she wished to live apart from him. That was the crucial matter. "Do you ask so you might move to the country?"

Her eyes flashed with pain. "Please just answer me, Adrian."

"I do not desire a liaison with Lady Denson," he stated as emphatically as he could. "I have never desired a liaison with her."

She turned her head away. "I do not know if I can believe you. I saw you with her."

He rubbed his face. "Lydia, how do I convince you?" He leaned forwards suddenly. "Perhaps appearances deceived you. Your parents were deceived when they passed you in the theatre. They did not see your distress."

Her eyes narrowed. "That was different."

"Not so different," he said. "Lady Denson sets her cap at first one gentleman, then another. I am merely the next in line, and my value has increased with the rivalry of a wife. She makes it appear to you that the contest is already won."

"You place the blame on her?" Her tone was accusing.

He shook his head. "Not entirely. I allowed myself to be distracted by her, but not for the reason you think. Not for a liaison."

"For what reason, then?"

He thought about it. "I do not know precisely. Habit, I presume." He gave a wan smile. "A woman calls a rake's name and he responds."

She waved a dismissive hand. "This is a silly discussion. I do not care about Lady Denson. You will have many Lady Densons, I expect. A man does not change just because he marries."

Adrian tried to think of continuing the life he'd led, the life of a rake. Of leaving her side to play cards the whole night, to be off to the races or hunting or travelling whenever the whim struck him, to set up a new mistress and be seen with her about town.

None of it appealed.

He leaned over to her, trying again to convince her that he spoke the truth. "Listen to me, Lydia, and please believe me. I do not want Lady Denson or any other woman. I am ready to be your husband and Ethan's father."

She looked at him with scepticism. "You were forced to marry me."

"I was not forced," he countered. "I chose to marry you. I chose to make love to you that night and I chose to marry you. You were the one who did not have a choice."

She met his gaze. "I chose to seduce you."

That fateful choice. "Perhaps we can look on that as a fortunate choice, the choice that brought us together. Perhaps even that event is subject to perception. We can see it the way we want to see it."

Her parents had perceived the very worst of her. If people erroneously perceive the very worst, why could they not turn it around and see the very best?

She gazed at him very intently. "What do you propose, Adrian?" Her voice turned low.

He returned her gaze with as much sincerity as he could

convey. "Let us decide to enjoy this marriage of ours, Lydia, as we did once, so briefly."

Her breath quickened and her eyes flashed with fear.

He backed away. "This is not coercion. It is not a dictate. I speak the truth when I say I want a marriage with you." He paused. "But if you do not want me, tell me now. I'll find you a home in the country if you wish it."

He waited for a long time for her answer.

Finally she said, "Very well, Adrian. We will try this a little longer, but next time I ask to leave, you must promise to let me go."

It was his turn to pause. "I promise to let you go," he finally said, "if you so request it."

He extended his hand to seal the bargain with a handshake. She held back at first as if reconsidering, but eventually she did clasp her hand to his. Her hand was soft and warm and he was reluctant to let go.

They stared into each other's eyes, hands clasped but still, as if they'd become bound together. It was what he wanted, Adrian thought. He wanted to be bound to her.

Lydia felt captured in his gaze, so intent, so unwavering, so earnest. She could feel the air moving in and out of her lungs. If she could trust her judgement, she would say she saw truth in his eyes, but she could not trust herself.

She *perceived* him to be telling the truth, that was it, but perception was not truth, not proof of what was real.

Her senses told her the strong grasp of his hand was real. His smooth palm, the spattering of hairs on the back of his hand. Those were real.

Her eyes darted away, but landed on the bed in the centre of the room. Its covers were turned down and she could imagine how cool they would feel against her bare skin. How warm he would be in contrast.

The air rushed into her lungs at a faster rate.

She gazed at him again. His eyes were dark and yearning now, an emotion she, too, well understood.

She ought to snatch her hand back and run to the safety of the bedchamber on the other side of the connecting door, but she did not wish to let go of his hand, the hand that was making her senses sing, making her body flare to life in a manner it only had done with him.

He bowed his head and let her hand slip from his. She felt bereft. He expected her to leave.

She started to turn away, but caught sight of the bed again. She turned back.

"Do you wish for a real marriage, Adrian?" Her voice felt raw in her throat.

His brows rose. "What do you mean?"

"Do you intend to assert your marital rights?"

He stood perfectly still. "I would do nothing you did not wish me to do."

She averted her gaze. "And if I wished it?"

"You have only to ask," he replied.

She turned and looked at him through lowered lashes. "Must I always ask?"

A smile flashed across his face. He gently touched her hair and plucked out the pins, one by one. Her hair tumbled onto her shoulders. He pulled the blue ribbon from her curls and used his fingers as a comb, smoothing the tangles. The sensation was so lovely Lydia sighed with the pleasure of it. Next he pulled away her shawl, almost tentatively, as if half-expecting her to flee after all, but she did not wish to flee.

It made no sense for her to want his lovemaking after such a dreadful evening, but his touch never failed to ignite her desire, to fan it into a white-hot heat. Her desire was as real as the sensation of his fingers in her hair, his hand on her skin.

His hand slipped down her neck to her breasts, skimming

the stained silk fabric, making her need more urgent. He searched for the complicated fastenings of her bodice, making her wish he would just rip the fabric away.

She stilled his hand and undid the bodice, pulling the gown over her head.

"You must have another gown made like this one," he murmured to her, caressing her neck and quickly untying the laces of her corset. "You looked beautiful in it."

She could only hope his words were not mere flattery.

He unlaced her corset with ease and soon she was free of all clothing but her shift.

He took her hand once more. "I am asking this time, Lydia," he murmured, leading her to the bed.

"Yes," she breathed.

He lifted her hand to his lips, placing his kiss in her palm like a gift.

She untied the sash of his banyan and slipped her hands underneath, feeling the firm muscles of his chest, the peppering of his hair. She rested her hand against his heart and felt it beating.

This was real, not perception.

His scent filled her nostrils, clean and male and, like an aphrodisiac, instantly enveloped her in carnal desire.

He released her hand and lowered his head to place his lips on hers, his kiss gentle, reverent and real.

Uncertainty plagued her, but there was nothing uncertain about Adrian's touch, his lips, his waiting body. She wrapped her arms around his neck and pressed herself against him, savouring the taste of him, the feel of him.

He splayed his hands around her waist and lifted her onto the bed, shedding his banyan and climbing up next to her. She rid herself of her shift and met him on her knees for another, less gentle, more demanding kiss.

He stroked her naked skin, his touch familiar from their

too-brief moments of bliss, like revisiting a place with happy memories. He kneaded her skin, ran his thumbs across her nipples and lowered his mouth to her breast, his tongue hot and wet.

He laughed against her. "I believe you taste of milk."

She kissed the top of his head, holding him as he tasted her again.

His lips were not perception, nor his laugh, nor the rigid male part of him that told of his desire for her.

He laid her down and entered her. She vowed to savour every sensation, every tangible thing, not only the growing urgency he created as he moved inside her, but also the sheen of perspiration on their skin, the sound of his breathing, the press of his weight upon her. She felt the smooth fabric of the bed linen against her back and the rough texture of the hair on his legs.

All real.

Lydia abandoned herself to the experience, feeling her need grow with each stroke, feeling it build as his breath came faster. Sounds, uniquely his, escaped his mouth. He brought her closer and closer, yet made her want to beg him to hurry.

Her release came in a sudden burst and she cried out. While she still throbbed with exquisite pleasure, he spilled his seed, and she felt truly joined to him, as if they were for ever connected.

But that was perception, she thought, as her pleasure ebbed and reason returned. *Illusion.*

He slid off her and nestled her against him while she felt his heartbeat and breathing return to normal. His lips found tender skin on the back of her neck.

"Stay with me tonight," he murmured.

She did not think herself capable of leaving him.

The room was light with the first stages of dawn when Adrian opened his eyes, suddenly aware that Lydia was no longer at his side.

She was moving about the room, gathering her clothing. "Lydia?" He'd hoped she would not leave him.

She started, but turned to him. "Ethan's crying," she said. "I must go to him."

Crying? Adrian strained to hear and could just barely make out Ethan's sounds.

She disappeared through the connecting door.

It was not until breakfast that he saw her again, but for her to share breakfast with him seemed like a huge step forwards.

As their lovemaking had been.

He almost dared to hope all would be well between them.

She was filling her plate from the side board, when Bilson brought in the morning newspapers. Both he and Lydia froze. She sat stiffly, pouring her tea as Adrian picked up *The New Observer* and looked for the section filled with gossip.

He looked up at her. "It is not so bad. A mere rehash of the christening and a promise of more tomorrow."

Lydia frowned.

He put the paper down. "Remember. It is all perception. We act as if the newspapers do not even mention us, and the stories will be discounted. People will believe what they see."

"Or they will see what they wish to see," she added in a strained voice.

He skimmed through the other papers, but they merely mentioned that he and Lydia were in town and expected to rejoin the social scene. Had the reporters known that he and Lydia were to attend the theatre in Richmond? he wondered. It had certainly seemed as if all the *ton* knew.

He gazed at Lydia as she sipped her tea. She was distant again, reserved. Nothing like the warm, passionate woman who had shared his bed and his lovemaking the night before. He wondered if that warm, passionate woman would return to him tonight. He could only hope.

At least her anger had gone.

"How is Ethan this morning?" he asked.

Her expression revealed a ghost of a smile. "He is well. Hungry and dear as ever."

"I must pay him a visit." Adrian had missed spending time with his son.

"He will probably be awake soon," she said.

It was practically an invitation.

He was emboldened. "After I visit him, would you like to walk around the house with me and talk about what you might want to change about it?"

She looked up at him. "The house is adequate as it is, Adrian."

He gave her a wry smile. "I should like your advice on changing it. Everywhere I look I think I am in my parents' home."

She glanced down at her plate, spreading butter on a piece of toasted bread. "Very well. If you wish."

If he went slowly, he said to himself, he might be able to break down her careful reserve.

They passed a pleasant morning spending time with Ethan and walking around the house, discussing pieces of furniture, wall paper and curtains. It was a bit difficult to draw out her opinion, but if he was patient, she shared her ideas.

In the middle of their tour she stopped him.

"Do you have the money to pay for all this?" she asked him.

"I do, Lydia," he answered her. "My allowance has always been generous and I have wealth of my own." In fact, he'd done a fair job of repaying himself the money he'd secretly given to her.

"But you gamble a lot," she added.

He faced her. "Not as much as I used to, and, I promise you, Lydia, I am not a reckless gambler. I never wager more than I can afford to lose."

They walked into a small sitting room at the back of the house.

She looked at him again. "You will tell me if I need to economise." She gazed away, seeming to survey the room. "My first husband spent extravagantly and left me in terrible debt."

"I remember." He turned away so that she could see nothing on his face of how well he knew about her debt.

She was quiet for a long time while Adrian pretended to examine items in the room.

Suddenly she swung back to him. "It was you!"

He looked up. "What was me?"

"You. It was you." She shook her head. "Of course it was you. You were the only one who could have known of it."

"Known what?" His heart pounded.

She met his gaze. "I thought my sister had rescued me. Restored my finances, but at the christening she denied it." She glanced away and back again. "Very vehemently denied it. I could not imagine who would have put out so much money for me, but, now that I think of it, you were the only one who could have possibly known how desperate matters were."

He simply stared back at her.

"Tell me, Adrian." Her voice turned more serious. "Was it you?"

He paused, but finally answered her. "Yes."

"How?" she cried. "Why?"

He shrugged. "I had a great deal of money and you were in need. You'd let your servants go and were conserving candles. I surmised that your circumstances were desperate. I followed it up with Mr Coutts who sent me to Mr Newton."

"They told you of my debts?"

He nodded. "I believe they were very anxious to see restored to you what ought to have been your due."

She continued to gape at him.

He added, "Your parents were abroad and it seemed no one else had assisted you, so I did."

She swung away. "That was an outrageous thing to do."

So much for gratitude. "You were not supposed to know."

She shook her head. "I am so beholden to you." She made it sound like an evil he'd done her.

"Lydia, there is no obligation to me at all. It was a secret gift and I would not have told you, except that I promised to always answer your questions with the truth."

She raised her eyes to his. "You saved my life."

The discovery that he had been her benefactor only seemed to increase her discomfort with him. They ended the tour of the house and she made the excuse that she needed to be with Ethan, who was sleeping.

Adrian told her he was going to White's to meet Tanner, but that information seemed to create even more distance.

Baffled, he walked out of the door of the townhouse and the reporters rushed towards him. He'd forgotten about them. They were yelling questions at him all at once, about Lady Denson, about Lydia. He pushed through, resolving to hire some burly fellows to keep them away. He was surprised he had not thought of it before.

When he reached the street he spied Reed at the fringe of the group, just watching, arms across his chest.

Adrian felt he ought to walk over and put a fist in the man's face for whipping the gossip about Lydia into a frenzy. He'd do it, too, if he could be certain Reed would not use it for more scandal in the paper.

Reed was not among the reporters who followed him to White's. Adrian ignored them, knowing they could not cross the threshold of that private club. Let them hang about outside all day, if they so wished.

Tanner awaited him at a corner table. He had an extra glass of brandy waiting as well.

Adrian pointed to the glass of brandy as he joined him. "What would you have done if I had not shown up?"

Tanner grinned. "Drunk it, of course."

Adrian took a sip. "Glad I came."

Tanner's expression turned serious. "I am also glad you came. What happened last night?"

Adrian frowned, wondering how much to tell. "A great deal happened." He began with the events in the theatre.

"Not a good evening after all," Tanner said when he'd finished.

Adrian lifted his glass to his lips, intending to tell Tanner at least a little of how it was between himself and his wife.

Tanner spoke instead. "I've heard talk here today, Adrian. A version of what you have described, except they are saying you ran off with Lady Denson at the theatre last night, while your wife cavorted with a wild crowd."

Adrian rose from his chair. "It is not true!"

Tanner bade him sit. "Of course it is not true, but three people have made a point of telling me about it and asking for more details."

Adrian glanced around the room and noticed that the other gentlemen were looking his way. "This is the outside of enough. Who is spreading such lies?" The answer came to him. "Crayden. The weasel. I'll wager a pony he is the one. He was at the christening and at the theatre, and he was watching both Lydia and me. I will deal with him immediately." He started to rise.

Tanner put a stilling hand on Adrian's arm. "Wait. Will that not cause more scandal? Why not allow me to handle Crayden, Pom? I would consider it an honour."

Adrian sat again, thinking of Tanner's proposal. "It would give me great satisfaction to throttle him myself, but I fear you are correct." He released a breath and drummed his fingers on the table. "There must be some way to counter the gossip. I wish there were some way I could keep it from Lydia." He glanced up at his friend. "How the devil do I tell her about it?"

Chapter Nineteen

Their infant forgotten at home, the notorious Lady C—
and her new husband sought entertainment in Richmond, attending the theatre, where, it is authoritatively
said, Lady C— dressed as a harlot, and, during the intermission, romped shamelessly with an unidentified gentleman. Her husband, meanwhile, was spied in a
passionate embrace with Lady D—, his latest paramour.
—*The New Observer*, November 11, 1819

The next morning Lydia entered the dining room for the
single purpose of reading what was written in the papers. After
Adrian had returned from White's the previous day, he'd
warned her that the events of that night had become public
knowledge and would likely appear in this morning's paper.

She'd spent a sleepless night and not in Adrian's bed. She
had all but made her request to move to the country. He had
begged her to give it more time.

Adrian was seated with the paper in his hand.

"Is it very bad?" she asked him.

His face looked ashen. "It is highly exaggerated."

She extended her hand and he placed the paper in it.

She read it.

"It is horrible!" She threw the paper down, the words *scandalous*, *romping* and, worst of all, *passionate embrace* spinning through her head.

Adrian skimmed the other papers. "These also write of the event, somewhat more moderately."

She stared at him, more wounded than she could ever expect. "What was this *passionate embrace*?"

He looked up. "It was not a passionate embrace."

But some sort of embrace, she surmised. Lydia's throat felt tight. And she'd almost believed his protests.

"Lydia." His expression was a plea. "Believe me."

It felt hard to breathe. "I cannot stand this, Adrian. I have been through this nightmare once. It is even worse now."

"It must pass," he insisted. "It cannot go on. We must stay the course, Lydia. Show them the newspapers are false." He leaned towards her. "We should go to the shops today. Ride in Hyde Park. We need to be seen together."

They already had accepted an invitation to a musicale at Lord Heronvale's, but the idea of facing anyone, whether at the shops, in the park or at an evening event, made Lydia feel sick.

Nonetheless, within the hour they were bound for St James's Street and Piccadilly. At Adrian's insistence they left through the front door.

As they stepped out, a footman accompanying them, the reporters rushed forwards, shouting questions. The footman pushed the men away. Lydia noticed Reed standing nearby. He had not approached them.

"I shall hire some men to keep them from our door," Adrian said. "But today we make use of them. They have seen us leave the house together."

Some of the reporters followed them, but the footman kept them from coming close. They soon crossed Old Bond Street, pretending to glance into shop windows. The streets were crowded, and people Lydia did not recognise turned around to point at them. People she knew pretended not to see them at all. Adrian kept up a conversation with her as if nothing were amiss.

"Shall we look for furniture next week?" he asked. "Perhaps we should add some chinoiserie, like the Regent has used in Brighton."

She mumbled replies to his questions as they strolled towards Piccadilly and tried to appear as if they were a contented married couple.

They stopped in Hatchard's Bookshop, where Lydia retreated behind a bookshelf in the corner. She heard someone approach and took down a book, pretending to read. Two ladies stood on the other side.

"Can you imagine?" one of them said. "How can they show their faces?"

"Did you see her?" the other one replied. "She is said to be quite beautiful, although, living as she does, her looks will never last. He certainly is handsome." The lady sighed. "A terrible rake, they say."

The first lady added, "Lady Denson is no better than she ought, but you knew he had to eventually succumb. What rake would not? Imagine being married to a man like that."

Her friend responded, "I suppose if you live the same sort of life, you would hardly notice."

"They must condone the practice of free love like that Shelley fellow," the first lady said.

"Well, I predict their marriage will not even last as long as Lord Byron's, but I'll wager she is the one banished to the Continent, not he." The two ladies giggled.

Lydia stepped out from behind the bookshelf, making it obvious she'd heard everything they said. The ladies gasped. They had spoken as if they knew everything about her.

She nodded to them and walked away with as much dignity as she could.

Adrian had remained in the front of the bookshop near the window so that he would be visible to passersby and anyone entering the shop.

He smiled when he saw her, a pained smile. "Did you find a book?"

"No, but I'm ready to leave." She was more than ready.

He insisted they visit Fortnum and Mason next door.

"We are not rushing away," he whispered to her.

They browsed through the store with its dried fruit, preserves and its newest novelty—tinned foods. Adrian selected some jams for their table. Finally they could walk back, the footman trailing behind with the packages.

Some of the reporters continued to track them, noting their every move, Lydia suspected. It made them even more of a spectacle. As they walked, she noticed that the women they passed gazed at Adrian.

Finally they reached Curzon Street. The reporters who had remained came towards them again, but they managed to get in the townhouse.

As soon as they stepped into the hall, Bilson hurried up to them. "Your father has called. He is waiting in the drawing room."

"My father?"

Lydia put her hand on the banister, eager to retreat to the peacefulness of the nursery and her baby Ethan. Adrian stopped her.

"Come with me," he said. "This is bound to involve us both."

She started to protest, but both Bilson and the footman watched to see what she would do. She nodded and followed Adrian to the drawing room.

"Good morning, Father," Adrian said when they entered the room. "We have just returned from the shops."

"Are you mad?" His father, who looked as if he'd been pacing, turned to face them. When he saw Lydia, he gave a disapproving frown. "Going to the shops after all this." He inclined his head. "I would speak with you, son."

Adrian gestured to Lydia. "You have neglected to greet your daughter-in-law."

"It is of no consequence, Adrian," Lydia said.

"It is common courtesy." He turned to his father and waited.

Lord Varcourt finally bowed. "Good morning, ma'am." He glanced back at his son. "I would speak with you, Cavanley. Now." He looked at Lydia as if to dismiss her.

Adrian held her arm. "Does this involve my wife?"

His father snapped, "Of course it does. Is your head buried in sand, boy?"

"Then she shall stay." His grip became firmer.

"Adrian—" Lydia protested.

Adrian leaned to her ear. "Whatever this is, hear it from my father's mouth, rather than from me later."

"Do not whisper," his father snapped.

"Just tell us what this is about." Adrian's voice was impatient.

His father pulled out a piece of paper and shoved it at his son. "This was in the print-shop window."

They had not passed a print shop on their walk. Lydia looked to see what it depicted.

It showed a caricature of her in a drunken orgy with a group of men, and Adrian in a lewd embrace with Lady Denson. In the corner was a baby, naked and wailing.

Lord Varcourt huffed. "They are in great demand, the fellow said."

Lydia pressed a hand to her stomach.

Lord Varcourt glared at his son. "Your mother had an attack of the vapours about all this. She's quite ill over it."

Adrian shoved the print back at him.

His father moved away. "I do not want the thing."

Adrian pointed to the print. "This is all fabrication, Father. It is not true."

His father gave a sardonic laugh. "Nonsense. It must be true. Or true enough." He snatched it back. "Look at it. It is too specific to be fabrication." He threw it down again and it fluttered to the carpet. "Besides, everyone knows Lady Denson—"

Lydia flinched at the lady's name.

Adrian broke in. "There is nothing to know about Lady Denson."

"Witnesses saw you kissing her," his father countered.

Lydia backed away.

"What they saw was not me kissing her," Adrian shot back.

Lord Varcourt snorted.

"It is abominable that you speak of such matters in front of Lydia," Adrian went on.

"You wished her to be present," his father reminded him, but his father did turn to Lydia and add, "I do beg your pardon, ma'am." He actually sounded as if he meant it.

He faced Adrian again. "Please, son, this is getting out of hand." He put a hand on Adrian's arm. "Go to Cavanley House as soon as possible. Stay there until the newspapers forget you. Leave now and you could be there before nightfall."

Lydia could only think, *a kiss is a kiss.*

"We will stay," Adrian replied.

"Then you are an idiot," his father muttered.

Adrian stiffened. "It will pass if we simply all ignore it."

"Son—" Lord Varcourt looked earnest "—it will only get worse."

Lord Varcourt is correct, Lydia thought.

His father sighed and bowed to Lydia. "Good day, ma'am." He walked past Adrian. "Heed me, son." He strode out the door.

Adrian glanced at her.

She lifted her chin. "You neglected to tell me the part about kissing Lady Denson."

"It only looked like I kissed her." He sounded defensive.

She laughed. "Perception again?"

"Yes," he said tightly.

She backed away. "I believe I have had enough, Adrian. Your father is right. This is only going to get worse, and it is already too far out of hand." She gestured to the outside. "Your father offers Cavanley House. Send me and Ethan there."

He did not answer her.

"Adrian." She gave him a level stare "You promised I could leave if I so desired."

"Give it more time, Lydia," he said. "Give *us* more time. This Lady Denson thing is nothing—"

She put up her hands to stop him, feeling as if she wanted to weep. "Do you not see, Adrian? It has gone too far. Whatever the newspapers say is what people will believe. Even you and I believe it."

"I do not believe what the papers say." He looked offended.

"You believed there had been some former suitor of mine at the christening. You believed it because the newspaper said it."

He glanced away.

"I cannot dismiss what happened with you and her," Lydia whispered. She cleared her thoughts and spoke in a stronger tone. "In any event, we cannot ignore the fact that this affects other people as well. Our families—"

"Do not say it." His eyes flashed. "Your family has behaved abominably to you. They should rally around us. Instead they believe the lies."

She shook her head. "We cannot entirely blame them. Everyone believes the stories about us. You saw it. You saw them staring at us and whispering about us."

And gossiping between the bookshelves, she thought.

Lydia crossed the room and picked up the caricature. She

brought it back to Adrian. "Look. They have started on Ethan, too. Do you wish your son to grow up with this sort of attention?"

His eyes turned pained.

"Very well." He sounded resigned. "We will go to Cavanley House."

Her heart pounded at what she was about to say. "Leave Ethan and me at Cavanley, Adrian."

He stared at her. "You do not wish me to come with you?"

She gazed at him. He was her champion, rescuing her every time she needed him, even when she had not known it. It was impossible not to love him and loving him made all the difference.

Loving him made not trusting him, worrying about every woman who looked at him, so much worse. She'd been betrayed by a man once, she could not bear being betrayed again.

Especially by Adrian.

She took a breath. "You promised that if I asked, you would send me away, Adrian." Her voice seemed as if it came from another person. "I am asking now."

He stared back at her, looking as if she had slapped him across the face. Finally, he shook his head. "Cavanley is only about a four-hour carriage ride away. Pack your things. I'll escort you there today and get you settled." He looked at her with pained eyes. "I will not stay."

Samuel remained at the edge of the group of reporters, who were all buzzing about the Cavanleys' walk to the shops and what Cavanley's father might have said to him, what made him look so angry as he pushed his way through them a short time ago. They began taking wagers as to what entertainment the couple would attend that evening, or whether they would go out at all.

None of it mattered to Samuel.

He stood in front of the house because he had nowhere else to go.

He and Phillip had had a row after the morning paper appeared. Phillip had tricked him and switched the story he'd written with one Phillip had written from his mysterious source. Phillip had done it all in secret.

Samuel had stormed out of the newspaper office and had come here, where Mary was near.

He stared at the windows of the upper floors, hoping to see her peek out. He'd not had even a glimpse of her, but he could hope.

One of his colleagues laughed and money was passing hands.

Samuel felt someone walk up behind him.

"Samuel?" a sweet voice said.

He spun around. "Mary!"

She was not dressed for out of doors, wearing a cap, but no bonnet, an apron still covering her dress. He took her arm and led her away from the other reporters.

"I came through the garden, Samuel, and I'll be dismissed if my lord and lady see me talking to you."

"Why did you come, Mary?" he asked.

She handed him a crumpled copy of the morning newspaper. "I want you to stop writing such things about my lady."

"Mary, I—"

The story had sickened him. Having seen Lord and Lady Cavanley together, he could not imagine those events occurring. He could imagine Lady Cavanley looking wounded and shamed.

And he could imagine the look on Mary's face, the look she showed him now.

How was he to tell her he had not written the story and have her believe him?

"How could you write such things?" She looked down at the newspaper. "I can read, you know. I fetched it after my lord and lady left the house." Her eyes rose to meet his. "I am asking you to stop this. It is hurting them very much."

"I cannot stop it, Mary," he said truthfully, wanting to explain.

Her eyes flashed. "At the christening, you professed to care about me. If you do care, you will stop this."

"Mary." He took a step towards her. "I cannot stop the stories. I do not have the power to stop them."

Her eyes widened and she made a mournful sound. "I thought you would not agree." She turned away. "I have to go back." She paused before turning away. "I will not be at Gunter's on Saturday after all."

He watched her hurry around the corner, his spirits plummeting to new depths.

Any chance he might have had for her forgiveness was gone because of a story another man had written.

Chapter Twenty

Sent by his father into exile to the family estate, Lord C— and his scandalous wife have no new antics to report. Lady D— has been seen soothing her wounded heart with a certain wealthy nabob, Mr G—.
—*The New Observer*, November 26, 1819

Adrian had been true to his word, remaining only one day to make certain Lydia and Ethan were settled at Cavanley. So close to London, the Cavanley staff had read all the newspapers and did not precisely greet them with open arms. He hated to leave her in that atmosphere, but he kept his promise to her.

He'd not returned to London, though, but had ridden on horseback through the countryside, staying at inns, trying to sort out the disorder of his life.

His first impulse had been to drink and play cards, but the liquor tasted foul and the card games bored him. Some tavern maids eyed him hopefully, one offered herself blatantly, but Adrian could not bear the thought of bedding a woman not his wife. Not Lydia.

There was no returning to the life of a rake for him, but, without Lydia and Ethan, he had no other life at all.

On the third day, perhaps forty miles from London, he rode by a house, once a fine Tudor manor house, now crumbling and abandoned.

Like him.

The house called to him like the mythical Sirens. He saw it not as it was but as it could be. He almost laughed. There in front of him was a task he wanted to complete, a useful way to spend his time. He would purchase this property and bring it back to its past glory, make it into a home.

He'd been waiting for his father to bestow upon him a property to manage and all this time all he had to do was purchase one.

The property included the house, some equally dilapidated outer buildings, and, best of all, land that ought to be growing crops.

Adrian rode back to London to make the arrangements to purchase the property from the family who'd not had funds enough to support it. When he arrived at the townhouse, he sent a note around to Tanner to tell him he was in town, but would remain secluded most of the time. When the footman who delivered the note returned, Tanner was with him.

Tanner and Adrian sat in the library, sharing a bottle of brandy, and Adrian told Tanner how things stood with Lydia, how the newspaper had spoiled what they might have had together.

"I cannot see any remedy for us," he told Tanner. "If we had been left to ourselves, we might have had a chance." He lifted his brandy and took a long sip.

Tanner's forehead creased and his eyes followed the brandy glass. "What will you do now?"

Adrian gave a knowing smile and held his glass high. "You fear I'll succumb to the pleasures of the bottle again." He lowered the glass and stared at its contents. "I tried. The first night I left her, I'd planned to do exactly that." He smiled wryly. "The innkeeper's brandy was vile, however."

Tanner's expression remained wary.

Adrian shook his head. "Truly, I hated that muzzy-headed feeling. I stopped before imbibing too much."

"I am glad," Tanner said. "It solves nothing."

"I felt the same about playing cards," he added. "The thought of sitting at a card table bores me."

"By God!" Tanner feigned alarm. "What will you do with yourself?"

Adrian smiled again. "It took me a few days of wandering, but I have found something to interest me."

Tanner frowned again.

Adrian laughed. "Do not fear. It is not a woman."

Tanner relaxed. "You read my mind. If not a woman, then what?"

"A property." He leaned forwards. "In Berkshire. Not far from your estate, come to think of it."

"And?"

Adrian took another sip of brandy. "And I have taken steps to purchase it. It is in sad shape, but that is the joy of it. There will be much work to occupy me there. It can be restored to something fine again, I am certain of it, and once it is done, perhaps…" He let his voice trail off. He did not say that perhaps Lydia and Ethan would come to live with him there.

"It sounds splendid, Pom."

They discussed the cost of renovating, the possible uses of the land, how many workers he would need. Tanner wanted to see the place and they talked of when that might be accomplished.

When Tanner poured them each a second glass of brandy, he changed the subject. "I should apprise you of my dealings with Crayden."

Adrian averted his gaze. He felt the twinge of jealousy upon hearing Crayden's name. On his long rides over the English countryside, he'd obsessed over the fact that

Crayden had once been Lydia's suitor. His father had told him so long ago.

He turned back to Tanner. "Go on."

Tanner paused, even though Adrian had given him permission. "He, of course, denied being the person who informed the newspaper of what happened in Richmond. Or at the christening. I do not believe him."

"It must have been Crayden." Adrian narrowed his eyes.

"I did discover that Crayden is dipping his toes in the River Tick. He owes a great deal of money and is having difficulty repaying."

Bilson entered.

"A man to see you, m'lord," he said. "I told him you were occupied with Lord Tannerton, but he insisted I tell you he is here. He was certain you would wish to see him."

"Who is it?" Adrian asked.

"Mr Reed, sir."

He and Tanner exchanged glances.

"What the devil can he want?" Tanner said.

Adrian said, "How the devil did he know I was here?"

Bilson's complexion reddened very slightly.

Adrian stood. "Bilson, did you inform Reed I was here?"

The butler lifted his chin. "I did take that liberty, m'lord, but it was with good reason."

Adrian's anger flared, but he held it in check. "Show Mr Reed in," he said tightly. "I will deal with you later."

Bilson bowed. "Very good, my lord."

When Mr Reed walked in, both Adrian and Tanner were standing, ready to face him. Adrian's muscles were taut with anger, and it would not take very much from Reed before he let that anger off its leash.

When Reed appeared, however, he looked dreadful, pale and gaunt and with dark circles under his eyes.

"Thank you for seeing me, my lord." Reed bowed to both men.

"Are you ill, Reed?" Adrian asked, forgetting his anger.

Reed glanced at him in surprise. "Why, no."

Adrian waved a dismissive hand. "Never mind, then. Get on with it. You wished to see me."

Reed bowed his head. "I fully understand the harm I have done you and Lady Cavanley—" he began.

Adrian broke in, "I doubt you know the extent of it."

Reed nodded. "I do not ask for your forgiveness, because I do not deserve forgiveness. I do wish to convey how profoundly I regret the words I wrote about you."

"It is my wife you maligned," Adrian snapped.

"I know it." Reed winced as if in physical pain. He pulled a letter from his pocket. "There is no reason you should agree, but I would beg you to send this letter to your wife, as your own letter, so she will open it. Not a letter in my name."

"You expect me to allow you to write to my wife?"

Reed looked chagrined. "Well, I have written a brief note to your wife, but the letter is really for Mary."

"For Mary!" Adrian stepped back in surprise.

"Who is Mary?" Tanner asked.

"Lydia's maid." Adrian still felt dumbfounded. He turned to Reed. "What do you want with Mary?"

Reed stared at his letter and silently handed it Adrian. "I did not seal it. Please read what I wrote to Lady Cavanley and to Mary."

Adrian unfolded the paper, and Tanner looked over his shoulder to read along with him. The note to Lydia was an apology and a plea to make certain Mary read his letter. The letter to Mary was a profession of love, primarily, but in it Reed also apologised to her and made a complicated explanation of not being the author of stories that had appeared since the christening.

He ended the letter saying, "I no longer write for the newspaper, but whatever employment I may find, my standard of behaviour shall always be, 'What will my Mary think?'"

"You no longer write for the paper?" Adrian and Tanner said at the same time.

"No." Reed gave a wan smile. "My brother pays some society fellow to feed him information and my brother writes the stories."

"I'll be damned," said Tanner. "Crayden, again. The cursed fellow is selling his lies to the paper."

Adrian stared at the letter, rereading Reed's profession of love.

"My lords," Reed said, "if I could print a retraction of the vile things that were written, I would do it, but I no longer have any control over the paper."

"Your brother won't agree to it?" asked Tanner.

Reed shook his head. He looked at Adrian. "Will you send the letter in your name?"

Adrian's mind was spinning. If the newspaper created this story, the newspaper could kill it as well.

He glanced at the letter again. "You must print that retraction."

"I said I cannot, sir." Reed protested. "My brother—"

"We'll get your brother's co-operation." His plan was already forming, a plan that might just put everything to rights.

"You will never convince my brother," insisted Reed.

"I know a surefire way to convince him," Tanner said.

"What is it?" Reed asked.

"Bribery," Tanner and Adrian said together.

Tanner grinned. "Bribery will work on Crayden as well."

"You are going to pay them to be silent?" Reed sounded shocked.

"Well," Tanner admitted, "perhaps it is a bit more like extortion. A lot more, actually. Wait until I get my hands on Crayden."

Adrian's excitement increased. "We'll have your brother print the retraction. We'll expose Crayden. Get him to admit he was lying." He gave the reporter an intent gaze. "But you must print an interview with me as well."

Reed looked as if his head had been twisted around, but he only murmured, "The issue will sell very well."

It was six days before they could accomplish it all, but Tanner's extortion did the trick. Neither Crayden nor Reed's brother wanted to be exposed for printing lies about peers.

Both Adrian and Tanner were at the office of *The New Observer* when the first copies of the Special Edition came off the press.

They each read it over carefully. Tanner grinned. "This should do the trick."

Adrian glanced over to see Reed waiting for him. "We are off, then. Wish me luck."

Tanner clapped him on the shoulder. "Good luck."

Chapter Twenty-One

Editorial. Falsehoods have abounded in the pages of this newspaper, your editor has learned, all the perfidy of one man, Viscount Crayden. Crayden sold to this paper an exclusive view of society events, but it has lately been discovered that he sold sensational lies. Peruse the whole story in this issue, we beg of you. An exclusive interview with Lord C—, husband of the notorious Lady C—, finally provides the true story
—*The New Observer*, December 3, 1819

Lydia leaned over Ethan's cradle and watched him shake a rattle, making excited cooing sounds at the same time. He'd changed so much in these last few weeks. Lifting his head, kicking his legs, grasping the rattle.

She'd found the rattle in a box on a high shelf in the nursery and all she could think of was that Adrian had probably held the same rattle in a tiny hand. He'd probably shaken it just as energetically.

Even though Adrian had been true to his word and left her, his presence was everywhere at Cavanley. A box of baby clothes was discovered in the attic. She knew they had been

Adrian's. The nursery contained his toys and books. The servants related stories about him, prompted by Ethan, his little son who looked so like him. Worst of all, there were portraits of him throughout the big house. Miniatures on side tables or forgotten in drawers. Paintings of him. With his mother when a mere toddler. An impish-looking schoolboy. A rascal of a youth. And one full-length portrait that must have been painted when he was in his twenties. He stood next to his horse, his hand casually on the saddle, a young man in his prime, full of virile energy and so handsome she could not help but stare. His image stared back, so real he looked as if he really could see her and as if he might break into an amused smile at any moment.

That portrait haunted her. She could not sit in that room, because it felt as if his eyes were always upon her. She avoided even entering the room, and yet, three times already she had woken during the night and carried a lighted candle down the white marble staircase to gaze at the portrait.

Once away from him and the relentless newspaper stories, Lydia realised what she had thrown away. He had always done the right thing by her, every time. She'd allowed the newspapers and the gossip and her own fears of betrayal to colour her perceptions of him, about what she knew in her soul about him.

And now it was too late.

A maid entered the nursery. "Newspapers from London." The girl's dimples twitched on her cheeks.

Odd for the girl to bring the papers up to this room. They were usually left in the library. Lydia avoided reading them, except skimming them for mention of Adrian.

"The messenger said you must read them right away, m'lady," the maid said.

The messenger? Why must she do what some messenger said?

"And the housekeeper wishes to see Mary, my lady." The maid looked as if she were a cat who had eaten a canary.

"Me?" Mary said from the corner of the room where she sat mending.

"Indeed," the girl replied. "You are to come right away." As she turned to leave, she pointed to the newspapers. "The messenger said to read them!"

Mary followed her out of the door.

"Oh, Ethan," Lydia sighed, "I do not wish to read newspapers."

"Oooo," said Ethan and he shook the rattle.

The servants at Cavanley had been cool to her from the moment she arrived and watchful around her. Lydia supposed it was because they had read all the London gossip about her. Perhaps there was some mention of her the servants wanted her to see.

Or mention of Adrian.

She stepped away from the cradle and walked to the table where the maid had left the papers. *The New Observer* was on top.

Would she never escape that paper? "Special Edition," it said. She picked it up and glanced at it.

"What?" Not believing her eyes, she held it closer to her face.

The Special Edition was about her and Adrian.

She read about Lord Crayden fleeing to the Continent, his creditors pursuing him. She read about *The New Observer* paying him for his sensational news stories. *The stories are completely false,* the newspaper now said.

She read about "Lord C" with even more interest. "Oh, Ethan," she exclaimed.

Adrian had given the paper an interview, to tell the true story about Lord and Lady C. In the paper he stated he had married her for love and was now grieving the necessity of them being apart. It said that Adrian had loved her from the first time they had met, but that her marriage to Wexin had made her frightened of love and marriage.

This "true" account was not entirely true. She knew Adrian had not *loved* her from that first moment, but now it seemed possible that he might have loved her later on, perhaps when he restored her widow's portion and gave her back her home.

The account put a touching, beautiful interpretation on everything that happened. Even if not wholly true, it made for a very romantic story.

"Perception," she whispered, "can be positive."

She put down the paper and moved across to Ethan, who greeted her with a shake of the rattle.

She scooped him up in her arms and twirled around. "Ethan," she cried, "we are going to London. We are going to see your papa!" She must go to him this very day. Tell him how wrong she'd been, tell him she loved him, too.

A voice came from the doorway. "Does the newspaper meet with your approval, then?"

She turned.

Adrian stood there, framed by the doorway, looking as if his portrait had come to life.

"Adrian."

He stepped inside the room. "I know the account is not entirely true, but it paints a prettier picture than had been painted previously." He paused and his eyes burned into her. "The part about me loving you—that part is true."

"Oh, Adrian." She closed the distance between them, their son still in her arms.

He enfolded them both in an embrace.

"I have missed you," she said. "I have been so entirely wrong about everything."

"You have not been entirely wrong. You were right about facing the newspapers. We ought to have stayed away." He kissed her, careful not to squeeze Ethan. When his lips reluctantly parted from hers, he added, "I do not believe I ever told you that I love you, that meeting you and marrying you and fathering Ethan are the best things that have ever happened to me."

He took Ethan from her and lifted him high in the air. Ethan broke into a huge smile and made a noise that sounded like a laugh.

"He smiled at you." She wrapped her arm around Adrian and leaned her cheek against his shoulder. "You made him laugh." She pulled Adrian over to the cradle. "Come see what else he can do!"

She took Ethan from Adrian and placed him in the cradle, holding the rattle near his hand. Ethan grabbed it and shook. "Oooooo!" he cried.

Adrian laughed and reached in the cradle to run his finger over Ethan's soft cheek. "Clever boy."

Lydia hugged her husband from behind. "You are the clever one," she murmured against his back. "To use the newspaper this way."

He turned around and held her in his arms. "I could not have done it without help. Reed helped write the article. He gave me the idea, really."

"Reed?"

Adrian grinned. "Reed is the urgent reason the housekeeper summoned Mary."

She was mystified.

He laughed. "Lydia, Reed was Mary's suitor. He courted her at first to learn about you, but he fell in love with her. Wrote a lovely letter telling her. That is what gave me the idea."

She gaped at him. "Mary and Reed?"

"I hope they are this very minute doing what I am about to do."

He leaned down and kissed her again, a soft and reverent kiss, a kiss full of hope.

Hope surged through her, not the glimmer of hope she'd experienced from time to time since meeting him, but a torrent of hope that their lives would always be as happy as this moment.

"You've created a beautiful world for us, Adrian. No man could ever have achieved a more beautiful world." She gazed into his eyes. "And I love you for it. I will always love you for it."

His eyes filled with emotion and he wrapped his arms around her, holding her as if he never wished to let her go.

Epilogue

Lord and Lady C— continue to summer at Nelbury House, Berkshire, where they are expected to remain for several weeks. —*The New Observer*, August 24, 1821

"Curr'cle, Mama! Look. Curr'cle!"

Ethan, who had just turned two years old the week before, pulled on Lydia's skirt and excitedly pressed his nose against the parlour window.

A shiny new curricle pulled by two snowy-white horses made its way up the carriage path. Lord Tannerton held the ribbons, and Marlena sat next to him with little William on her lap.

Ethan, however, only had eyes for the dashing vehicle. "*Two* horses," he added knowledgeably.

"Yes, I see," Lydia replied, mimicking his enthusiasm. "Two *white* horses."

"*Black* curr'cle, Mama. Black."

Lydia was amazed at this small creature who was her son. He seemed to learn new things every day.

"Let us go and meet our callers, shall we?"

Ethan would have run had Lydia not caught his hand and held him to a fast walk to the hall.

This was Tanner and Marlena's first visit to Nelbury House, the Berkshire property Adrian had purchased. The Tannerton estate, only two hours away, was palatial in comparison.

Lydia could not love her house more.

Adrian had spent the last year and a half seeing to the restoration of the old Tudor property. There was still much to be done, but at least enough of the house was habitable for them. They already had tenants on the property, a small flock of sheep, and enough swine and poultry to make this a working farm. Adrian and Lydia and Ethan moved into Nelbury House a few days after the King's coronation in July.

In the hall Dixon stood ready to attend the visitors.

A smile tugged at Dixon's lips at sight of the eager Ethan. "Your father is already outside, Master Ethan."

"Papa?" Ethan tugged harder.

Lydia smiled. "The father is as eager as the son, is it not so, Dixon?"

"Indeed, my lady." Dixon opened the front door for them.

Dixon, Cook and Thomas, the footman, had come to Nelbury House with Lydia from her London townhouse, still as faithful to her as they'd been in her darkest time.

Lydia and Ethan stepped outside.

Adrian stood shaking hands with Tanner, who clapped him on the back. Adrian glanced over at her and smiled. Lydia's heart leapt as it always did when she saw him. Tanner's tiger drove the curricle to the stable, and Thomas carried in the few items the Tannertons had brought with them, gifts for Ethan among them, no doubt.

Little William tried to pull away from his mother to go and chase the chickens that had escaped their coop. Marlena held tightly on to William's hand.

Lydia bent down to Ethan. "See. William has come to see you."

The carriage was safely away, and Marlena released William, who dashed after the chickens.

Ethan ran after him. "Curr'cle, William!"

Marlena embraced Lydia. "It is good to see you."

Lydia returned the hug. She was becoming accustomed to the friendship Marlena unfailingly offered. "Welcome to our home."

Another carriage turned into the property and both Lydia and Marlena dashed to again grab the hands of their little boys.

"Papa's gig," Ethan informed William excitedly.

William ignored him in favour of the chickens.

"This must be Mary and Samuel," Lydia said. Mary and Samuel were coming for a visit of several days. "Adrian's coachman has fetched them from the London coach."

Lydia's joy over her life with Adrian was increased by knowing that Mary, too, had found happiness. Mary wed Samuel Reed over a year ago and had her own pretty set of rooms near Lincoln's Inn Fields. Mary also was expecting a baby.

Lydia turned to Marlena. "I do hope it does not offend you that Samuel and Mary will also dine with us. We had little notice that they had changed their day to arrive."

A Marchioness had every right to object to sharing a meal with a former maid, but Adrian had insisted Tanner and Marlena would not stand on such formalities. Lydia sent a message informing Marlena just to be certain.

"We do not mind at all," Marlena assured her. "In fact, I believe Tanner wishes to discuss business with Mr Reed."

Tanner had purchased *The New Observer* newspaper, making him boss over the Reed brothers. Tanner quipped that it seemed the easiest way to keep *The New Observer* from printing gossip about them.

Lydia's name still appeared in the newspapers, although in a kinder manner. What entertainments she attended, what clothing she wore, what shops she patronised, all found their way into the columns. Her mother actually liked her daughter receiving this kind of attention. Lydia's status as a leader of all things fashionable gave her entire family a certain cachet and had done much to mend the breach between them. Secure in her husband's love, Lydia could even forgive her family their superficiality. It helped that her parents genuinely doted on Ethan.

"Gig, Mama!" Ethan cried.

The gig pulled up and Mary almost did not wait for it to stop. Samuel assisted her down from her seat.

"My lady, it is so wonderful to see you!" Mary curtsied, but Lydia gave her a one-armed hug, the other arm busy holding Ethan.

"We have missed you, Mary."

"Mary!" Ethan cried, pointing to the carriage. "Papa's gig."

Mary scooped him up and kissed him on the cheek. "Are you not clever to know that?"

Samuel stepped over to Lydia. "Good day, my lady. It is an honour to be here." He always looked at her with apology in his eyes.

"You are most welcome here, Samuel." As far as Lydia was concerned, Samuel's devotion to Mary was enough to redeem him to her.

Adrian's voice rose. "Let me take you on a quick tour of the property, before you brush off the dust of the road."

Lydia smiled. Her husband could not wait to show off all that he'd accomplished.

He provided all the details as he led them around to the back of the house from where the outer buildings and the vegetable garden were visible. In the distance were the white sheep grazing on a hillside.

After the tour, Ethan's nurse took the boys to the nursery, and the adults sat down to their meal, Dixon overseeing and Thomas and another newly hired footman serving.

As the lively meal progressed, Lydia took in the sight, the Marchioness being so kind to Mary, the Marquess arguing politics with a newspaperman, her husband showing himself a happy, contented man. Her breast swelled with emotion.

Adrian looked over at her and smiled. She knew his thoughts were much like her own, grateful for the company of friends at their table, grateful for their new home, for their son, for each other.

The talk at the table seemed to fade, and it felt as intimate as if she and Adrian were alone. He lifted his wine glass to her. "I love you," he mouthed.

Tears of joy stung Lydia's eyes. She nodded in reply.

Their friends conversed, oblivious to the toast Lydia and Adrian drank to each other and to their bright and happy future.

Lydia could imagine how Samuel, had he been paying the least bit of attention, once might have written about it in *The New Observer*:

Lord and Lady C— shockingly ignored their dinner guests to pass longing looks at each other. Dear Readers, are we to assume that the rake and the notorious widow have found happiness at last?

* * * * *

Here's a sneak peek at
THE CEO'S CHRISTMAS PROPOSITION,
the first in USA TODAY *bestselling author*
Merline Lovelace's HOLIDAYS ABROAD *trilogy*
coming in November 2008.

American Devon McShay is about to get the Christmas surprise of a lifetime when she meets her new client, sexy billionaire Caleb Logan, for the very first time.

Silhouette
Desire

Available November 2008

Her breath whistled out in a sigh of relief when he exited Customs. Devon recognized him right away from the newspaper and magazine articles her friend and partner Sabrina had looked up during her frantic prep work.

Caleb John Logan, Jr. Thirty-one. Six-two. With jet-black hair, laser-blue eyes and a linebacker's shoulders under his charcoal-gray cashmere overcoat. His jaw-dropping good looks didn't score him any points with Devon. She'd learned the hard way not to trust handsome heartbreakers like Cal Logan.

But he was a client. An important one. And she was willing to give someone who'd served a hitch in the marines before earning a B.S. from the University of Oregon, an MBA from Stanford and his first million at the ripe old age of twenty-six the benefit of the doubt.

Right up until he spotted the hot-pink pashmina, that is.

Devon knew the flash of color was more visible than the sign she held up with his name on it. So she wasn't surprised when Logan picked her out of the crowd and cut in her direction. She'd just plastered on her best businesswoman smile when he whipped an arm around her waist. The next moment she was sprawled against his cashmere-covered chest.

"Hello, brown eyes."

Swooping down, he covered her mouth with his.

Sheer astonishment kept Devon rooted to the spot for a few seconds while her mind whirled chaotically. Her first thought was that her client had downed a few too many drinks during the long flight. Her second, that he'd mistaken the kind of escort and consulting services her company provided. Her third shoved everything else out of her head.

The man could kiss!

His mouth moved over hers with a skill that ignited sparks at a half dozen flash points throughout her body. Devon hadn't experienced that kind of spontaneous combustion in a while. A *long* while.

The sparks were still popping when she pushed off his chest, only now they fueled a flush of anger.

"Do you always greet women you don't know with a lip-lock, Mr. Logan?"

A smile crinkled the skin at the corners of his eyes. "As a matter of fact, I don't. That was from Don."

"Huh?"

"He said he owed you one from New Year's Eve two years ago and made me promise to deliver it."

She stared up at him in total incomprehension. Logan hooked a brow and attempted to prompt a nonexistent memory.

"He abandoned you at the Waldorf. Five minutes before midnight. To deliver twins."

"I don't have a clue who or what you're…"

Understanding burst like a water balloon.

"Wait a sec. Are you talking about Sabrina's old boyfriend? Your buddy, who's now an ob-gyn doc?"

It was Logan's turn to look startled. He recovered faster than Devon had, though. His smile widened into a rueful grin.

"I take it you're not Sabrina Russo."

"No, Mr. Logan, I am *not*."

* * * * *

Be sure to look for
THE CEO'S CHRISTMAS PROPOSITION
by Merline Lovelace.
Available in November 2008 wherever
books are sold, including most bookstores,
supermarkets, drugstores and discount stores.